My Sister's Keeper

Also by Nora Kelly:

In the Shadow of King's
Bad Chemistry
Old Wounds

and she's gone, and no one can take her place. But we're also here to celebrate her life. She only lived for twenty-seven years—' Libby's voice quavered. 'The world will never know what she might have done had she been allowed to live longer. But she did a lot with the time she had.'

Tony had moved inconspicuously to one corner of the square from which he could get a good angle on Libby. He kept the camera on her.

'Denise Reed is going to play a song for Rita, and then we will light the candles. After that, anyone who knew her and wants to say something about what she meant in their life is welcome to speak to us. In this way, we can all know her better before we say goodbye.'

Libby stepped back and Denise moved to the centre. The guitar hung comfortably from a wide strap around her neck. As the first chords trembled in the hushed church, Denise murmured, 'Rita told me she loved this song when she was a child, and even after she grew up and left her church, it still had a special power for her.' And in a small, clear voice she began to sing *Amazing Grace*. Gillian wasn't surprised, knowing what she did about Rita's background, but she thought others might be. She glanced covertly at the audience. The potent melody was doing its work—many eyes were blurred with tears already. Jane had her tissues out. Jacobsen, though, sat stony-eyed; Paul Smith looked uncomfortable. She turned slightly to see the other man. He was staring straight in front of him, rigid in his seat. Gillian suddenly realized why he looked familiar: he resembled Rita. He must be Rita's brother, John.

Where is Bacon, she thought frantically. Why isn't he here? She should tell him right away—but she couldn't get up and leave in the middle of the memorial service. And what if the man left? What could she do? Follow him? She looked carefully around the room again. Maybe Bacon had sent someone else—someone young who wouldn't be conspicuous. She tried to find a face with the watchful stare she had endured in Bacon's office. Other people were looking furtively about, too. Of course, she thought, they're wondering if the murderer is here. Rita's brother caught sight of Tony moving behind the seats, panning across the faces of the listeners as Denise sang. He looked startled. Then he dropped his head, concealing his face.

Amazing Grace drew to a close, and a long silence fell, broken only by muffled sniffling. A vivid picture of Rita as she used to arrive in the history office appeared in Gillian's mind: her face whipped pink by the wind, her untidy dark hair flattened by the impression of her helmet.

At last Libby stepped forward and lit the candle. The flame burned blue and then gold, perfectly steady in the still air of the church. No one spoke. Marnie moved to the table and picked up a second candle that had been lying hidden among the flowers. She lit it from the first one and held it. As she did so, Libby began to speak, to tell the story of Rita's life.

'Rita was born in London, England,' she began. Gillian's eyes swivelled to Rita's brother. His hands were gripping his knees as he stared at Libby.

'Her family was working class,' Libby went on. 'Her mother had crippling arthritis. Her father ruled the family with violence. He beat the children with a belt, especially Rita, because she wasn't obedient. He didn't want her to finish school, but to stay home and take care of her mother and the younger children. She had two sisters and two brothers.'

A violent scraping sound broke the narrative. John Gordon shoved his seat aside and walked rapidly out of the church, head down, looking at no one. All heads turned. There was an audible hiss of breath, and people began to whisper. Marnie's candle wavered in her hand. Libby's face was white. Gillian saw Tony's camera turn and follow Gordon. She shifted agitatedly and half got to her feet. Then, as Gordon strode towards the door, another man rose from the back row nearest the door and followed him. The door swung open and banged shut. Gillian belatedly recognized the young policeman who had perched on a chair in the background and taken notes when she was interviewed by Bacon. She sat back, gasping with relief. Bacon was not missing his chance.

Libby threw her a look of agitated inquiry from the centre of the room. Gillian moved her arm in a reassuring gesture and felt sweat soaking the silk of her blouse.

'Who were they?' Laura muttered in her ear.

'Rita's brother and a policeman.'

Laura's eyes widened.

Jessie looked sharply at Gillian. 'What's going on?'

'Tell you later.'

Shakily, Libby resumed speaking. The room quietened down again, but Gillian's attention was fragmented. Others, too, looked this way and that, wondering what more might happen. But there were no further disturbances. Libby left the microphone, and one by one the members of the Feminist Union came forward and gave their testaments of friendship. There were touching stories and funny ones. Near the end, Marnie told them about taking Rita camping for the first time.

'She'd been here for a couple of years already, but she'd never been in the wilderness. We drove to Garibaldi in my old clunker. I had camping gear, and she borrowed a sleeping-bag from somebody. So we hiked in for a few hours and camped. She liked it, but she was kind of unnerved. Every time there was some little rustle or crackle, she'd say, "What was that?" She stayed awake half the night, she *knew* that every noise was a bear. So. The next day we hiked out on another trail and only made it back to the parking lot after dark. We had some oranges and extra chocolate bars left and we were leaning against the fenders, munching, and Rita was feeling sort of relieved that we were back in civilization. For her, after all those trees, seeing an unpaved parking lot was like Columbus seeing land. I was looking in the trunk for another orange when Rita spotted an old man in a shabby coat poking through the garbage cans by the edge of the lot. Without a thought, she went right up to him and tapped him on the shoulder and asked him if he wanted a chocolate bar. He turned his head to look at her—and there was her bear.'

Gillian laughed and then cried. Each member of the group had lit a new candle. There were more than a dozen burning now in glass holders among the flowers. She forgot to be watchful.

Other people spoke. Honeycutt said a few words about her scholarship; Frances and later Gillian both talked briefly about her presence in the department and at the university.

A young woman stood up. She was fair and delicate, very pretty. Gillian had seen her around the History Department. She had a vulnerable look that made Gillian want to enrol her in karate classes. Her voice was nearly inaudible.

'I just wanted to say this because Rita did something for me.' The room went silent in a new way, the audience caught by a different tone, a constricted tension in her voice. She halted, then took a big breath and began to speak very fast. 'There was a professor I had who was hassling me.' She stared fiercely at the floor, and her next words came out in a choked burst, as if one part of her was trying to stop the other from speaking. 'I mean sexual harassment. I didn't know what to do. I was too scared to tell anyone.'

She looked up then and said more easily, 'Rita found me crying in the ladies' room and I told her, because I was so upset. She said I should go see the Dean—I should, like, file a complaint. But I didn't want to. I just couldn't. So I was going to drop the course. She was angry at me, but then she said if I really couldn't, she'd go talk to him and tell him she knew. She thought that would make him stop. She was right. He left me alone.' She blinked rapidly. 'That's all I want to say.' She sat down, her face flushed.

Gillian was riveted. Who was she talking about? It was probably someone in the History Department. Rankin? What was her name? After a slightly shocked silence, while people were obviously wondering what to do or say, someone else stood up to speak, but Gillian paid no attention. If anyone in her department had harassed this woman, she was going to find out about it.

The gathering wound gently to a close. At the end, Denise and another woman played a duet on guitar and flute, and then the members of the Feminist Union gathered in a circle and blew out the candles. It was over.

Gillian made a beeline for the blonde head of the undergraduate.

'That was brave of you,' she said. The young woman was jumpy. She looked at Gillian and then away, and said, 'Rita told me not to be ashamed. And I'm not, not exactly, but it's weird. It's real hard to talk about. It would be easier if the guy was a stranger, you know? Then nobody would think it was your fault.'

'I'm Gillian Adams. What's your name?'

'Why?' She suddenly looked apprehensive.

'Well, we're all connected to Rita. And I've seen you around the History Department.'

'I know. I'm Nina Vargas.'

'Are you a history major?'

'No, minor. I'm majoring in economics.'

'If I may ask, were you being harassed by someone in the History Department?'

Nina shook her head quickly. 'I don't want to say.'

'Can you tell me when it happened?'

'No. I'm sorry, but it's nobody's business. I just wanted to thank Rita—to kind of make it up to her that I couldn't go to the Dean the way she wanted me to—that's why I said something. She gave me an article by a woman who was raped and wrote about it, using her real name, because she said hiding it made it seem as though the woman had something to be ashamed of. But I don't want the whole thing dragged up again. It's over.' She jerked her head away, like a skittish horse. 'I have to go.'

Gillian stepped back a little, giving her room to pass. Jacobsen was standing a few feet from them, eavesdropping intently. As she looked up, he backed hastily and fumbled with the buttons of his coat. Gillian opened her mouth to apologize to Nina, but she was already hurrying towards the door. Paul Smith was waiting there and followed her out.

CHAPTER 24

In the parking lot outside the church, a small crowd was milling about. Gillian could see a television camera and microphones. She joined the group and asked one of the spectators what was happening. The police, she learned, had arrested a man who'd threatened someone outside the church.

'He ran through my neighbour's back yard,' the woman said, pointing up the road. 'But the dog squad got him.'

John Gordon, Gillian thought. Did that mean the police already knew he was the killer?

On Monday Gillian found time to go to the administration building and look at Nina Vargas's student record. She was in her fourth year now and would graduate in the spring. She was taking eighteen units—an honours load—and was doing well. She'd taken a number of history courses: one in her first year, one in her second, two in her third year, and now two more. Gillian noted them down. It would be a simple matter to crosscheck the department records. But Gillian knew who several of the professors would be already. Right now, Nina was in one of Rankin's classes.

When Gillian checked, she found that Nina had been in one of her own classes—not a seminar, but one of the big lecture courses that Gillian shared responsibility for. She had also taken courses from Jim Jacobsen, Verne Palmer and Ham Ridgeway, and a sophomore-level course from Rankin. Which of them was it? Jane and Allie remembered nothing helpful. Could it have been Jacobsen? She hadn't been watching him while Nina was telling her story, but he'd been determined to hear what she said to Gillian afterwards.

Frances said, 'There's nothing we can do unless she's willing to confront him. Even then, we can't promise any redress, or even protect her from retaliation. No doubt that's why she doesn't want to risk it.'

'Can't we do anything about professors abusing their power over students? We have a harassment policy.'

'We don't know what happened. But suppose we did. We have a policy, yes, but the university's willingness to act on it hasn't been clearly demonstrated. There are no mandatory penalties attached. The real problem, though, is that the policy requires the victims to negotiate face to face with the accused—who are usually much more powerful than they are. The grad students are especially vulnerable. How does a woman "negotiate" if she's being groped by a man who's on her thesis committee, or who determines whether or not she gets funding for research?'

Gillian had much else to do, and she set the problem aside for the moment. She had two papers to referee, and final corrections to make to her own paper on Disraeli before it could be published as part of the proceedings of the conference in London. She went about her business at the office for the next few days, but she found herself scrutinizing the colleagues on her list, looking for some sign. A sign of what? she asked herself irritably. Nerves—or did she think she was going to catch one of them suddenly looking like the picture of Dorian Gray?

She heard nothing from the police for a day or two. Then she had a call from Frank Bacon. She was at home, soaking in the bathtub before frying a trout for dinner and settling down to a couple of hours of reading and taking notes for her fourth-year class. She leapt out of the tub and stood shivering in the hall, clutching a towel, with cold little rivulets running down her neck from the ends of her hair.

'I've had a chat with your boyfriend,' he said cheerily.

Boyfriend! Of all the stupid words. She hadn't had a boyfriend since college.

'I thought I might drop by later this evening, if you'll be at home.'

'I'll be here. I should be finished working by nine,' she answered, wanting him to know that academics also worked long hours, just in case he was one of those who thought that all they did was teach a few hours a week.

He arrived at nine-ten. Gillian had already poured herself a Scotch, an expensive single malt she had bought the day before the memorial service.

'A drink?' she inquired.

'That would be very nice. It's been a long day.'

She poured him one, neat, without asking if he'd like ice. He swallowed some absent-mindedly, started to speak, and then stopped in surprise. He looked around for the bottle.

'This is good. What is it?'

She handed it to him.

'The Macallan,' he read. 'I had a friend who knew a lot about whisky. Harvey Bates, VSOP, we used to call him.'

'What happened to him?'

'Liver cancer. He was gone in six months.'

Gillian had lit a fire a few minutes earlier, and now she set a couple of larger logs over the blazing kindling. The light leapt and flickered over the rows of books. Behind the sofa, where Frank Bacon sat sipping his whisky, the curtains were pulled against the dark, wet evening. It was the very end of November, and the nights had lengthened until they almost seemed to swallow the days. Bacon was silent while she tended the fire.

'I take it this is not a social call,' she said when she sat down again.

'Strictly business,' he answered, but his manner wasn't as impersonal as it had been at the police station.

What did that mean? Was it merely the effect of domestic surroundings?

Bacon lowered his head and looked at her from under his brows, much as he had in the police station. But now the look wasn't threatening, or possibly her expectations and therefore her interpretations were different. 'Your Detective Chief Inspector Gisborne. He's been very helpful. We got the family checked out in record time.'

Ah, she thought. He's just curious about me because of Edward.

'But I want to go over your visit to Mary Mayhew. Everything she told you about the family. We've got John Gordon—you know that? He's being charged with the B&E at Rita's place. It'll be in tomorrow's paper. He had a medallion on him like the one she lost.'

'How did you guess?'

'Didn't. Gordon wasn't sensible. He ran when we wanted to talk to him.'

'Do you think he killed her?'

'I couldn't say one way or the other—not yet. He wasn't behaving rationally when he came out of the church. Said the memorial ceremony was insulting to his family. There was a fellow from the church—keeping an eye on things, I guess—unlucky enough to be standing at the bottom of the steps when he came out. Gordon called him a few things I won't repeat, and ranted about putting a stop to the service. He was grabbing the fellow's coat when my man Woods intervened. He identified himself as a police officer, and bam—Gordon was off. Ran like a rabbit.'

'But you got him.'

'Sure we got him. Where was he going to go? He went crashing through a few suburban back yards, that's all.'

'So why did he run?'

Bacon shrugged. 'Panic.'

Gillian drank her whisky and waited.

'Afraid of being put away again. That's what he said after we told him all about himself.'

'Do you believe him?'

'Why not? Nobody likes to be locked up.'

Gillian reached for his empty glass.

'Thanks.'

He waited until she gave it back before he spoke again.

'He claims he didn't know Rita's death wasn't an accident until we told him.'

'Really?'

'It's possible. You can walk down the street any day and find somebody who doesn't know who's Prime Minister.'

'So he doesn't read the newspapers. But he knew about the service.'

'Right. He got that off a bulletin board at UPNW.'

'How did he find Rita, anyway?' Gillian could hear rain gurgling in the downspouts. It was pouring outside.

'He says his sister Ruth told him. She says she didn't—that he must have found out some other way. But she admits he visited her a couple of months ago. We've got nothing to connect him to Rita's death, so we can't hold him long.'

He looked at Gillian's troubled expression. 'You see why I want to go over the ground again.'

⟞⚷⟝

It was after ten when Bacon left, but Gillian could not sit at home. Her mind was racing in circles. What to do? She thought of calling Edward, but he might not be home, and a telephone conversation wasn't what she really wanted. At any time in the past fifteen years, at any time like this, except in the past few weeks, she had called Laura. Now she hesitated. Was it too late in the evening? A craven excuse; Laura was a night owl. She was afraid they would have one of those stiff conversations they had had since their fight, the ones that left her feeling bereft. But she'd been at least as stiff as Laura, so…What about their argument? Fundamentally, they agreed. It was tactics they had quarrelled about: not enough to wither a friendship. What hurt was that Laura hadn't respected her reasons. But she had hurt Laura in the same way. And she had withdrawn: all this turmoil about Rita, and she hadn't been talking to Laura. Laura must be acutely aware of that. To her, it would be as if Gillian had been carrying a sign saying KEEP OUT. It was up to Gillian to make an overture now. They would find a way to talk about their differences. They had to. Avoiding it, as she'd been doing, afraid of widening the breach, was only keeping them apart. It was no good letting things drift. She dialled Laura's number.

'Are you busy?'

'No, just reading. Is something wrong?'

'I'm fine. Don't worry. I've just had a visit from the police and I can't sit still. I've missed talking to you.'

'Why don't you come over?' Laura said.

'Are you sure? It's late. We could meet tomorrow.'

'Of course, you idiot. Come right now. I've been horribly depressed ever since we squabbled. I'm longing to see you.' Laura laughed, the tension flooding away. 'Besides, I'll die of curiosity if I have to wait till tomorrow.'

Gillian drove the dozen blocks to Laura's house automatically. A light rain was falling now. The car pulled into the driveway like a horse recognizing a familiar stable. The carriage lamps were on, and Gillian walked quickly through the light-spangled drizzle towards the front door, but before she reached the bottom step the door opened and Laura, in a green quilted dressing-gown and fuzzy slippers, flew out. Her eyes were bright.

'Oh my dear,' Gillian said.

A minute or two later Jack came into the hall. 'I thought I felt a draught,' he said drily, holding the door. Laura and Gillian let go of each other. Gillian's hair was clinging to her forehead.

'Christ, I'm wet,' she laughed.

'I've made tea,' Laura announced. 'Now, tell.'

Gillian told them everything that had happened during the past week, starting with her visit to President Bingham and finishing with Bacon's visit to her. Since they continually asked questions and went back to earlier parts of the story, it took a long time.

'What's Bacon like?' Laura asked.

'An old hand,' Gillian said. 'Smart. He's been a cop for twenty years, I guess, so he has that leathery toughness they get, but he doesn't strike me as dehumanized. He looked at me once or twice in a way I thought was a bit personal, and I thought for a second he was giving me the eye, but he's just nosey about Inspector Edward's squeeze.'

Laura rolled her eyes up. 'You haven't gone and seduced another cop, have you, Gillian? This is getting to be a bad habit.'

'It would be, wouldn't it? You'd start wondering if I had a leather holster fetish or something.'

'Do you like him?'

'I don't know a thing about him. Laura, calm down. When I met Edward, I was panting with lust as soon as I set eyes on him. I breathe perfectly normally around Frank Bacon.' Gillian's eyes danced. 'He's not my type—even if he is a cop.'

'There's a terrific guy in my office,' Jack chose that moment to inform her. 'Got divorced last year, so he's probably ready to meet someone new.'

'What is this? Byng and Blaine, Matchmakers, Inc.? Let's leave sex out of it and get back to crime.' She caught a furtive, guilty glance passing between them. She groaned.

'You can have me to dinner with him sometime, just so you can say you tried,' she said, 'but not till this is over.'

Jack grinned. 'I think I'd better go to bed. I'll leave you two to have a nightcap. Now, the gist is, the police have Rita's brother; he's a looneytune and probably guilty, but that doesn't solve your problems on campus. Right?'

'Right.'

'So you're still at square one with the harassment?'

'If the police think John Gordon did it, I doubt they'll be very interested in some piddling little boys scaring women students.'

'And what *do* they think?'

'Bacon didn't say, of course.'

'Of course.' Jack put his arm around her in a brief hug. 'Sorry if I put my foot in it.'

'That's all right. It's a very nice foot.'

'Not when he comes to bed late,' said Laura. 'Then it's a damned cold foot.'

'Tonight you'll be the late one for a change,' Jack replied. 'Good night, you two. I'm going to light the blue paper.'

Gillian chuckled. It was what Jack always said on the occasions when he went to bed first, leaving them to talk until all hours. Everything really was all right.

'You don't still think that's funny, do you?' asked Laura. 'You're as bad as Jack.'

The first time Gillian had heard him say it, she'd been mystified.

'His father always said it when *he* went to bed,' Laura had explained. 'In England, the instructions for fireworks always say "light the blue paper and retire immediately". Get it? His father thought it was funny for fifty years.'

Now Gillian thought: what would Edward say every night if there were someone to say it to? If they lived together, would she find herself re-enacting long-forgotten parental rituals? She would never know. Edward didn't want to know—he shunned domesticity. She wasn't sure whether or not she wanted to hear Edward's version of lighting the blue paper. Sometimes, solitude was a luxury.

Laura opened a cupboard and pulled out a bottle of single malt. 'Somebody gave us this. I've been waiting for you to try it with me.'

'While you're pouring, do tell me why couples want to pair off everyone else.'

Laura glanced quickly at her, and, reassured that she wasn't offended, grew merry.

'Let me remind you of Austen's dictum: "It is a truth universally acknowledged, that a single man in possession of a good fortune—"'

'"—must be in want of a wife",' Gillian finished up with her. 'But if the woman isn't in want of a husband, what then?'

'We're just doing our bit for society. The couple is the fundamental economic unit of the state.'

'I think I qualify as a unit all by myself,' said Gillian, entering into the spirit of this, happy that they felt safe enough for playful argument again. 'I have a job, I own a house, I pay taxes. I even employ people—to mow my lawn and fix my car. If I had a husband, he might do those things, and the economy would shrink.'

'Hah! You pay taxes, but you don't procreate,' Laura said, pointing her finger in the general direction of Gillian's belly and passing her a glass. 'No children, no future.'

'Well I'm not going to start procreating now, even if you do marry me off.'

'It was Jack's fault, anyway,' said Laura. 'I said his partner was a dish, and he said then let's introduce him to Gillian.'

'I see. Jack's afraid you're going to run away with his partner and ruin his law firm.'

'That must be it. Have some more of this. It's good.'

Sometime after that, Gillian gathered her courage and said, 'We have to talk about our quarrel—straighten things out.'

'I know we do. But do we have to dissect our souls tonight? It's late, and I think I've had too much to drink.'

'You're right. We need the sober light of day. But I want to make one apology now. When we disagree, I may think you're dead wrong, but I shouldn't cast aspersions on your motives. I'm sorry I did.'

Laura pushed a stray lock of blonde hair back from her face and looked up, meeting Gillian's eyes. 'People do have honest differences of opinion, but in the heat of political argument even friends forget that.' She smiled, and added lightly, 'Even us feminists. As somebody said, "There's a lot of human nature in women."' Then she was serious again. 'I wasn't very respectful either. I'll accept your apology if you'll accept mine.'

Gillian sighed with relief. They'd found their footing. 'You know what? I thought I'd never be able to drink that bottle of champagne, but I've changed my mind.'

'Good. I'll come over to your house, we'll save the world, and then we'll pop the cork.'

Chapter 25

It was nearly three when Gillian got home, and she dragged her way through the next day. None the less, she arranged to meet Libby at five-thirty at the student union bar. The noise level there was such that one need have no fear of being overheard.

Libby looked better than she had before the memorial service, not so wan and pinched. She unwound a blue and white scarf from her neck and accepted a beer.

'I'm mourning,' she said, when Gillian asked how she was. 'But I'm not in shock any more. The memorial helped—all those people remembering Rita together. That was beautiful. But I'm totally weirded out by this thing with her brother. Did he kill her?'

'If he did,' Gillian replied, 'the police will find out. He's too much of a mess to commit the perfect crime.'

'It's so weird,' Libby said. 'Here I've been thinking the whole time about those guys at UPNW, and it turns out this sicko brother could be the one. I hope they put him away forever.'

'Didn't Rita say anything to you about seeing him here?'

'Yeah. The police asked me that too. I would have told you when you came over that time, but she'd said she didn't want anyone to know about him. And of course then I didn't put him together with what happened to her. One night she came over and told me a whole lot about when she was a kid—stuff I'd never heard before. She usually didn't like to talk about it. I knew about her father, but she hadn't told me what her brother did before they put him away.'

'I think I know,' Gillian said quietly. 'You mean about the abortion and the knife attack?'

'How do you know?' Libby was startled.

'Mary Mayhew told me.'

'Oh, yeah, right, Rita said she knew. So what happened was, he showed up on her doorstep one night—like with no warning. There he was.'

'What did he want?'

'He said he wanted to talk to her. She told him there was nothing to discuss—that he should stay out of her life forever. She didn't let him in. She told me he'd gone back to England after he tried one more time. She was real nervous until he left.'

'I see. You mean she didn't say anything about this until she thought he'd gone.'

'No, the dummy,' Libby said bitterly. 'She thought I'd worry—hover over her or something. She couldn't stand that.'

'Why did she think he'd left?'

'I guess he said he was going. The second time he came and she wouldn't talk to him, he just said he was sorry he'd bothered her and told her he'd leave.'

'But he didn't go back. He's been here the whole time.'

'It's really freaky—what was he doing?'

'Finding out about her life. I don't know. Finding out what she wouldn't tell him.'

Libby shuddered. 'Spying? You think that's why he broke into her apartment?'

'Maybe. Or he may have been angry at her for refusing to reconcile. He must have wanted something from her very badly to have come this far without any guarantee of seeing her.'

Libby frowned. 'He was looking for closure, I think. That's why he came to the memorial.'

'But it just opened up the old wounds again.'

'I don't care,' Libby said defensively. 'That kind of family violence is devastating. It was in Rita's life, and it shouldn't be hidden—that lets it keep happening.'

'I wasn't attacking you,' Gillian said mildly. 'Listen, there's something else I want to talk to you about.'

'What?'

'The Carver. I'm still trying to figure it out.'

'But I don't know anything about that.'

'Did Rita ever mention anything about delivering a letter to the Dean's office? Or maybe an envelope?'

'Nope. Do you mean the thing that's supposed to be in her file?'

'Yes. Nobody in the Feminist Union wrote one to the committee, so far as you know?'

'Of course not. What would we do that for? It could only've screwed her up.'

'What about the forms for the grant? Did she ever say anything about them? About taking them to the office?'

Libby thought. 'Well, she talked a bit about what a pain the application was, and all the recommendations and bits of paper she had to have signed. She did say there was some form she had to get from a prof, and he kept forgetting to fill it out so she had to ask him three times. She only got it at the last minute.'

'Who? Which professor?'

'A guy she didn't like. Ridgeway.' Libby stared at her. 'Why? Do you think he gave her the letter?' Her brown seal eyes grew rounder than usual. 'Wait a minute. Wow! I think she told me he gave her the form so it wouldn't be late. He was leaving early and it was too late for the campus mail. Yeah, I'm sure she said that. He signed a bunch of stuff at the last minute, for her and Paul, and she took it to Stanley's office. She didn't say anything about envelopes, but the candidates aren't allowed to see the forms, so—'

'Ridgeway!' Gillian sat bolt upright. 'But why?'

Libby frowned, puzzled, and then shrugged. 'I don't give a shit about the Carver, anyway. I mean not right now. I just want to know who screwed around with Rita's motorcycle.'

'I feel the same way,' Gillian said. 'But the police are dealing with that. It's their bailiwick. Investigating the Carver problem makes me feel as if I'm doing something.'

'Hey,' Libby said as they were putting on their coats. 'Who was that at the memorial who said Rita helped her out when a prof was hassling her? I've seen her around the department, haven't I?'

'Yes. Nina Vargas. She's a fourth-year student. Minor in history. Did Rita ever say anything about her?'

'She never told me her name. Last spring she said she knew an undergraduate who was having trouble with one of the history profs, but she'd made Rita promise not to tell anyone. She didn't want everyone talking about it. Rita was furious about the whole thing, but she said you couldn't force a decision like that on a woman. In the Union we talked about asking all the women in the department if they'd ever had any trouble—we had the idea that we might find a few who'd be willing to bring charges together. Like a class action. But we didn't actually know anyone else in history who'd said they had a special problem—just a lot of women who were pissed off by Rankin's sexist comments. And Marnie knew a couple of grad students in English who had, so we decided to start there. It was going to be a pilot project that we could duplicate in other departments if it worked. We were planning to talk to Frances Romano about it after the Rayne thing was finished. But Rita told the history prof that if what's-her-name—Nina— had any more trouble, we'd be after him...I have a feeling Nina's going out with Paul Smith—I've seen them in the bar a couple of times.'

They stood for a couple of minutes under the projecting roof of the building. A wind was blowing; it was a warm wind from the south, but the rain was coming at them in wild sideways gusts.

'Where's your car?' Gillian asked.

'Over by the gym.'

'I'll walk with you.'

'You don't have to—'

'It's no trouble. The gym's all the way at the other end of the lot, and they haven't put the new lights in. I'd ask you, if it were my car.'

As they plunged into the wet darkness, Libby said, 'Some of those engineers are really gynophobic. I'm still getting phone calls. They say horrible, graphic things. I gave the tape to the police, and they're checking it out.'

They splashed through the lot towards the car.

'Do you think Rita's brother's a real psycho?' Libby asked.

'I wish I knew.'

⟝⊶⟞

Gillian was baffled by John Gordon. It seemed to her that he wouldn't have stayed around if he'd killed Rita. He would have gone right back to England. He would have had his 'closure', as

Libby put it, and been anxious to get the hell out of the country. An accident was different. That would have been an awful blow, if he'd still had hopes of getting through to his sister. Maybe he was hanging around to find out more about what had happened to her. What could you say about probabilities if he was crazy? And did he know anything about motorcycles? That was a point. Whoever did it knew a lot. But the police would be covering that angle.

She ate a light dinner at the faculty club and put in an appearance at a sherry party for a visiting lecturer. Then she remembered a book she had wanted to bring home with her and went back to the office for it. While she was there, she took out the list she'd made of Nina Vargas's courses. Last spring, she'd been in Carole Stein's seminar and Ridgeway's third-year course on the rise of the modern state.

So. It was Ridgeway. Rita had told Ham Ridgeway she knew he was harassing Nina. Gillian thought about Ridgeway's bilious humour and thin, almost concave torso, and marvelled. She would have put her finger on Rankin and his overt sexism (and sexuality), or even Jim Jacobsen, whose thickset body and bullying disposition fitted her image of a man who would harass a vulnerable student.

Rita had told Ridgeway the Feminist Union would be after him if there were more trouble. Maybe she'd even mentioned their pilot project. There might be more skeletons in his cupboard. In any event, he'd had a very good reason to want Rita off campus— not sitting as an equal at department meetings for the next two years. A much stronger reason than dislike of her politics or 'turbulent' personality, as he'd called it. So he'd written a letter to spoil her chances, knowing full well, as a member of the Carver committee, how that committee would deal with it. He would also have known Cynthia's routine, known that there was virtually no chance the letter would be opened in front of Rita and that Cynthia would remember where it came from. And he'd had the opportunity. Libby had told her that.

But what could Stanley do about it? At least she now was certain she knew what had happened. There was some satisfaction in that. But the administration would be reluctant to act. The circumstantial evidence she had was compelling, but it probably wasn't enough to force the issue. And what if Ridgeway denied everything? Rita was dead. She didn't want to badger Nina Vargas. For the moment, she couldn't think of anything useful to do except to tell Bacon. Maybe his lab would find Ridgeway's traces on the letter. Then the administration would have to face facts.

She wanted to call Birdie in Point Roberts, but she knew she should inform Bacon first. Dutifully, she dialled his office, but he was out. She left her name and the message that she had some additional information about the Carver Fellowship and went home.

As soon as she got there, Murray called.

'Hey. I've just been to the faculty club. Rumours are rife. What happened at the memorial service? Did a student say a professor had molested her?'

'Not exactly. Listen, Murray, this has to stay under your hat. There can't be any gossip about it right now.' She told him about Ridgeway, the phone cradled on her shoulder while she fixed herself a drink. Murray wasn't encouraging.

'If Nina goes to the sexual harassment committee, you may see some action there, but I don't see how you'll persuade the president's office to do anything about the Carver. If Ridgeway took them to court, and they lost, they'd have egg on their faces. They'll be scared to death he'll sue. And remember—he'll be around. In the department. You'll have to live with him.'

'Jesus, Murray, I know.'

She was depressed when they hung up.

For the next couple of hours she roamed restlessly about the house, unable to work or even read the paper, which was full of dire news about dioxin-contaminated shellfish near the pulp mills. She called Laura but resisted the impulse to analyse the Carver developments in detail, in case Bacon was trying to reach her: a useless piece of self-restraint, since he didn't call until the next morning.

But he was interested in her story.

'Woods told me about Nina's show at the memorial service. So you've figured out it had to be this Ham Ridgeway. Exactly what is sexual harassment on the campus?'

'Anything from making off-colour comments to rape—and everything in between such as touching, threatening if sex is withheld, or offering rewards for sexual favours.'

'And we don't know what he did.'

'No. Just that it was enough to bother Nina Vargas so much that she was going to drop an important course, and was afraid to speak out about it.'

'And could Rita have been blackmailing him?'

'Never. She wasn't that kind of person.'

'Hmm. Well, I don't see exactly where this leads us—if she couldn't bring charges without Nina's cooperation, he was safe enough.'

'Yes, but how much pleasanter life would be for him without Rita's critical eye upon him. He just didn't want her around, so he sabotaged her grant application. Could you examine that letter and find out whether he left any marks on it? I need some concrete proof.'

'We might take a look at it. But first I'm going to have a chat with Nina Vargas.' He paused, thinking, and Gillian could almost see the computer screen lighting up inside his head. 'OK. Thanks. I'll be in touch.'

CHAPTER 26

On the last day of November Gillian and Frances had dinner together.

'Call it a working dinner,' said Frances when she telephoned to invite her, 'because there are several things I want to discuss with you, but let's go somewhere offcampus. The faculty club walls have ears, and I can't hear myself think in the student union. I've been meaning to get to know you better for about five years, so how about now?'

'Sounds great.' Gillian laughed. 'When we're really good friends, can I borrow your clothes?'

Her hair, she'd noticed, needed cutting, and she made a point of seeing the hairdresser before dining out with Frances. She liked her hair when it was weightless, like smoke curling about her ears, not when it grew longer and heavier and fell forward over her temples. Going out with Frances was a little like being in Paris: you felt obliged to live up to a standard of elegance that you otherwise didn't bother with.

Frances had booked dinner at Umberto's. She sat back with a relaxed air as they waited for their drinks. She was wearing a beautiful silk sweater in teal blue, and jade earrings. I must ask her where she found that sweater, Gillian thought. 'It's still the best of all his restaurants,' Frances was saying. 'And his empire started here, so I thought it would be a good place to discuss the plans for ours.'

The waiter appeared with their dry sherries.

Frances picked up her glass. 'Women's studies.'

Gillian touched her glass to Frances's. 'Women's studies. Is there news?'

'Some. But first I have to tell you that I'm pretty sure I will *not* be resigning.'

'That's great news. But why? What's happening with the engineering students?'

'Well, nothing concrete yet, but I'm positive Frost won't be able to smooth it over. Remember Joe Wiegand in civil engineering? He was in the protest march and rushed into the building when we saw the posters?'

'Of course I do.'

'Joe found out who some of the students were who had put up those posters, and he told them that dean or no dean, he was going to give their names to the sexual harassment committee unless they came forward themselves. So they had a little pow-wow, and the whole bunch—including the ones he hadn't caught—admitted to being involved. There were about thirty of them, and I think they had the idea that their numbers would protect them. And that Frost would too, of course.'

'That's logical. They've never been punished for anything before, have they?'

'That's right. And I have to say I don't know whether they would even have had their wrists slapped this time, but now what's happened is that the police have gotten involved. They've been grilling the engineering students, checking into the things that were happening to Rita and the Feminist Union—in case there's a link to the murder.

'I don't know whether someone hoped to get off by identifying the ringleaders, or whether some of the guys were shocked because they thought they were just goofing around and then Rita got killed. Whatever, somebody panicked or had a guilty conscience, or was too naïve to stonewall the questions, because the police now know that they joked about killing her. And the police know about their dirty little tricks, too—who did what to whom and when.'

Another waiter arrived and handed them their menus. He recited the specials of the day, in which Frances took a maddening interest. Gillian couldn't remember a word he'd said afterwards.

'Go on!' she said to Frances as soon as he turned away.

'I can't give you the names of the core group, but there were four of them who organized a kind of vendetta against the Feminist Union. They made the plans, and a larger group carried them out. The big thing that included them all was the posters and mooning the protest marchers, of course. But they started in right after the Triumph Day protest was on television and they got all that flak in the media. That was when they began making obscene calls to Rita and the others, and the same gang of four were the flashers in the parking lot.'

'What about the witch I found hanging in the History Department?'

'Yes, that was part of it. And there was some graffiti in the women's room on your floor?'

'"Feminists Must Die." But that appeared *after* Rita's motorcycle crash, you know. Even if some of them were shocked, not all of them were.'

'I believe that particular item was a freelance job—not planned by the central committee. Whichever one of them did it must be nastier than most of them. I think *all* the students involved felt extremely hostile to the Feminist Union, partly for spoiling the Triumph Day parade—the terrible publicity and the push to cancel the slave wagon—and partly for, as they see it, hijacking the Rayne money. I think they were after revenge—and they also thought they might be able to make the Union back off. But I honestly don't think most of them would have physically harmed the women.'

'You never know what mobs will do, and they were acting like a mob—at least that day we saw them in the windows.'

'That's true. But planned, deliberate, single acts are different. I'm sure most of those students would never have sabotaged Rita's motorcycle.'

'The question is, would one of them?'

'The police will find out, I hope. We can't accuse all thirty of them of murder. What I know already is that because of the investigation, Frost won't be able to clothe these incidents in decent obscurity. The media will have a field day with all these shocking incidents happening to a woman who was then murdered. Bingham will have to take action against the ringleaders at the very least. The police may even lay charges.'

'I suppose they could charge some of the group with vandalism. There's my porch light, for instance, and Libby's bumper. And indecent exposure is in the criminal code.'

'I'm all for it, if it will only change the attitudes around here. That's the only thing that matters.'

The waiter returned for their order. Gillian chose some pasta almost at random. When he had gone, she picked up the conversation again.

'You know, I find it almost impossible to picture a group of them plotting to commit murder. It's much easier to imagine a lone assassin—a "madman", as our society likes to call them. But I don't even know any more whether I'm realistic or naïve. I believe most men aren't murderous brutes—I just have to look at all the times in my salad days when I put myself in situations that would have been lethal if they were. Or think of men like my father. But these days so much about male violence is being revealed—even the government passes out leaflets telling us that one in six women is abused by her partner. I'm told that gang rape is a normal event in fraternity life. The Montreal Massacre was almost a year ago, but I feel as if it's in the air I breathe. I don't know what to say.'

'We're all shocked at what's coming out. And yet the women who come to my office to talk about their problems with sexism say it's actually gotten worse since Montreal. And I hear the same thing from my counterparts on other campuses. I'll tell you what I think: Montreal ripped the lid off. Now—after the massacre— nobody can pretend that the problem doesn't exist—not the way they did before. Nobody can pretend that sexism and violence aren't linked—and lethal to women. Men can't hide from it either. They either have to accept change or brazen it out. The ones who don't want to think about change are becoming very aggressive.'

'What will the administration do about the guys that were harassing the Feminist Union? Will they be kicked out of school?'

Frances grimaced. 'That's too much to hope for at this university. What they've admitted to didn't *literally* harm anyone— that's the way the president's office will see it. To kick them out of school—that might do real damage to their careers, my dear. They'll probably be put on probation, and the ringleaders will be suspended.'

Frances brightened. 'I did hear a very interesting rumour recently; at one of our sister institutions the *Dean of Engineering* has been put on probation—until the engineers clean up their act! Now that's what I call a real response to the problem.' A gleam of anticipation lit her eye. 'I must find out whether it's true—I'd love to recommend it to Bingham.'

'What about women's studies?' Gillian asked later, after the wine and their antipasto had arrived.

Frances looked mischievous. 'My dear, I think it's going to be all right. Frost wobbled a little on his pedestal, you know, when Jessie Rayne didn't come through for him. And I think it has actually occurred to Bingham that he can't afford to drop a million just because Frost will have a tantrum. Jessie isn't budging. I mean the more they talked to her, the more adamant she was about not giving the money to anything but women's studies. She's in a royal rage at Frost and Co. In confidence, there's also some talk about another interested donor. Not anything like as much money, of course, but still...Bingham's got the idea that women's studies are "sexy"—and will attract new funds: he's caught on that women are making their own money these days, and they have money to give away. He's talking about a new mandate for advocacy of women's issues on campus. I think I can predict that they'll squeeze women's studies into the budget. It could be up and running by nineteen ninety-two.'

'Hooray!' Gillian cried.

'A cautious hooray. We're not home free until the President goes public and we have the money in our hands. That's one thing I've learned.'

'A cautious but heartfelt hooray, then,' said Gillian, lifting her glass.

Gillian and Frances shared a cab home. Gillian dug her keys from the bottom of her bag before they left the restaurant, so she wouldn't have to hunt for them in the dark.

'This has been a grand evening,' she said to Frances as they waited for the taxi. 'Why has it taken us so long?'

'We all work too much. The 'nineties are going to be the decade to slow down. I'm looking forward to the day when people don't talk about how busy they are any more. I plan to set an example.'

They reached Gillian's house first, and the cabbie pulled up at the bottom of the drive. Gillian slipped Frances some money and made certain she had her umbrella. 'Let's do this again soon,' she said to Frances before stepping out into the dripping air under the trees. She waved as the taxi slid away, and started towards the house. The porch light was on; she hadn't forgotten it once since she'd replaced the broken globe. She sniffed. The smell of winter was in the air; the longest night of the year was not far away. The hedge loomed, a high, smooth black shape. It had been trimmed while she was away in England and looked quite handsome now, she thought, in its plain way, although she enjoyed imagining the effect on the neighbourhood of some startling topiary—pigeons, maybe, or dinosaurs. People would drive by and stare. She heard a noise behind her. A footstep, she thought, not quickly enough. She half turned, and then felt a violent blow on the back of her head. She thought she saw a flare of light, and then she lost consciousness.

⬥

When she came to, she was lying on her back in her driveway, and Frances was bending over her.

'Thank God, she's coming around,' Frances said to somebody. A blinding light flashed on and off. She couldn't speak, but her eyes must have blinked. 'That's the ambulance,' Frances said to her.

For the next short while, Gillian was intermittently aware of chaotic activity. She was in an ambulance, and Frances was there. She was in the hospital. She was asleep, or wasn't. She was making a noise. Her head hurt. Men and women loomed over her and mumbled and went away again.

When she at last began to put the pieces together, she discovered that she was in a hospital bed with a painful swelling on the back of her head. Frances was still there, or there again.

'What happened?' she asked feebly.

'Somebody hit you on the head,' Frances said.

'I can figure that out,' Gillian said, with a touch of asperity. Her head hurt dreadfully, but her brain was working again.

'Well, I can't tell you a lot more. I hoped you'd tell me. When we got there, you were lying in the driveway with a man standing over you. He hurtled into the bushes and I never saw who he was.'

'I didn't either. I heard a footstep, and then bam!'

'Maybe we could have chased him, but we had to take care of you.'

'Who's we?'

'Oh. The cab-driver and me. We came right back because you'd left your keys in the taxi.'

Gillian remained in the hospital for observation until Sunday afternoon. She had suffered a concussion, but her skull was intact; the first, glancing blow had not cracked it. Frances—and her own forgetfulness—had saved her from a second. Bacon stopped in to see her on Saturday.

'How are you?' he asked, looking concerned.

'Oh, I'm just dandy,' Gillian replied. 'I'm the first person on earth whose life has been saved by Alzheimer's.'

He chuckled. 'Yeah, it's a hell of a lucky thing you left your keys behind. Your friend Frances and the taxi-driver got there just in time. They called us right away, and we had a car there pronto, but I'm afraid your assailant still had time to escape. He probably had a car parked close by. Did you see anything at all?'

Gillian shook her head and then winced.

'Any idea who it was?'

'What about the guy who put that graffiti in the women's room?' she asked. 'Feminists Must Die.'

'Him? He's a weaselly little guy. Your pals say the guy they saw was tall. But we're not through with the engineering students yet.'

'What did he hit me with?'

'A classic blunt instrument. A sock full of sand.'

'You found it?'

'It was under the hedge, a few feet from where you were lying.'

'I wonder if it was the same creep who tripped me up with that pumpkin.'

'Oh yes, your Hallowe'en vandalism. It's possible. I don't have any information on that at this point. It still might be nothing more than a neighbourhood prank. But we'll check it out,' he added soothingly. 'And the car. Someone might have noticed it. People in your neighbourhood don't park on the street.'

'May I ask you something?'

'Ask away.'

'What about Rita's brother?'

'We've still got nothing to link him to the motorcycle.' Bacon shifted in his chair. 'If we can't find anything, we'll send him back to the UK.'

'You won't go to court because he stole that medallion?'

'I don't think so. There's not much point. He's not really a thief, is he? If he's anything, he's a nut. And if he's a nut, he's a British nut. We've got troubles of our own. Let them cope with him.'

Laura drove Gillian home from the hospital and helped her pack a bag. They had agreed that Gillian would stay with Laura and Jack for a few days, and that Laura would drive Gillian to campus and back. Laura had suggested it, and Gillian had accepted with gratitude. She needed not to be alone, and she wasn't sure she ought to drive. Suppose she blacked out? Or suppose her car was tampered with?

'Whoever it is, if he's the same one who killed Rita, he's getting more desperate—he's taking much greater chances now,' she'd said to Bacon, and he hadn't disagreed.

While she was choosing clothes in a slow, indecisive sort of way, and Laura was folding and packing the suitcases, the telephone rang. It was Rita's sister, Ruth.

'Oh!' Ruth said, sounding surprised. 'You're there at last. I've been trying to ring you for days.'

'I've been in the hospital,' Gillian said, sitting down on the bed and trying to collect her wits. 'It's Rita's sister,' she mouthed at Laura, who stood arrested, a dressing-gown in her arms, and listened to Gillian's end of the conversation.

'Somebody attacked me in my own driveway,' she explained to Ruth.

'Christ! Are you all right?'

'I think so.'

'Who was it?'

'We don't know yet.'

'Well, look, the reason I'm ringing, the police have been here and asked me a lot of questions about John. My brother—and Rita's, you know? They told me he was over there in Canada when she was killed. They wanted to know did I give him her address. The fact is, I bloody didn't. But I don't think he killed her either. They said he broke into her flat and made a scene at the church and then ran away from the police. I don't know what they're on about, and I've been in a blue funk, wondering what's going on, so I finally thought I'd just ring up and ask you if you know what it's all about. Did you see him at the memorial service?'

'Yes. He didn't like what Libby said about Rita's family life.'

'Shit! Did she mention what happened between him and Rita? Do you know what I mean?'

'Yes. No, she didn't. She was talking about your father. But you'll see for yourself. She had the whole thing videotaped for you.'

'She must be daft.'

'She didn't know your brother was going to make a scene, did she? I believe she thought you'd like a record of the occasion—since you couldn't be there. A lot of people came and said wonderful things about your sister.'

'Oh, right. I see.'

'So you didn't know your brother was here?'

'No. He came to see me—I think he must have copied her address out of my book while he was here. But he never mentioned going. I know it sounds bad, but look, he's just a pathetic little worm, really. I used to hate him for what he did to Rita, but I couldn't keep on. He changed after he was in the home, I don't know if it was the drugs, or what, but he just fell to pieces. They let him out after a while, and he went home, and didn't do anything. Sort of lay about like an unmade bed. Then Dad would shout at him, and he'd curl up in a corner and stop eating. He was in and out of that hospital three or four times. But he's not been bad for the last couple of years. Got a job and all. He came to see me twice, he even talked about what happened back then—it's nearly ten years ago now. He said he was sorry.'

'Why did he come over here, then?'

'Because he wanted to say he was sorry to Rita. To beg her to forgive him, I'm sure of that. He's still religious, he goes to church and prays. If he went to see Rita, it was because he thought God wanted him to.'

'Then why didn't he ask you for her address? Why filch it without telling you?'

'One time, maybe a year ago, he said he wanted to write to her, but I told him not to. He knew I'd try to stop him going. Rita didn't ever want to see him again, she told me that. He asked me once if she was ever coming back, and I said no, she didn't want anything to do with the family, she'd been hurt too much. I think he thought he could change that by going to see her. He could heal her, maybe. But of course it was himself he was trying to heal…What's going to happen to him?'

'The police will put him on a plane home—if he didn't have anything to do with her death.'

'I'm sure he didn't. Anyhow, if the same person attacked you, it can't be him. He doesn't even know you.'

'That's true.'

Gillian promised to call Ruth as soon as she knew anything more about the police investigations and gave her Laura's number. Her head was throbbing.

'I need to take some painkillers and go to bed,' she told Laura, and they bundled a few more garments into her suitcase and locked up the house.

⋯

Gillian hadn't spoken to Edward while she was in the hospital; she'd remembered that he would be away that weekend, some conference or other. Even the police had succumbed to the bureaucratic ailment of their time and were dragged off to meetings and conferences at dull hotels where they ate beef and two veg and listened to speeches. It was Monday in London now, but she was too tired to stay up late, and her emotions were swooping about alarmingly; she thought she might start crying if she heard his voice, and be unable to stop. She would call him tomorrow afternoon.

In the morning she was feeling better, and Laura drove her to the campus. She looked all right, she decided, peering into the mirror before they left. A little wan, and her eyes were bloodshot, as if she'd been drunk all weekend, but she would pass. She wore dark glasses in the car; the light hurt her eyes although it was a cloudy day. Laura was to call her at noon to see whether she wanted to return to the house. Frances had already telephoned Libby to let her know what had happened and to tell her to warn the rest of the Feminist Union to avoid going anywhere alone at night.

Jane and Allie were both in the office. She told them what had happened. 'But please don't spread it around the department this morning,' she added. 'I don't want to be asked about it every five minutes. I'm leaving early, so you can tell them this afternoon.' Jane and Allie fussed over her and urged her to go home and rest. In fact, she was soon tired, and she decided to call Laura rather than wait until noon.

Laura said she would pick her up in about half an hour. While Gillian was waiting and fiddling rather aimlessly with her computer, Carole Stein tapped at the door, came in and shut it.

'I have a class,' she said hurriedly, 'but I thought I'd better tell you in case you hadn't heard yet. Jim Jacobsen's spreading a story that Ridgeway molested that student at Rita's memorial service.'

'How does he know?' Gillian asked, startled.

'He says Paul told him. What if it's true, Gillian? What can we do about it?'

'Not a thing—unless she goes to the harassment committee. And I don't know how much they can do—the policy's a bit toothless. If he denies it, then what?'

'Witnesses?'

'He's not that stupid.'

Carole left for her class. Gillian thought. Jacobsen had listened in on her chat with Nina after the service. Paul and Nina had been seen together. And Jim was Paul's adviser. He could have looked up the same information she had and questioned Paul. But if Nina hadn't wanted anyone to know, why had Paul told him? Jim's motivations were crystal clear, at least. Ham Ridgeway would never be department head if Jim could help it.

Laura gave Gillian a ride back to the house shortly after eleven. Gillian promised to take a long nap, but first she called Edward. It was evening in London, but he wasn't home. She left a message on the tape with Laura's number. An hour later, after she had dozed off under a fluffy quilt in the guest bedroom, he called back.

'Not much use to you, am I?' he said when she told him what had happened. 'I can't go home with you at night, I can't even make you a cup of bloody tea.'

'I know, but that's the way it is.'

'Do you want me to fly over?' he demanded.

'Of course I want to see you, but if what you mean is will I feel neglected if you don't, no, I won't. I'm all right. And I don't think this man will try again—he'll have precious little chance as long as I'm staying with Laura and Jack. Darling, I'm touched that you'd think of coming over.'

'It's ridiculous to live like this,' Edward said angrily. 'Why don't you come to London? We'll get married.'

'Edward, don't. You're making me cry, and my head hurts. You don't really want to be married, you're just suffering because you can't protect me. Even if I married you,' she said with a shaky laugh, 'I could still be hit by a bus.'

'I'm sorry I upset you,' Edward answered after a moment. 'You're right about the protective instincts, they're flailing wildly in all directions. But I'm not so certain that I don't want to be married. I think it's you who doesn't. We'll talk about it in the spring. At least you could think about a job in London.' He grew brisk. 'Now, tell me the rest. I want to know what you've found out.'

She sketched the story since she'd been to see Birdie.

'I think John Gordon's off Bacon's list,' she wound up, 'or he wouldn't be squeezing the engineering students so hard. And I think it must be one of them, because Rita's brother wouldn't have gone after me.'

'What about the history student—Nina, was it? Has Bacon questioned her?'

'I suspect so. He must have followed up on the story she told at the service. Maybe that's why Paul felt free to pass the information to Jim Jacobsen, who's his adviser and Ridgeway's enemy. And it might be useful. Something's got to be done about Ridgeway.'

'And you're assuming that the same person who killed Rita tried to do you in?'

'Yes, of course. Isn't it logical? I can't believe the two events are disconnected. But I suppose it doesn't have to be the same person if there are several engineers in the plot. But I find that just as hard to believe. It had to be the same guy.'

'And why do you think some engineering student would do that? Would kill Rita, and later would find out where you live and watch you and try to kill you too?'

'A grudge against the Feminist Union. They hate us. I've explained all that. He's got to be nuttier than the rest of them, but the police *know* they made jokes about killing Rita.'

'All right, it's possible—if your villain knows something about motorcycles.'

'Any engineer would, wouldn't he?'

'I think it would be fairer to say that any engineer would be able to find out. But they don't all "know" how to sabotage a motorcycle the way they all know the calculus.'

'OK. So?'

'I don't have the answer. I just have a sense that something is missing from your thinking. Why were you singled out for attack? Why not Libby, for example? Who else besides the ruffians in the Engineering Department might think the Feminist Union was a threat? Is the Union really the target, or the Rayne delegation, or do you and Rita have a separate significance? These may be important questions. The attempts to terrorize the Union have given you every reason to be suspicious, but don't forget to look at the problem from all angles.'

After she and Edward hung up, Gillian sat on the bed, huddled under the quilt. Edward knew the facts about the engineers, or most of them, but he wasn't living here in this poisonous atmosphere. Was she overlooking something important? Rita had been the most conspicuous member of the Union. But why was she, Gillian, next on the list? Was there a reason? If the Rayne delegation were the targets, then Libby or Frances or Marnie would be next. She had no access to the mad logic of the progression. All right. Suppose the targets were only Rita and herself. Then what? Or rather, then who?

Rita's brother certainly didn't fit. Dean Frost and his myrmidons didn't either. The Carver Fellowship was the other possibility. But why? Not to prevent Rita from obtaining it. To remove her from the department? But then why Gillian? To eliminate women from the department? Should she warn Carole? No, that was ridiculous. Talk about paranoia! The attack must have addled her brain. Back to the Carver. The only motive that made sense was the need to conceal the forgery of the letter.

That meant Ham Ridgeway. Could she make him fit? She leaned back against the pillows and stared up at the ceiling.

She'd assumed that all he'd done was dupe Rita with that letter, to ensure she left the campus. That he'd simply wanted her at a safe distance. What she hadn't considered was that once the judgement of the Carver committee came under serious scrutiny, Ridgeway—having written that letter with the simple intention of driving Rita away—was exposed to a new and much greater risk. The consequences of sexual harassment wouldn't amount to much, if Rita had persuaded Nina to complain. He'd lose his chance to become department head. He'd be humiliated. But he wouldn't lose his job. Not unless Nina took him to court and won. Even then, if the charge was anything less than outright rape, the university would be unlikely to fire him. But what if he were found to have falsified Rita's letter? That would be another story. Molesting a student might be regarded as a peccadillo; it would be beyond the pale to tamper with the Carver Fellowship. If that could be proved, he'd be done for.

But why would he have feared exposure so much? The committee didn't bow to outside pressure. They wouldn't reopen the file. That was the point. Yes, that made his original risk very small. But later there was a distinct possibility. He couldn't have foreseen that. He didn't know there would be a row over the Rayne money, and protest marches and headlines in the newspapers.

Gillian sat up.

And there I was, she thought, pushing as hard as I could, with all this unexpected hullabaloo attracting more and more attention to Rita and the mysterious Carver decision. It must have looked to him as if the letter were about to explode in his face.

And I said I was going to force a public explanation. The whole department must have heard me.

'God,' Gillian whispered. She was thinking rapidly. Rita would have been asked to explain the letter—and she would have denied writing it. The committee might not have believed her, but how could he afford that risk? He couldn't prove he *hadn't* done it, and once the question was raised, maybe she could prove he had. With Rita out of the way, he was safe. Or he thought so until Gillian became so obstinate about the Carver.

This had to be the answer. Now that she saw it, it all made sense. She let out her breath, which she hadn't been aware she was holding.

But why hadn't she seen this possibility earlier? Partly because she had learned about the letter while she supposed Rita's death to be an accident. The Carver Fellowship had seemed to be a separate problem: someone wrote a letter to ruin Rita's chances, no problem to solve except who had done it. She hadn't revised this logical sequence after she learned that the death wasn't an accident at all. And why not? Because the engineers' activities had preoccupied her. With good reason. And then it hadn't occurred to her that her own actions could be a strand in the web. Maybe she hadn't wanted to let that thought arise.

Gillian felt cold and pulled the quilt more closely about her shoulders.

There was another reason she hadn't figured it out sooner. A painful one. It had been easy to assign the lethal hatred of a killer to 'the engineers'. The engineering students who had hounded Rita had behaved abominably, but that was not the point. The point was that she hadn't wanted to look elsewhere. She'd wanted them to be the whole problem. Their misogyny was on public display, and they sneered at all the things Gillian cared about. They conformed to their own mean prejudices and thought they were flouting convention. They were the Other. It was easy to despise them, so comfortable to assume that they were what women had to fear: that you knew who your enemies were, as Paul had said. They'd acted as a mob in public, and she'd responded by refusing to consider their individuality. 'They' had been guilty when she didn't even know their names.

How reluctant she had been to believe that a humanist, someone in the arts, someone in her own department, someone supposedly civilized, who sneered now and then but had learned to mask his hostility, who didn't bellow obscenities or tell jokes about murdering twelve-year-old girls after fucking them, that such a man, known to her, would kill. She saw in her blindness something akin to that of women who rejected feminism, hoping instead for a safe harbour in the arms of the 'right' man.

Or perhaps it was simply hard to believe that a person she knew had done it. It usually was, she supposed.

She should call Frank Bacon. She had given him all the pieces of the puzzle she'd collected, and he had pieces of his own. Perhaps he'd figured it out by now. Like Edward, he was trained to look at all the possibilities. But he didn't know the university world as well as she did. Besides, the police could find out whether Ridgeway knew anything about motorcycles. She would call him. But she would rest a little first. She was terribly tired.

Gillian slept. When she woke again, the afternoon light coming through the little rectangular panes of the bedroom window was already dim. She padded downstairs and put the kettle on. Laura had left a note; she had gone shopping and would be home soon.

As she was rummaging in the cupboard for the Earl Grey tea, the doorbell rang. She felt a sudden stab of fear. Outside, the daylight lingered, and Laura would be back at any minute, but now she was alone in the house. She wasn't going to open the door without seeing who it was. She tiptoed to the dining-room, where there was a bay window, and cautiously peeped out from behind the curtains. She was startled but relieved to see a police car in the driveway, and Frank Bacon's big grey head visible through a screen of shrubbery. She went to let him in.

He accepted a cup of tea and inquired politely after her health. Then he said abruptly, 'I came to tell you we've arrested Ham Ridgeway.'

'For Rita's murder.'

'No. For the assault on you Friday night. But we're banking on getting him for both. It's the only way to figure it that makes sense.'

'How do you know who it was?'

'Your taxi-driver remembered that when your assailant fled, he was limping. We had a description of Ridgeway that included the information that he limped. And then we found a little sand in his car. We compared it to the sand in the sock that hit you. It matches. And we think we have a witness who can identify the car.'

'Do you know why he was after me?'

'Only with twenty-twenty hindsight. We figure he thought you were on to him. Everybody else was concentrating on the engineers, but you kept hammering away at the Carver scam.'

'It's ironic. I *was* on to him about the Carver, but I never connected it with the murder. I thought it was an engineer.'

'He waited too long, anyway. Once you'd been to Bingham and Stanley about the letter, it was too late—but that was what must have panicked him. When he found out what you were doing.'

'How did he?'

'Stanley told him last week that there was some doubt about the letter's authenticity.'

'He couldn't have believed he'd get away with it.' Involuntarily, she put her hand to the tender place on her head.

'Yeah. He lost it, all right.' Bacon scratched his head and sighed, like a melancholy old bear. 'He had a position to protect. With that type, it's hard to see how they start down the road, if they have any smarts, but once they start, they can get caught up in something that goes out of control.'

'How will you get him for Rita's murder?'

'The first thing is to find out whether he has any experience of motorcycles.'

'You should ask Dick Rasmussen,' Gillian said. 'He and Ridgeway were college room-mates, and Dick told me their whole crowd used to race motorcycles in the desert until they had a couple of accidents.'

'Hm. I expect we'll find that's where Ridgeway got the limp.'

⟶⟵

That week was the last week of classes before exams and the Christmas break.

On Wednesday, December 5th, President Bingham officially announced the administration's intention to establish a women's studies department, with courses to be put in the calendar for 1992-93. Jessie Rayne handed him the cheque. At the sherry party afterwards, in an atmosphere of conviviality somewhat modified by the now public news of Ham Ridgeway's arrest, Gillian made an announcement of her own. She was starting a fund for a Rita

Gordon Memorial Scholarship in women's studies, she said. And she wrote out a cheque then and there.

'It's strange how things work out,' she said to Laura afterwards. 'Nothing is ever simple. If sexism weren't such a burning public issue, the Carver committee would never have opened that file, and, who knows, Frost might have gotten the Rayne money, and there would be no women's studies department. But Rita would still be alive.'

'And if there had been no Montreal Massacre—if those fourteen women were still alive—sexism wouldn't be such a burning public issue.'

'Tomorrow is December 6th. If you're going to the memorial service at the student union, let's go together.'

'Yes.' Laura drew Gillian's arm through hers. 'We'll go and remember them.'

Printed in the United States
43751LVS00002B/463-486

My Sister's
Keeper

Nora Kelly

Poisoned Pen Press
Scottsdale, AZ

Poisoned
Pen
Press

Copyright © 1992 by Nora Kelly.

First Trade Paperback Edition 2000
Missing Mystery #16

10 9 8 7 6 5 4 3 2 1

Library of Congress Catalog Card Number: 99-068779

ISBN: 1-890208-28-0

Poisoned Pen Press
6962 E. First Ave. Ste 103
Scottsdale, AZ 85251
www.poisonedpenpress.com
sales@poisonedpenpress.com

Printed in the United States of America

PROLOGUE

The ivory tower was not built by barbarians. A university is a civilized place, or so we suppose. Campus warfare, though fierce, is conducted on paper; the rules are fair. How peaceful it looks, as the light shines from the library windows. No one is in danger here. We are seduced by the signs of order: the clipped lawns, the books arranged in rows, the bellstruck hours. Reassured, we bless the rude freedom of ideas and expect a safe place to send a daughter or to say things people don't want to hear.

Great expectations. But at Gillian's university, the fall term had detonated them. Now people stood about in the ruins and estimated the length of the fuse. It had all begun in September, or the previous spring, if you looked only where the law led, but Gillian was a historian and looked further back: to December of 1989, and then to the past two decades—in fact, she said, to the whole sad story of what used to be called mankind.

CHAPTER 1

The sudden thunder of boots on the steel treads of the library stairs announced the end of the hour. Gillian closed her volume of Hansard and drew a deep breath. A passing student stirred a sluggish current of air, leaving a few molecules of locker-room to find their way to Gillian's nose.

'A university should be a place of light, of liberty, and of learning.' Thus Disraeli, demolishing the Irish University Bill in 1873. As she checked her quotations, she marvelled once more that the Bill had reached second reading: imagine proposing a university at which philosophy and modern history would be forbidden subjects! It was a weird tribute to Gladstone's eloquence that the Bill had been debated at all. She gathered up her notes and threaded her way through the narrow aisles to the nearest stairway. No longer at liberty to learn, or, more precisely, to hunt down *op. cit.* and *loc. cit.* in these bygone forests, she went in search of light.

It was a glorious afternoon. Emerging from the gloomy deeps of the library stacks, Gillian blinked at the blue sky and the long shafts of September sunlight. Virginia creeper flamed against the library's granite walls, and the lawn was deep green under the golden leaves of the chestnut trees. She meant to return to the history department office, where there were the usual pressing matters requiring her attention, but half way there she abruptly changed direction.

The Green, a dismal bog in the winter months, was dry and springy underfoot. Brown-limbed students lay here and there, leaning on their elbows, pretending to read; a shoal of cyclists drifted silently along the edge, flashing tropical colours against the grey stone of the old arts building. Gillian crossed the lawn and made her way around the building, now inhabited by a wing of the administration. She crossed Bluff Road, the main artery linking the east and west gates. A broad strip of lawn and luxuriant clumps of rhododendrons lay between the road and the bluffs. Behind the building, interrupting the flow of green, was a neat little rose-garden. To her surprise, there was no one in it. The stone benches, warmed by the sun, were empty, and the late blooms offered up their sweetness for her solitary pleasure. The garden sloped gently to the south, and a few roses blossomed throughout the autumn. Now it was Indian summer, the most beautiful time of the year. Soon it would be over, and the rains would come. She sat down on one of the benches and gazed dreamily into the distance. The flat, green river delta, a patchwork of fields and pastures retreating before an onslaught of sub-divisions, spread out from the foot of the steep scarp that formed the south-western boundary of the university grounds. The river's northern arm was a glittering ribbon. Beyond it, to the west, the wide blue water ran away to the edge of sight, to blue-green layers of islands and the misty peaks of the Olympic Peninsula. And beyond that, beyond sight, was the blue yonder—nothing but ocean and sky all the way to Japan.

Gillian gave herself up to the luxury of doing nothing. The first flurry of the fall term was past. The new students had lost their bewildered look, the timetables had settled down, the initial epidemic of meetings seemed to be abating. She had had two solid hours in the library today—not bad for a head of department in the last week of September. She cherished hopes of finishing her paper on Disraeli for the conference in London next month. What a pity that she would only have a week there. By the time she had recovered from the eight-hour time change, she'd be on her way back. She hadn't seen Edward since July, and after the conference she wouldn't see him again until the end of spring term. A ridiculous life, but they were apparently stuck with it. If they had met when they were younger...but now there was too much at stake. She wouldn't care to give up her job, her friends, her house and garden for a cramped flat and a man who was never home.

'Policemen don't work nine to five,' was his refrain when she commented on his hours. Neither do academics who publish as well as teach, she thought, but when we take time off, it's *off*. We don't vanish on two minutes' notice in the middle of a holiday because 'something's come up'. And it was quite impossible to imagine Edward living anywhere but London. 'Rotting out there under the rhododendrons' was his picture of life on the west coast. Well, it wasn't hers. *Earth has not anything to show more fair*...Wordsworth had said that about London, but today she found it apt to the prospect before her.

She kicked her shoes off and swung her stockinged feet in the sun. The heat seeped through the navy linen folds of her skirt. Tucking a stray wisp of her short hair behind her ear, she felt a slight beading of sweat at her temple. It was a wonderful luxury, to be too hot in late September. She tilted her face to the sun and closed her eyes. Her palms pressed on the warm, gritty stone. The texture was pleasant, the solidity soon noticeable to her spare frame. She shifted her weight and looked at the pink stippling of the skin and then turned her hands over. Her only ring, a smallish square-cut emerald set in a plain gold band, flashed green fire. It had been her great-grandmother's, and her grandmother's, and her mother's. It was hers now; her mother's hands had grown thin with old age, and she had given the ring to Gillian during their last visit. It fitted perfectly; Gillian had inherited her mother's hands as well as her long bones and dark cloud of hair. The network of fine lines engraved on her skin showed clearly in the bright afternoon light. It was a sight that at times depressed her, a sign of age and the body's decay, but now it struck her as appropriate: she was used to seeing the ring on a hand weathered by life, not on a girl's smooth finger.

A jet took off from the airport a few miles away. It droned loudly overhead and then faded eastward. Gillian's thoughts ceased to wander and focused on the variety of noises that penetrated her sanctuary. A nearby car roared over a *basso continuo* of distant traffic. Something—a ventilator?—hummed loudly on the roof of the administration building. Voices faded in and out again. If you shut off these sounds, she supposed, you would only uncover layers of noise that were now masked. The city was never quiet. In fact, it seemed noisier than ever nowadays, with car alarms whooping in the dead of night every time a cat jumped…Not to mention the plague of boom cars thumping and whining through the streets. Even in the inactive hours before dawn you heard screeching sirens and the distant rumble of trains, and the peculiar shuddering noise of the fridge. There was somebody shouting now. In fact, a lot of people shouting. Let them shout. She fixed her eyes on the view. Perhaps she would leave early this afternoon and read that article in *Past and Present*. It would be pleasant to sit in her study at home, with the last of the afternoon sun coming in. She thought the shouting was growing louder. It *was* louder. Whatever it was was coming closer. Damn it all, why must people shatter a perfect hour with that infernal howling?

She stood up and made her way back to the garden entrance and along the side of the building. A wide walkway ran past the front steps. The road, empty of cars now, swept by the administration building and angled away to connect to the road from the main gate. The gate was rustic but imposing: two tall columns of yellow cedar surmounted by a lintel, stripped bare and left to weather. Beneath this allusion to the mighty forests of the coast (and the mighty forest industry) was a spectacle.

'Oh Lord,' Gillian muttered. She'd forgotten that today was Triumph Day.

A parade of soap-boxes rumbled slowly towards her. A mob of red-jacketed young men, shouting boisterously, seethed about the vehicles, flooding the road and the grass verges. Rolls of toilet paper rocketed upward from the throng, unwinding as they descended. The trees were festooned with the pale streamers.

A crowd of students had gathered at the gate to watch the procession, and more were coming across the lawn. Spectators craned out of the open windows of the administration building. Close by, a large young man with a videocamera on his shoulder was walking backwards parallel to the line of vehicles.

'Gillian Adams?' asked a voice at her shoulder. She turned and saw a vaguely familiar face, a tall, tanned man with thick blond hair and spectacles. He was…he was Ham Ridgeway's old college room-mate, who was doing some research here during the fall term. Economic history, Ham had said. What was his name? Rasmussen, something Rasmussen.

'…er, hello, Dr Rasmussen.'

'Dick. What's going on?'

'Triumph Day, I'm sorry to say. The engineering students' annual frolic.'

He inspected the approaching swarm. 'What's the matter with it?'

'Among other things, it's always been a nasty display of sexism,' said Gillian.

'Really?' He looked amused. 'But I detect the Medusa stare of feminist disapproval. Haven't you turned them to stone?'

A cardboard cylinder sailed past their heads.

'Obviously not. Actually, I don't know what they'll do this year. Nobody does.'

'Why Triumph Day? Have they won a race?'

'No. They race each other in those chariots, and the winner then rides his at the end of the parade. The parade is their tradition—like a Roman triumph, the Romans being such great engineers, you see. They ride under the arch and all round the campus, and the mob follows them, hurling obscenities and toilet paper. They've been doing this for decades, and warding off all protests with the sacred word "tradition".'

The lead chariot was abreast of the building now, closely followed by several others. Far more sophisticated than the soap-boxes Gillian remembered from her childhood, they were wildly and absurdly various, cobbled together from bathtubs, kayaks, car parts, electric fans, tricycle wheels, and domestic detritus of every kind. They were loud and gaudy and improbable. The students clustering along the parade route stared and laughed and kept well clear of the road, where a squall of toilet paper and beer was raging.

The crowd was a lot smaller than it had been in the past, but in the past there had been considerable advance publicity for the event. This year there had been none. Most of the audience was male, Gillian noticed, but there were women in the crowd, too. She tried to read the expressions of the faces nearest to her. There were people laughing raucously, but nobody was relaxed. Tension was strung along the road like telephone wire. Heads turned to look towards the gate, as if waiting for something to happen. A few young women looked scornful. Others were giggling—new students, maybe, who didn't know what came next...or denied the implications.

'It's a tad anachronistic,' Dick observed, 'at least to a stranger.'

'Most natives think so too.'

'Then why does it go on?'

'Just because it always has,' Gillian said impatiently. 'Besides, applied science is the richest faculty on campus. Bob Frost—the Dean of Engineering—knows how to get money. He has a lot of pull, and he's a fan of "the tradition". And it's a display of his power, in a way, since so many efforts have been made to stop it. He and the president and a couple of the heavy-duty governors are buddies. We—the faculty, I mean—don't have a vote on the issue. Like many other things, it's in the hands of the administration.'

The man with the video-camera panned across the confusion, then he sped away to the main gate, where a huddle of darker figures moved suddenly into a gap in the scarlet-hued parade and spread out. Forgetting Dick, Gillian moved towards it, skirting the leading edge of the crowd, which was making too much noise to notice what was happening further back. Now she could see. A line of pickets had blocked the entrance to the university: they were women. Maybe a dozen or fifteen of them. They had linked arms across the road. Some of the engineers who had passed through were turning back, screaming at the picketers. More surged forward from beyond the gate, and a scuffle broke out as one or two tried to force their way through the line. On the other side was the tail of the parade: a sort of wagon, pulled by students, and last of all, the winning chariot, obscured by the crowd except for the flag of triumph that fluttered over their heads.

Gillian hurried towards the gate, but before she could reach it, a red wave engulfed the line of women. A din of angry voices rose. Through its unintelligible roar, Gillian heard women chanting in unison: 'No Go! No Go!' And contrapuntal male yells: 'Break the line! Break the line!' And then one voice braying above the rest:

'Shoot the bitches!'

She craned around the heads in front of her but could barely see what was happening. She glimpsed the line as it swayed and broke. Then the protesters were shoved roughly off the road, and the engineers pushed the wagon through. There were three women in it, huddled nervously together, clutching the wagon's sides for support. They wore heavy make-up and harem pants; gold tassels dangled from their breasts, and gold bangles glittered up and down their arms. They were chained to the wagon by wrist and ankle.

'Who are they?' Dick asked in astonished tones. 'They're not students, surely?'

'Those are the captives,' Gillian replied. 'The so-called "slave women". I believe that in Rome they walked in the dust, but that's neither here nor there. No, they're not students. I'm told the engineers hire them.'

'Oh, hookers,' Dick said, relieved.

Gillian scowled, but his eyes were on the women and the milling crowd. 'They rode along stark naked a few years ago. That's been stopped, at least. The other prisoners—the ones pulling the wagon—are students,' she added. 'They're captured in the dorms.'

Six young men, roped together and lacking the red jackets sported by the engineers, jerked the wagon along the road, as the engineers gave it a hard shove from behind. Dark patches of sweat blotched their T-shirts, and their faces were crimson with effort or perhaps embarrassment. They moved on. The winning chariot, trailing clouds of toilet paper, rolled through the gate and down the road, the red flag, emblazoned with a large E, fluttering behind. A rearguard of engineers straggled after the flag, turning to jeer at the dishevelled picketers. Ahead of them, the women in the wagon had recovered their poise. They waved at the camera like homecoming queens.

Gillian turned back towards the gate, a little stunned. The drama was over; it had only taken a couple of minutes. The parade marched on. Probably the students on the far side of the Green—gathering now to watch the parade cross the campus to the Applied Science Complex—didn't even know what had happened. She glanced at the faces around her, where a volatile mix of excitement, anger and fear was vividly registered. A few students had rushed towards the mêlée, but most had shrunk back, separating themselves from the engineers and the women alike.

Gillian walked towards the scattered picketers regrouping on the grass. The women had been shouldered to the edge of the crowd, and several had been thrown bodily on to the kerb. Most were on their feet already, feeling for bruises.

'I didn't think they'd be so brutal in front of the camera,' one said, rubbing a bruised elbow.

'They weren't brutal, by their standards,' another retorted, tucking in her shirt. 'They broke the line and pushed us and called us whores and dykes, but they didn't beat us up.'

'Someone punched Linda.'

A few feet away, a dark-haired protester was hunched over, clutching her chest and groaning. Another crouched beside her.

'Are you OK? Are you OK?' she kept asking.

Gillian bent down. 'Do you want a doctor?'

The hunched woman shook her head without looking up. Her friend encircled her with a protective arm. 'Assholes!' she shouted after the departing parade.

CHAPTER 2

Gillian straightened up, but hovered for a moment, reluctant to leave the two of them sitting on the kerb. They looked so vulnerable—young women of nineteen or twenty, just starting their lives. She heard a voice she knew. Looking about, she saw, on the opposite side of the group, Rita Gordon, a graduate student in the History Department. She was speaking directly to the camera.

'This campus stinks of sexism. Look at those men hanging out of the windows of the administration building. You think this farce would have gone on this year if the president and the deans weren't all men? But this is the last time. The parade's toast.'

Students who had watched the confrontation from a distance now pressed closer to listen. The camera wobbled a little. It must be a film student who held it, Gillian decided; he looked too young to have a job, and professionals came with crews wearing baseball caps—dink hats, they were called here—and jackets with writing across the back. Here there was only someone holding a microphone—another student, judging by appearances. Gillian wondered whether they had come to film the parade or the protest. She wasn't surprised to find Rita speaking for the group. Rita was remarkable; her brain burned like a blacksmith's forge, melting down the old, hammering out the new. Her energy and her way of brushing aside the cobwebbed orthodoxies that came her way had turned more than one seminar on its ear. She had just passed her thesis examination and would receive her degree formally at convocation in the spring. She was also an outspoken feminist.

'This is 1990,' Rita was saying, 'and half of all students are women. This is our campus, too. But women are sexually harassed by male professors, and the administration does nothing to stop it. We've got date rape. We've got pornographic jokes in student publications funded by the university. All these problems are symptoms of the sickness called sexism. The mandate of this university, from the day it was founded, has been to educate both men and women. Yet here, in this place where we are supposedly equal, we are expected to endure—in fact to enjoy—the public degradation of women as objects owned by men. It has been, we are told, a "tradition". So has footbinding. So has slavery. Tradition is no excuse for injustice.

'This is 1990. A year after the Montreal Massacre. We know that misogyny is lethal. Women will not be silent. Women will not be "good". It is not time for us to be patient. It's time the university paid more than lip service to equality.'

The protesters clapped and cheered, joined by a cluster of students who had watched the events at the gate. Dick bobbed up again at Gillian's elbow.

'A real rabble-rouser, eh?'

'She's the best student our department has seen in years,' Gillian said tartly.

'Ah. Building the ovary tower.' He cocked his head. 'What's that accent she has?'

'English.'

'Really?' Dick blinked at her behind his gold-rimmed glasses. 'The English girls I've met were never that shrill.' He surveyed the group. 'Anyway, the show's over, I guess. Looks like all the Amazons survived. I'm glad they didn't need rescuing—for a moment there I thought it might get ugly.' He waved a casual hand at the big library clock. 'I should be going.' He moved off, and Gillian gladly forgot him.

'Did you get it all, Tony?' Rita was saying to the cameraman.

'You bet.'

'Brilliant. Let's go.'

Rita set off briskly, followed by several others. The women scattered, and their audience drifted away. At the far end of the long green lawn that was the centre of the campus, a red blot beneath the trees marked the progress of the parade.

Gillian retraced her steps. As she passed the administration building, she noticed that the faces were gone from the windows. They'll have telephoned the president's office, she thought, but it's a little late for damage control.

Frances Romano, the Dean of Women, dashed down the steps.

'Gillian! What happened? I've been stuck in a meeting, and I could *not* get away.'

'It's all over.'

Frances halted at the foot of the steps, and Gillian recounted what she had seen.

'God in heaven,' Frances exclaimed. 'It's a mercy no one was badly hurt.' She stepped into the road and looked towards the gate. Gillian glanced about. Hardly anyone was left at the arch. The muffled din of the parade continued from beyond the far end of the Green. Agitated clusters of students were standing here and there on the paths or walking rapidly away; others, still recumbent on the turf, pointedly ignored the recent disruption. Frances peeled a squashy wad of toilet paper from the sole of her shoe. 'I've been trying to use back-channel diplomacy to put a stop to this slave-wagon business for the past three years, and I really had hoped that this year…But I've gotten precisely nowhere. Now we'll find out what some bad publicity can do. Rita and the others are to come and see me if they get into trouble over this.'

When Gillian belatedly reached the history office it was full of people.

'Did you hear about what happened at the parade?' Jane burst out as soon as Gillian walked in.

'Yes, I saw part of it.'

Gillian liked Jane Riley. They were temperamental opposites, and Jane's bouncy extroversion at times made Gillian want to shout 'Sit!' but she frowned at this as prejudice springing from her own reserve. Jane had been around the History Department for fifteen years. She was quick, knew the established routines by heart, had useful connections with staff all over the campus, and possessed the virtues of loyalty and resilient goodwill, the latter indispensable in a department lumbered with several egotistical and cranky full professors. She had a persistent fondness for voluminous clothing in strident shades of purple and orange, and made her own garments in blissful disregard of current fashion. Her emotional life was generally a shambles, as she rescued one man-in-a-mess after another, only to be dumped in a matter of weeks or months.

'Good for those girls,' she said vigorously. 'I don't know how they dared. I'd have been scared to death.'

Women, Gillian thought automatically, but kept quiet. To Jane, all students were girls and boys, a linguistic habit that had proved ineradicable.

Besides Jane and Allie Moore, the two secretaries, three of the faculty and a couple of graduate students were clustered in the office. Vernon Palmer paused in the act of collecting his mail from the bank of pigeonholes near Jane's desk. He was bearded and tweedy and came equipped with pipe, like a professor doll. He was fifty-four and a full professor. 'And tomorrow it will be all over the papers. The administration really ought to put a stop to it,' he said testily.

'Are you advocating censorship, Verne?' asked Charlie Rankin, who was leaning on the counter. He wore blue jeans, a white shirt, and a tennis tan, and he had a brown velvet voice which he used to great effect on his female students. At forty-eight, he carried no excess weight and was fond of alluding to the large waistlines of his colleagues.

'If you call it censorship to forbid this silly slave business, then yes, I am,' Vernon replied. 'It's causing more fuss each year, and it's embarrassing.' He nodded to Gillian and walked away.

'Good God, another convert to feminism,' said Charlie, rolling his eyes. 'We macho types are becoming an endangered species. You'll be sorry when we're gone.' He leered at Allie, who leered back.

'I'm not worried,' she said. 'They've got wonderful breeding programmes at zoos nowadays.'

Charlie snorted. 'Couldn't you get us some new secretaries?' he asked Gillian. 'Ones that blush?'

'Don't you have a two-thirty class?' asked Jane.

'As a matter of fact, yes. Something to do with Sherman's march. Do you know, I've got sixty-five girls in a class of less than a hundred? If I were those engineers, I'd be nervous.' He lounged off. The two graduate students had kept clear of the crossfire. Allie turned on them.

'OK, you guys, what's your opinion?'

'I've never watched the parade,' said Chris Lowell warily. 'It sounds pretty stupid.'

Paul Smith shrugged. 'Some people who are targets of hate propaganda don't want it banned because they think it's safer to fight it out in the open. At least you know who your enemies are.' He scooped up some papers from the photocopier and followed Chris out towards the elevators.

'What do you think, Carole?' Gillian asked her sole female colleague in the department.

'Let's ban those damned red jackets—then maybe they'll stop acting like a mob.' She was scanning the newspaper that lay on Jane's desk. She looked up irritably. 'No, seriously, I hate this sort of issue. The kind that pits freedom of expression against the struggle for equality. I don't want to burn books on the Green— not even kiddie porn or the *Protocols of Zion*. But I don't think they have the right to rub our noses in their dirt. If the President had any backbone, he wouldn't let them drag their slave wagon all over the campus. By the way, have you seen this?' She tapped the front page of the newspaper.

'Battered Wife Told to Sponsor British Husband,' Gillian read over her shoulder.

Carole glared at Jane and Allie. 'Can you believe it? The Immigration Department wants this woman to go on taking financial responsibility for a man who put her in hospital for four days!'

'Why don't they deport him?' Jane asked indignantly.

'You probably get points for being a wife-batterer—you know, like one of those skills that the Canadian economy is looking for,' Allie said.

'I doubt that,' Gillian replied. 'We're hardly short of them.'

It was a warm evening. Gillian went out to the garden and snipped a few sprigs of mint. Then she crushed the leaves with some sugar and groped among the bottles in the liquor cupboard for the remains of the Jack Daniels. Having achieved a rather sketchy mint julep, she settled down to watch the evening news. She dozed through the sports but snapped awake when the local news came on. 'At the University of the Pacific North-West,' the announcer intoned, 'women attempted to block the main gate during the Triumph Day parade this afternoon.' Well! Rita must have hiked the film straight down to the station.

She had a much better view than she'd had earlier; the camera had been closer to the action. There was the line of women linking hands. Now the charging engineers. The screen was filled with identical jackets, an image like one from a football game or a war. Clothing makes the mob, Carole Stein had suggested. The engineers were closing in. They burst through the chain of women like a red tide. A beer bottle smashed to the ground. There was a blurred, snarling face and a glimpse of the frightened slave women in the wagon. Then a shot of a protester falling to the ground.

The telephone rang. Gillian crossed the room, her eyes on the screen. It was Laura. 'Turn on your television!' she said without preamble.

'I know, it's on.'

Laura Byng, a professor in English, was Gillian's closest friend. They held on, watching for a minute or so in silence, until the story was over.

'Well,' said Laura, 'the administration is going to shit itself.'

CHAPTER 3

For the next several days, the protest was a hot topic. The head of the ESS—the Engineering Student Society, which organized the annual parade—dismissed the incident with a perfunctory apology, but this failed to quench the fires of indignation. Those who had been offended by the slave wagon were outraged by the bullying behaviour of the engineers. Those who had warned that something was bound to happen were pointing out that something had, and demanding to know what the administration was now going to do about it. What were the Dean and the President waiting for? A full-scale riot?

The story was front page news; furthermore, it refused to die, as a scalding editorial in the afternoon paper was followed by letters, columnists' opinion pieces thumping the ESS and the administration, and then more letters. The televised images of the slave women and the protesters and the howling engineers attracted scathing comments from across the country. According to Frances Romano, the board of governors had let it be known in the president's office that they were not pleased, and several alumnae had telephoned to announce that contributions to university coffers would not be forthcoming should this sort of thing continue.

Gillian was cheered by the publicity. A few years earlier, the events would have attracted little notice. A brief story in the paper, a few comments on the letters page about strident feminists with no sense of humour, and back to business as usual would have been what one could expect. Now, suddenly, the parade was no longer taken for granted. It had made the transfer from the list of unimportant problems to the list of serious, newsworthy problems. Things that had to be stopped. So maybe the 'tradition' would be finished at last. About time, too. It was galling that it had gone on so long. But it was only a blatant and obnoxious expression of attitudes that ran deep on campus. She hadn't been as aware of this before she'd spent that sabbatical in Cambridge in the early 'eighties. There, she'd found herself among college fellows who were still stewing over whether to allow female guests at dinner. The shock had been considerable. Coming home, she had at first been relieved by the differences, by the progress women had made. The percentage of women on the faculty was higher and was still rising; more graduate students were women—almost a third of the Ph.D. students now; it seemed inconceivable that the cost of bathrooms would be offered or received as a serious argument for the exclusion of women from important educational institutions; the blatant insults that persisted at Cambridge were not tolerated here.

But these comparisons, however favourable, had attracted her attention to problems that had previously escaped her notice: the permanent effect had been to alert her to the obstacles women still faced. These were everywhere, tangible and intangible. Progress was infuriatingly slow. The strife was constant, the atmosphere electric. Sometimes, especially lately, Gillian had imagined that the air in classrooms and committees was breathless and strange, like the prelude to a cyclone. Peculiar eddies of feeling whirled up and subsided. The temperature kept rising.

It had reached flashpoint in Montreal in December 1989— the Montreal Massacre. A man had murdered fourteen women at the Ecole Polytechnique because 'feminists had ruined his life'. And what had changed since then? Probably the parade would still be classed as harmless fun if it hadn't been for the massacre. Violence against women had entered the public discourse. Assault, rape, wife-beating—they were condemned in the newspapers every day. But they still went on. The war on women, it was called now.

There had been no slave wagon in the parade that year, but no promises of a permanent ban, although strenuous efforts had been made to obtain one. Frances had tried her best, and hundreds of women, including Gillian, had signed petitions or written to the president's office, to no avail. The administration, the engineers, and in particular Bob Frost, the Dean of Engineering, were immovable. It remained to be seen whether the protest and embarrassing fuss would supply the necessary leverage. In Gillian's opinion, the protest had been a shrewd move. A new coalition of women students—the Feminist Union—into which Rita had recently poured her considerable energies, had organized it, she knew that. They were fed up with the routine failure of their private skirmishes with authority. Public pressure—and an overall strategy—were needed if women were to move closer to real equality. Gillian agreed. Lobbying and personal appeals had failed to stop the slave wagon; it was possible that the tactics of the Feminist Union—now that sexism was news—would shift the balance.

She sighed. Those two hours in the library on Triumph Day had been the only breathing space she'd had since term started. She'd had enough of meetings. But a committee of the Feminist Union was coming to see her this afternoon, about something to do with a proposal for a women's studies programme. If a new push was coming, she would do her share. She was not optimistic, however, What could they have in mind? There was no money. That had been the administration's impregnable barrier to all previous proposals.

Rita had made a good speech at the protest. Remembering, Gillian was furious all over again. How *could* the slaves have been brought back? It looked like a deliberate effort to regain the status quo ante. A slap in the face, that's what it was. What had Paul Smith said about the parade? 'At least you know who your enemies are.' Cold comfort.

❦

Jane and Allie seemed to be taking an informal poll of the department. As she passed in and out of the office, Gillian kept catching snatches of commentary.

'For where two or three are gathered together, there is the parade in the midst of them,' said Ham Ridgeway, with heavy sarcasm. 'I should be grateful that the 'sixties are long dead, or I'd have to be relevant and discuss it in the classroom.'

He enunciated the word 'relevant' with precise distaste, like a Victorian doctor identifying a social disease.

Jim Jacobsen, the other senior member of the department, splayed the pages of a journal on the photocopier and mashed the lid down.

'When the media lose interest, so will everyone else. The universities don't even exist so far as the media are concerned—until something like this happens. Then the paparazzi have a field day.' He opened the journal to another page and Gillian heard the spine snap. He was a heavy, clumsy man, and objects fought back.

'Degenerate princes called themselves Cæsar and Augustus until the fall of Constantinople,' said Eric Kittredge mildly. 'The persistence of Roman images in our culture is interesting, don't you think?'

Jacobsen merely grunted. Kittredge, whose historical interests were Germanic and intellectual, was one of the department's recent appointments; Jacobsen had campaigned for another Canadian historian and had lost because Charlie Rankin and the rest of the American historians had sided with the European faction led by Ridgeway. Each of the last two appointments had been a tussle. Carole Stein—that had been a worse fight. Ridgeway hadn't wanted her; the boys' club had beat the bushes for at least one other French social historian with Carole's qualifications. Their candidates were lustreless, and she had a book being published by Yale, but even so it had been a near thing. Gillian had fought hard to get her. Angry words had been spoken, and she'd been accused of sacrificing departmental goodwill to feminist politics. Jacobsen, a sore loser, had backed Carole just to spite Ridgeway. At least that was what Gillian surmised. The next appointment—when the budget allowed it—should probably go to a Canadian historian; some areas were well represented, but Canadian social history needed someone new. Gillian expected another dust-up. Ridgeway still wanted to be department head; Jacobsen did too.

'Some of the kids in my tutorials are really disgusted by the parade. They want the admin to fine the engineers—take away their society's funds,' said Paul Smith. He was tall and lanky, with a trim beard, faded blue jeans and a Nietzsche sweatshirt. He had finished his thesis (Canadian history, railway politics) in June, but he was still waiting for the external examiner to fly in for his defence. It would be a formality, Gillian had been told; the committee was very happy with what he had done.

'The rest of them don't say anything,' he went on. 'I can't tell what they're thinking.'

This accorded with Gillian's experience. Her fourth-year class, who had been reading about the abolition movement, quoted Wilberforce. They were quite ready to ban the slave wagon, an interesting difference, she thought, from her own student generation, which would have argued hotly about freedom of expression. On the other hand, her first-year class, though it included a ration of the articulate and indignant, was largely silent on the subject. In Gillian's experience, students rapidly sensed what views were welcome in each class, and most often kept quiet when they disagreed.

In the middle of the afternoon Gillian shut herself in her office and tried to print out a draft of her paper for the conference in London. If it hadn't been essential to her sanity as department head, she might never have started to use a computer. But there had been no way round it, and now she was glad. Typing on the computer had been an instant delight: moving paragraphs about, inserting afterthoughts, altering sentences three or four times without retyping her pages. Printing was different. She had a fast new printer now, and was using a new program that was supposed to be a dream with footnotes, but she still hadn't made it work properly. After the third telephone call, she asked Jane to take messages and began yet again to read the baffling instructions for the printer. What in God's name was a hexidecimal dump? The writer of this hefty volume seemed to assume she would know. The parade receded from her consciousness.

⚓

An hour later she was scarcely wiser, despite the heap of shiny manuals that obscured the surface of her desk. She glared at the page emerging from the backside of her printer.

'Goddammit,' she said aloud. 'Now what's the matter with the footnotes?' She glanced back at a page in the topmost manual. 'Insert dot D...I *did* that.'

The end of the page slid over the roller, and the printer, humming while it worked, began a new one. The offending note on the completed page had not appeared at the foot where it belonged and where she had carefully instructed it to materialize.

It had printed itself squarely in the middle of the third paragraph, bracketed by graphic symbols that were not supposed to be printed at all.

'What do you want?' Gillian snarled, swatting viciously at the printer's Off button.

Jane tapped on the open door. 'Your four o'clock meeting has arrived,' she announced, eyeing the dishevelled pile of computer manuals and the sagging accordion of paper beside the desk.

'Thank God,' replied Gillian. 'My bloody printer's going to be the death of me. I've never seen such diabolical idiocy in my life.'

Three graduate students filed in, the last closing the door behind her.

'I suppose *your* computers always print the footnotes exactly where they're supposed to go,' Gillian said.

Rita Gordon, leading the trio of women, tilted her head to look at Gillian's pages. 'You should use an Apple. It's easier.'

'So I gather. But this is an IBM office. My disks must go to Jane and Allie and back again. In the future, I'm told, they'll sail across the office like frisbees on a summer afternoon. One has to be compatible to survive.'

Gillian glanced out of the window at the patch of lawn, ten storeys down, where the frisbee players had been at play only a few days ago. The autumn rains had begun right after Triumph Day. Now the rhododendrons stood in sombre clumps, and the clean geometry of grey pavement and green grass was smudged with muddy diagonals of footprints. On the half-naked branches of the trees, disintegrating strands of toilet paper hung like grey fungus. The afternoons were growing shorter.

Gillian switched off the computer, and in the sudden quiet looked at her visitors.

'Please, have a seat,' she said. 'Now, what's up?'

'Women's studies,' answered Rita. 'It's our big project.' She dropped into one of the chairs across the desk from Gillian. The other two, Libby Hosmer and Denise Reed, sat down on either side of Rita. All three were in their twenties; two were graduate students in the History Department and one in Music. Libby was Gillian's own student, and the one best known to her, but she'd had Rita in a seminar, and was familiar with her graduate work as well as her energetic criticism of the university and the department. Denise, the music student, she had only encountered in an undergraduate course several years earlier. As head of the department, Gillian made an effort to know something of all its graduate students, but the undergraduates were too numerous. The current crop of MA's and Ph.D's afforded her much satisfaction. None of the twenty-four, so far as she knew, was in undue difficulty. The women, in particular, were an interesting lot, filling more than their share of verbal space in the seminars and turning in short, sharp papers. The men were a little duller. It was curious, Gillian thought, how the uncertainty that used to be such a marked characteristic of women students, was—in this group, at any rate—more frequent, if less pronounced, among the men. The men didn't preface their comments with 'this may not be important, but...', the hallmark phrase of women students who lacked confidence, but there was something tentative about the tone of their remarks, as though they expected to be criticized rather than admired. Certainly there were fewer arrogant pricks around than there used to be. Here, anyway. No doubt they were still thick on the ground in Cambridge. She must remember to ask Laura whether she had noticed a similar phenomenon in the English Department. Not that the men were inadequate. Far from it. They were smart and diligent, and most of them would find teaching positions sometime in the 1990s, when the coming undergraduate bulge was predicted to coincide with the retirement of the professors hired during the 'sixties bulge. Yes, a good crop.

Rita, however, was exceptional. That overused word, 'outstanding', really applied to Rita. She sat across from Gillian: a ragamuffin, skinny, dark, with nails bitten too short and hair long grown out of its cut, unprepossessingly attired in loose black cotton pants and a sweater like a burlap bag. She had small, glittering, deepset eyes, a prominent nose, and a fierce, concentrated way of holding her angular body. A *belle laide* in France, Gillian imagined, but plain in any English-speaking country. Her scuffed boots had left tracks on the carpet. None the less, she was formidable. Other students might read as voraciously, might remember as aptly, but she was as quick in argument as a trial lawyer, and despite her bleak and impoverished childhood in east London wrote well and easily. She had already published two papers in significant journals.

Having finished her thesis over the summer, she had applied for the Carver Fellowship, and Gillian expected her to get it.

The Carver post-doctoral grant, $25,000 a year for two years, was awarded every third year to a new-minted Ph.D. in English or history. Carver Fellows were expected to produce a book by the end of the two years, or at least several articles. They were required to teach one course and could request additional travel money for research and attendance at conferences. It was a lush fellowship and attracted, as it was meant to do, a number of excellent Ph.D. students who might otherwise have flitted mothlike towards the bright lights of the east. The committee consisted of the president of the university, the Dean of Arts, two senior members from the relevant departments, two well-known academics from other universities, and, through an old Carver connection, an important personage from the Oxford University Press—seven men in all. Rita was not their cup of tea, but they would choose her anyway.

Rita pushed her ragged bangs off her forehead and began to speak. Gillian could still hear the London twang in her voice, though its edges had been filed smooth by years away.

'You saw the demo at the Triumph Day parade? That was the Feminist Union's first action.'

'And you certainly got everyone's attention. Did you plan that television coverage?'

'Of course,' Libby replied. 'The engineers tried to pull a fast one. They didn't want any publicity—like people in the media screaming and yelling about the slave wagon—so they wouldn't even say if they were going to have it. We couldn't let them get away with it. So we decided that if there was a wagon, we'd make sure there'd be a whole lot of screaming and yelling. We didn't want a professional crew; anyway, we figured they wouldn't hang around the campus just on the off-chance, so we got Tony Cardero to do it. He knows people at the station, but they would have grabbed the story anyway—it was great footage.'

Libby reminded Gillian of a young seal, or an otter. She had round brown eyes and a round head, and brown hair which she wore very short, like fur. She leaned forward in her chair, excited. 'Did you see the newspapers the next day? Both of them published anti-Triumph Day editorials. And wasn't Bingham totally lame?'

President Bingham had indeed come off rather poorly. The oil he had attempted to pour had looked too much like whitewash. The administration feared embarrassing publicity, and its overpowering impulse was to conceal trouble. Controversies, like fires, were to be put out, smothered with a blanket of subcommittees and administrative procedures. Vast quantities of paper could then be produced to demonstrate the seriousness of the administration's intentions. The President regretted the incident; he was sure that the engineering students had intended no harm…it had been ill-judged to revive the slave wagon, but after all the parade was an old custom…of course the rough treatment a handful of women had received was deplorable, but perhaps their demonstration had been a little provocative…surely they could have made their point without physically blocking the gate…Clearly violence could not be tolerated, and the administration would take steps to ensure that such confrontations would be avoided in the future, etc., etc.

The student newspaper had supported the protest, but the letters that were printed were divided. Three male arts students sent a letter that said the parade was offensive. A male second-year engineer said it 'went beyond the bounds of decency and common sense'. That one must have required some courage, Gillian thought. But two letters trotted out the old bromides in defence of tradition, and one chastized the protesters for their deficient sense of humour. Several letters from women in various branches of the arts and sciences condemned the slave wagon and the rude treatment meted out to the protesters. None defended the parade, but a student reporter quoted one woman as saying she didn't see any harm in it. Gillian herself had overheard another version in the snack bar. 'We aren't bimbos, you know. We wouldn't ride in that cart. But those girls aren't forced to—they do it for the money. So what?' Gillian had seen the crowd of onlookers, and she knew that such views were not uncommon.

'What's your take on faculty opinion?' Denise asked.

'Well, I don't hear everyone's,' Gillian replied. 'Most of the people I talk to are in arts departments, but I think that on the whole the faculty would just as soon see the last of the parade. You could probably persuade the association to pass a resolution.

I doubt they'll give you more active support unless inactivity is made very uncomfortable.'

'That's what we have in mind,' Rita said.

Gillian wondered what they were working up to. She had heard comments about the Feminist Union—referred to by a number of male faculty members as the Eff Yous. She was delighted that they existed, she had been interested to see what they would do. But she had assumed...what had she assumed? That the group had little to do with her. They were students. She was faculty. She was older, she was a loner, she was rather used to her anomalous position—the outsider in the establishment.

Libby handed her a sheet of paper. 'Here's our Christmas list.'

Gillian ran her eye rapidly over it. A women's studies programme. A sexual harassment policy with real penalties. The student handbook to be rewritten in non-sexist language. Course in sexism and racism to be added to core curriculum in all faculties. Anti date-rape measures. Free day-care. No university funds for pornographic publications. No more Triumph Day slaves. And last, but definitely not least, affirmative action.

'Not a modest list, is it?' she said drily.

Libby and Denise smiled, but Rita was indignant.

'Nothing on this list is impossible. Every item already exists on one campus or another. We're living in the dark ages here.'

Gillian looked at the list again. 'When you say affirmative action, how are you defining it?'

Rita passed her a folder. 'Read that. It's our basis of unity statement, plus definitions, our policies, and an outline of our plan of action. But to answer your question, we mean second-wave affirmative action. First wave—you know, "if qualifications are equal hire the woman" has only led to tokenism. Men hire a woman or two and then go back to hiring men—and they use the one woman as a shield against charges of sexism. Why go through that? It'll just delay the real change that's needed. What we want is to hire women until we have parity. Full stop.'

Gillian laid the folder on her desk. 'I was going to say you've left out the moon, but you haven't. What in particular do you want from me?'

'Our top priority is a women's studies programme. We know some feminists don't agree because they think it'll be a ghetto, but we think it's essential. And we aren't just making the demand, we're trying to get things started. We're going after serious money,' Rita answered. She paused, and then sprang her surprise.

'We're going to ask Jessie Rayne for an endowment, to get women's studies started.'

Gillian was startled. 'The coal queen? I thought Bob Frost had that money all sewed up.'

'That's what he thinks,' Rita said. 'But we have reason to believe that she's approachable. Her family's been donating to the university for a couple of generations now, but Queen Jessie might like to put her own stamp on the philanthropic tradition. She went to Cambridge, you know, right after they let women take degrees—and she quotes *A Room of One's Own*.'

'Really? How do you know?'

'Spies,' said Rita, with the first glint of a smile.

'I see!' I'd like to meet her, Gillian thought. 'And what about the engineers?' she asked. 'They aren't going to be overjoyed, exactly. They'll think you're poaching.'

'We know that. They'll do whatever they can to discredit us.' Rita leaned forward in her chair. 'That's one reason why we need your help. We want some women with clout. You're a head of department. Jessie Rayne should be impressed. We'd like you to come to the meeting.'

'She's already agreed to a meeting? Well, well.' Gillian thought for a moment. 'Have you asked any other faculty members?'

'Not to join the delegation. But we're asking for letters of support. We'd like to have official support from the faculty of arts, or for that matter from any of the faculties, but we don't expect much until we have something more tangible from Ms Rayne.'

'What about the administration?'

'The Dean of Women,' said Libby, 'is with us all the way. We've just asked her, and she'll be on the delegation.' She flipped the pages of a small notebook. 'The Dean of Arts, I quote, "supports women's studies in principle, and will of course be an enthusiastic participant in the negotiations if Ms Rayne should offer financial assistance", but he prefers to wait for "the situation to develop a little further" before he takes an active role.'

'In other words,' said Rita scornfully, 'Dean Stanley would love the money, but he won't stick his neck out.'

'We thought he might,' Denise put in, 'because we all know how much he hates Dean Frost.'

'Yes,' said Gillian, 'but the President's a scientist, and he and Frost are thick as thieves. The arts are poorer every year relative to the sciences, and Stanley has to fight for every penny. He'll avoid unnecessary friction if he can. He'd think it was foolish to raise Frost's hackles without a good reason—he'd see you as a bad risk.'

'What about you?' Rita looked challengingly at Gillian.

CHAPTER 4

Gillian, alone in her office, absent-mindedly cleared her desk, thinking about the meeting that had just ended. She wrote a couple of letters, killing time until the traffic thinned out. Of all things, to find herself defending Dean Stanley, that pusillanimous oilcan. But it was something that happened when Rita was around. She made no allowances, and the next thing you knew, your own realism—as you saw it—landed you in a corner with people you usually tried to avoid. What an uncomfortable presence she was. 'What about you?' she had said. In other words, Dr Adams, do you think we're a bad risk too? Are you afraid to raise hackles? Well, was she? There would be a meltdown in the department. Half of them would be anxious about money: worried that the same old pie would have another slice cut from it. After all, Jessie Rayne might get women's studies started, but the rest of the money would come out of the university budget. And then there were the foes of women's studies; they would reassert that 'women were already appropriately studied within the usual disciplines'. But worse, her association with the Feminist Union would enrage those faculty—and that was most of them—who bridled at any suggestion of hiring policies that favoured women. Of all the items on the list, affirmative action was the one that would provoke the fiercest opposition. Gillian knew that from past experience. She looked at the list she had been given. Rita was right, she thought, we are in the dark ages here. We have to fight tooth and nail for a women's studies programme in 1990 when at most universities they had been in place for years. As for affirmative action, it had been uphill work to induce the department to hire Carole even though she was better than her competition. The Feminist Union was talking about second-wave affirmative action, but here at UPNW, the first wave hadn't even wet their toes.

Outside, the light was fading. Gillian tucked her copies of the proposal and the correspondence with Jessie Rayne into her briefcase. Even Rita had agreed that she should read them before giving her answer, and they would serve to rescue her from her previous plans for a riotous evening alone in bed with her computer manuals. She locked the door to her office. The secretaries had gone home, and the main office was bleakly empty under the fluorescent light. Down the carpeted corridor, several open doorways indicated that various department members were still at work. In another hour they would all be gone, settling down to dinner at home, or drinking at the faculty club. The department, like others all over the continent, was middle-aged. It was a good thing that people like Rita came along, Gillian thought as she waited for the elevator. We're all too comfortable for our own good. With her Carver Fellowship, and the course she would consequently be teaching, she would be part of the faculty for the next two years. Life would be interesting.

The elevator descended crankily, as if it too wanted to be finished for the day. Rita still calls it a lift, Gillian remembered idly. She still calls gas petrol after seven years here. I wonder if I'd still say elevator if I lived in England...I know I'd say washcloth— I can't imagine saying face-flannel. My language has become a mongrel breed of English anyhow; I don't speak pure American any more, but I don't speak British English, or true Canadian. I scramble them all. I say 'sneakers' and pronounce 'missile' as if it were a prayer book, and prehistoric American slang like 'nifty' and 'baloney' pops out of my mouth, but I use bloody as an intensifier, call university forms bumf, and think Rankin fancies himself. I used to say 'apartment', but now I sometimes say 'flat' and sometimes 'suite', the way they do here. When I sleep late, I sleep in. It's a good thing there aren't three sides of the road to drive on.

She stepped out into the soft, dusky air. It wasn't raining, but beyond the shelter of the overhang the pavement was wet. A few lamps lent a dim and intermittent illumination to the network of paths. Students could be seen at the rear entrance to the library across a wide, dark swath of lawn. Gillian followed her path past the library and the English building. Branches arching high over the path dripped on her hair. Her car was in the lot sandwiched between the faculty club and the applied science complex. She cut along a gravelled path and threaded her way among the puddles in the unpaved lot. A cold glare from the engineers' windows quivered on the water.

'Why don't you buy a sticker for the new parkade,' Laura had said, twice now. 'It's dry, well lit, and your car's under cover.'

'And it's further from the history building, and it costs ninety dollars a term,' Gillian had answered both times. Besides, she hated the parkade. It was the ugliest thing on campus, and that was saying something. Before it had been erected, the Gillian Adams prize for worst building had been awarded in alternate years to the English Department, which occupied a four-storey stucco slum tarted up with ersatz Spanish motifs, and the Chemistry Department, which held a gigantic concrete bunker against the encroaching ambitions of Biology and Physics. The original rectangle of granite buildings around the Green, pleasantly proportioned and now festooned with creepers, was kind enough to the eye. The rest of UPNW was a shoddy architectural sampler without a single dreaming spire to its name. But the view was unsurpassed. Set down at the straggling southern edge of the city, the campus had had a rural flavour until a decade or so ago, and people who by virtue of seniority, luck or politics occupied offices with south-facing windows could still look at the same wide blue water that the Indians used to see from the bluffs. Those whose offices looked in other directions saw a mounting wave of office towers in the distance, or a wall in close-up. Gillian's office had two huge windows at the south-west corner of the new arts building—one good reason to be head of the department. Her five-year term was up next year. She expected to be asked to renew, and she would have to decide whether that was what she wanted.

She drove slowly through the dusk, joining a stream of rush-hour traffic beyond the gates. The campus wasn't very large. A Klondike fortune had bought the land and endowed the library, a bit of romantic history dramatized in bronze near the main gate, where a prospector stooped with his pan over a yard or two of stainless steel river. The story was preserved in more detail in the Klondike Archive on the top floor of the library, and in another form in the benefactions of the Rayne family. At least it was said that UPNW had been chosen owing to the mining connection. The engineering and geology departments were the richest on campus, thanks to a mountain of coal discovered by Cyrus Rayne in the 1880s. Their buildings were big, and their equipment was elaborate and up-to-date. In the faculty of arts, the showers of wealth were referred to as Acid Rayne.

The drive from her office to her house took about fifteen minutes, except during the morning rush for eight-thirty classes. Gillian hadn't taught one of these for years, but she was often on campus by eight o'clock. If she didn't arrive until nine, the day usually went out of control. Although she frequently worked in the evenings, she liked to escape the office and go home to read and write in the quiet of her own house.

She pulled into the driveway and got out to open the garage door. Drifts of leaves lay under the trees on the lawn. The air was heavy with moisture. She had forgotten to leave the porch light on, so she had to walk back to the house in the dark and fumble her key into the side door. Nobody ever used the front door— nobody who knew her. In the age of the automobile, everyone parked in the driveway and used the side door. But the house had been built before cars were common. The garage was a separate building at the back of the lot, and in this old neighbourhood of large lots and big trees, the glaring street lights hardly penetrated the private green spaces hidden behind hedges and thick shrubbery. This was all to the good—so long as you weren't afraid of your own yard in the dark.

Gillian wasn't. Break-ins were hardly unknown, though they were less frequent than one might have expected, given that the inhabitants of this neighbourhood probably had more worth stealing than the average. But most burglaries took place during the afternoon, when people were away at work, not at six o'clock in the evening when they were apt to return home. It was late at night, when she was alone in the dark house, that she was sometimes afraid. She would lie in bed, sleepless, listening to the rain, thinking of the flimsy latches on the basement windows, of how the rain would mask the noise of footsteps, of screws tearing loose two floors below, thinking she should sell the house and move into an apartment, a place where people would hear if she called for help.

But now, arriving home, her house seemed a refuge. Inside, she shed her coat, poured a drink, and telephoned Laura.

'What about an impromptu dinner? Something's come up, and I need to talk to you about it.'

'Sure. Jack isn't home yet. I'll just put the pizza menu out on the kitchen counter. Did I tell you? It's my signal flag. It means fend for yourself.'

'Does he always order pizza?'

'I would rather not know.'

Jack Blaine, Laura's husband, was a lawyer. He often worked late into the evening, and Laura, after years of leaving dinners in the oven, had recently stopped cooking except on the rare occasions when he came home early, bearing gifts from the market. She ate food from the delicatessen and read journals she had previously never had time for. Their two children were now away at college, but it had been their recent summer vacation which had precipitated the change. Laura had piled her shopping cart high with food for four that then went bad in the refrigerator because the family was never home for dinner at the same time.

'I had to throw away some salmon,' she had recounted to Gillian, 'and that did it. I told them they'd all be sleeping with the fishes if it happened again, but Jason just said, "C'mon, Ma, this is 1990! Get a life! Buy a microwave." He drives me nuts, he's always keening "this is 1990" as if 1989 was before we had the wheel, but this time he was right.'

Gillian inspected the meagre contents of her own refrigerator. There was half the roast chicken she had cooked on Sunday, a lettuce, a bag of string beans and a small triangle of smoked salmon. After she had chucked a jar of tar-black pesto, a few withered Greek olives and a tub of cream cheese that had cracked like old plaster, there was little else. She stripped the browning outer leaves from the lettuce and began to make a salad.

Over dinner in the panelled dining-room, Gillian told Laura about her meeting with the Feminist Union and the Rayne scheme. They looked over the correspondence and what Libby had called the Christmas list. Gillian had opened a bottle of wine and lit candles; she liked to make dinner with Laura a festive occasion, even when the food hardly seemed to warrant it.

Laura leaned back in her chair and gave a meditative twirl to her wineglass. Her honey-coloured hair, threaded with grey, gleamed dully in the candlelight. She was forty-eight, two years older than Gillian, and plump where Gillian was thin, smooth where Gillian was weathered. Her opaque, milky skin hardly seemed to age. She had been twenty-five, she had once told Gillian, before she stopped having to show identification at bars.

'So they want a million from Jessie Rayne, and they want you to help them get it.'

'That's right.'

'But Applied Science and the Geology Department have been cultivating her forever. She's their golden goose.'

'I know. But it seems that the goose may have feminist feathers. God knows, coming from that family, she'd have to be tough or she'd be dangling at the tail of some trust fund, managing a clothing allowance instead of running the company.'

'Isn't there a brother?'

'Yes, but I've heard he doesn't have much to do with the mining company. Didn't he lose his shirt in real estate a couple of years ago?'

'So maybe *he* gets the clothing allowance.'

Gillian laughed and refilled the glasses.

'Anyway, Gillian, the thing is, do you want to be mixed up in this? You'll make an army of enemies, and your own department won't thank you for that. And they won't like their department head being associated with a bunch of radical feminists.'

'Radical? How radical are they?'

'Oh God, let's not argue about labels. In the general view of the faculty, they're radical. Look at this stuff. They spell "women" *wimmin*, for God's sake. People flip out when you invent new spelling and change vocabulary. They go ballistic. It's worse than spitting on the flag.' She gestured at the papers Gillian had showed her. 'And they want radical change. I don't mean women's studies, I mean that list you've got—all those demands at once, and especially affirmative action. And seeking legal advice about suing the university. I agree with most things they want, even women's studies, although I used to think that kind of ghettoization was a mistake—but you know I don't approve of the so-called second wave. It wouldn't have a hope in hell, and I think it would be terrible for the university if it did.' Laura's voice rose. 'Gillian, think. They're telling us to hire only women. If we want this to be a good university, with a good reputation, so we can attract talented grad students and faculty, we have to hire the best people we can get. We can't hire on any other basis, or nobody who's any good will want to come.'

'How do you know? Maybe some of the best women will make a point of coming here.'

'We can't base policy on that. What if they don't? We'll slide downhill. We're not Harvard or Oxford—they could afford to make a gesture, though of course nobody there thinks so, they just want to hire Nobel prize-winners. Here, women just have to compete with men for the places available. We hire the best or we're sunk.'

'And who defines best? Men do. The administration is male, eighty-six per cent of the tenured faculty is male. And most of the time they choose more men—not because the men are better, but because they're more comfortable with each other than with us. My department has only two women. Look at the science faculties. Look at Chinese and Russian studies. Hardly a woman! Thank God we don't have a forestry department or the figures would be worse. As it is, we're stuck at fourteen per cent, while talented women with Ph.D's are commuting eighty miles to teach part-time for peanuts. And what about full professors? Where are the women? What about salaries? Women are still fighting for equal pay—why do you think that is?'

'That's blatant injustice, I agree. We had a case in my department last year when Amy Lang was promoted. They tried to give her the promotion without the same increase in pay that the men got.'

'Well, Laura, how are we going to change things like that? We've *got* to have more women on the faculty. But women are only hired when they are so much better than the male candidates that it would be positively embarrassing not to hire them. And sometimes not even then. Imagine what would happen if Rita Gordon applied for a job here after her two years with the Carver Fellowship!'

'After the Carver? You think she has it sewn up? But they've *never* given that grant to a woman.'

'I know. But she's head and shoulders above the usual run of candidates. You've given me the run-down on the English students—you said a couple were excellent, but not remarkable. I know the students from my department. They *have* to give it to her.'

'If you're so sure, then why bother with affirmative action?'

'Because grants aren't the real hurdle. Grants are temporary. Jobs—permanent jobs, with tenure and promotion and the power to make decisions—that's what affirmative action is about. And I might add,' Gillian said with some heat, 'if you're so sure she won't get it, why aren't you *for* affirmative action?'

'I do support first-wave. When the candidates are equal, the university should hire women. I'm all for that. I signed that letter two years ago, remember?

'And remember the reaction? We had Stanley and a crowd of irate men telling us that hiring committees couldn't be restricted like that—there were "intangibles" that mattered. Intangibles. A penis may be unmentionable, but it ain't intangible.'

Laura laughed, reluctantly. 'Gillian, you know that I *hope* you're right about the Carver, don't you? I hope Rita gets it.'

'I'll bet you a bottle of champagne.'

'You're on. But the winner buys. If you lose, you won't even feel like drinking it, let alone buying it.'

'I won't lose.'

'We'll see.' Laura waved the argument away. 'But getting back to the problem at hand, I really don't think you should endorse the Feminist Union programme as long as it includes second-wave affirmative action. In the end, women will lose. If you hire people for political reasons, real standards go out the window. Inferior candidates will be hired, and then the men will say "See, women aren't good enough."'

'Oh, balls, dear. It's time we stopped having to be twice as good in order to make the short list.'

'*We* made it, Gillian. That means other women can.'

'I used to think that, Laura. Now I think we're unwitting buttresses of the status quo. The university can point to us and say, "See, we do hire women"—the implication being that they've scoured the earth and found only us. Listen, they're dying to get the woman question off their plates. They're sick of it—they yearn to think they've done enough. We're supposed to be happy with small-scale change and paper policies. You and I can't afford to be complacent. Unless we fight for other women, *we* become a key mechanism for keeping them out.'

Gillian frowned and shut her eyes, ambushed by an acute craving for a cigarette. She and Laura had quit together years before, but once in a while, usually in Laura's company, the ghost of the addiction came back to haunt her. 'Arguing with you was more fun when we smoked,' she said grumpily. 'Anyway, I'll quit making speeches. We're not going to resolve this tonight. Setting aside your own view of the Union, if they claim-jump the engineers and push their programme, it's going to be extraordinarily messy: a dogfight, from one end of campus to the other. Is it right, in my position, to go out on this political limb?'

Laura considered. 'Well, it depends on how you see your duties as department head, doesn't it? A lot of people would say that your political function is to keep the department bread as well buttered as possible. You won't do that if you're identified as an Eff You.'

'Oh. You mean the Dean of Arts is the cash cow, and I'm the departmental dairymaid? Hell's bells, I don't define my job that way, not if it means that holding unpopular political opinions is a dereliction of duty. Why did I take the job? Partly because there aren't any women at that level. They're as scarce as hen's teeth— I'm getting carried away with rural metaphors—and I'm not going to be trapped into a neutral stand on women's issues.'

They argued their way through the rest of the wine. Near the end, Laura said, 'You know, they may not ask you to be department head again if you do this.'

'That's possible...but I could see that as a blessing in disguise.'

'Quite a disguise,' said Laura. 'Even its own mother wouldn't recognize it.'

Chapter 5

The next morning Gillian left for work later than usual. She had lingered over her coffee, thinking out her decision about the Feminist Union and the Rayne committee before facing the office and its gnat-cloud of distractions. It was raining hard, and wet leaves were plastered to the driveway and the lawn. The garden was dreary. Between now and April she would scarcely look at it, except for the gnarled limbs of the elderly fruit trees, which had a bare beauty even on the darkest, soggiest days of January. When she had moved in, eleven years before, the trees hadn't been pruned in years, and suckers as thick as her wrists sprang from every branch. She had had a gardener in to prune them properly, and that year there had been hardly any flowers and no fruit. But since then the annual pruning had been easier, and in the spring the trees were lacy with blossom. She liked the hard, sweet pears, but there were far too many apples; misshapen and scabbed, suitable only for apple sauce she had no time to make. The flowering orchard breathed sweetness into her bedroom on damp April nights, and she hated to cut down old trees, but now the lawn was a mess, poxed with rotting apples. She would have to see if the teenagers down the street wanted to rake this year. She hadn't the time.

The long, yellowing leaves of irises and day-lilies, flattened by the rain, sprawled over the edge of the flowerbeds along the driveway. Gillian thought of her mother's well-kept garden and the burning colours of the fall. It was at this time of year that she most longed for home. But think of March, she reminded herself, when here the trees are coming into flower, while the east is a wasteland of frozen mud. Think of eastern cities when the snow melts, and the air reeks with the winter's deposits of dogshit. She was acclimatized now; she no longer missed the blazing summers and fierce winters of her childhood, she found these soft, undulating west-coast seasons kind.

She was caught in the rush hour, crossing streams of cars on their way downtown, creeping along in the middle of the logjam of students trying to make their eight-thirties. The rain bucketed down, and the car windows steamed up so that she could hardly see. The traffic slowed even more, then halted. Gillian peered forward, trying to see what was holding them all up. She could see nothing but rain and a glittering blur of brake lights. She dug into the glove compartment and found her Italian tape.

'*Crede che piovera oggi? Ha le soprascarpe?*' said the opulent voice of the Italian woman. 'Do you think it will rain today?'

'*Si. Credo che piovera oggi,*' Gillian said back. 'But I don't have any rubbers.'

'*Sulla Costa Ligure piove poco,*' the woman intoned. 'On the coast of Liguria, there is little rain.'

A mellifluent man's voice replied, '*Ma piacerebbe passare l'inverno sulla Costa Ligure.*' 'I would like to spend the winter on the Ligurian Coast.'

'*Mi piacerebbe—*' Gillian sang in bogus Puccini.

The traffic began to move. She passed two cars with buckled fenders. The drivers stood in the rain, writing down each other's licence numbers.

'Hmmph,' Gillian grunted uncharitably. 'They probably didn't have their headlights on.' It was one of the things that annoyed her on rainy days. It never occurred to half of the drivers to turn on their lights, although one glance through the rear window in weather like this should have told them how invisible they themselves were to the vehicles ahead of them. The accident rate went up and up, and so did the insurance premiums. In Sweden, she'd heard, there was a law now—your lights were always on, day or night. She would like to visit Sweden sometime, but Edward wouldn't. This was one of the disadvantages of transatlantic love— all her travel time and money was used up on trips to London. Edward at the beach was unthinkable, and when she suggested Venice, he only laughed and quoted Mitford. 'Abroad is unutterably bloody, and foreigners are fiends.' Well, she was going to Italy next year, with or without him.

By the time she reached the history office, Gillian was later and wetter than she liked to be. Allie greeted her cheerfully.

'Nice day, huh?'

'*Sulla Costa Ligure piove poco,*' Gillian replied.

'Hey, your Italian's getting better,' Allie said. 'You should come to class with me. You could learn really useful things, like the Italian for fucked-up. They never put those words on the tapes. No space left, I guess—they're all filled up with words like "hatstand".'

Gillian laughed. 'And what is the Italian for fucked-up?'

'*Fottuto.*'

'Good morning,' said Jane, coming in with a swirl of burnt orange skirts and a kettle of water for coffee. She had a pumpkin on her desk, Gillian saw. 'What are you making for Hallowe'en this year?' she asked Jane. Every year Jane made a few costumes for children in families on welfare. She chose a pattern and made up half a dozen copies. In past years she had made pirates, goblins and black cats.

'I'm making witches this year. Black cloaks and pointy hats.'

Gillian smiled. 'I was a witch when I was five. My mother made the costume. I even had a familiar—a tiny bat pinned to my shoulder.'

'I'm going to a costume party this year,' said Allie. 'I'm going as a garbage dump.'

'What?' said Jane and Gillian.

'I'm gluing bits of newspaper and plastic bags and orange peel and toilet paper all over a coat I got at the Sally Ann, and I've got a stuffed seagull to wear on my head. And on the back of the coat there'll be a sign that says "Recycle".'

Allie grinned at them and fished her cigarettes out of her bag. 'Ciggy break,' she announced, and went out. Gillian watched her blonde, bristly head disappear around the corner. This September, Allie had reappeared after her vacation with her hair cut short and gelled in points. She looked like a gilded hedgehog, Gillian told her. Quite fetching. Allie had rolled up her eyes.

'It's not supposed to be fetching. It's the opposite. Call me Spike.'

But nobody did, any more than they used her proper name, which was Allison. She was slight, with slanty eyes, and Gillian had heard friends call her Cat. So had Charlie Rankin, who had called her Kitten until she threatened to quit.

'No mail yet?' Gillian asked Jane.

'Not yet.'

'Just as well. I haven't answered yesterday's.'

She unlocked her office and went in, leaving the door open. Later, when the morning bustle of mail and coffee and telephone messages had passed, she would shut it and go over her notes for her ten-thirty class.

Jane brought her some coffee, and she drank it while she looked at her schedule. Only one meeting today, her class, and a noontime lecture by Keith Thomas, who was passing through. Kittredge should be meeting him at the airport about now. She had sixteen essays left to mark from the recent batch. She picked up a few at the top of the stack. 'British Imperialism and the...' 'Colonial Policy and the...' She sighed.

Outside her windows, the rain continued. The faculty straggled damply in, the mail came, the telephones rang. Voices murmured and grumbled in the history office. Through the general buzz Gillian heard Libby Hosmer's voice, louder than usual.

'It's such a piss-off,' she said. 'I just bought the car this fall, and I don't have any money to fix it.'

'What happened?' another voice asked.

'Somebody trashed Libby's rear bumper last night, and now the trunk won't open,' Allie said.

Gillian set down her pen and turned her head to listen.

'What a drag. Was it a hit and run?'

'I don't think so,' said Libby. 'It looks deliberate—like it was done with a crowbar.'

'But why? Why would anybody do that?'

'I don't know. I guess somebody didn't like my prochoice bumper sticker.'

⚜

Later that day, Gillian ran into Rita just outside the building. She had tried to reach her in the morning, to let her know she had decided, and had left a note in her pigeonhole, but Rita hadn't come into the office. They stopped under the shelter of the entryway. Rita was wearing leathers, and a motorcycle helmet dangled from her gloved hand.

'Not much of a day for riding,' Gillian observed.

'No. I haven't taken my bike out of the city for a week, now. When the rain stops, I'm going, even if I have to cancel my office hour. I can't go very often once the warm weather's over. I like to ride up the North Shore mountains, and when the clouds close in, I'm trapped.' She shifted from foot to foot, swinging her helmet restlessly.

'Did you enjoy Keith Thomas?'

Rita nodded. 'The well-turned lecture. If I had an accent like that, I'd be queen of Oxford.'

'Would you like that?' Gillian inquired, thinking of her own years at Cambridge.

'I like it here,' Rita said and changed the subject. 'Did you hear about Libby's car?'

'Yes, I heard. Do you think it was because of her bumper sticker?'

'Could be. But it could be because she was at the Triumph Day demo. The Union is coming out in the open now, and we're bound to be targets.'

'I've decided to join the delegation to Jessie Rayne,' Gillian told her. Rita's face lit up.

'Grand! We're trying for a date within two weeks.'

'All right,' Gillian said. 'But I have to warn you that I'm going to England for a conference next month, and I'll be away for a week.'

Rita wrote the dates down. 'We should see her before then.'

'That's fine. So long as you know my constraints.'

Rita's smile glinted. 'Now I know one of them.'

⊸T⊱

Shortly after that, Gillian called Laura.

'Have you made up your mind?' Laura asked.

'Yes.' Gillian paused. Laura would not be happy with her.

'Well?'

'I've raised the Jolly Roger.'

CHAPTER 6

That afternoon there was a departmental meeting at four-thirty. It was not a controversial hour in the History Department, but Gillian had heard that the four-thirty meeting was now an issue in the English Department, where there were more women and more young faculty with children who needed picking up from daycare. It was amazing, she thought, how a seemingly innocuous item—the hour of the meeting—could turn into another battleground. The full professors were refusing to alter a schedule that was enshrined by habit and had always been convenient for them. (Most of them, if they'd had children long ago when they were young had also had wives who were home at four-thirty.) The assistant profs, on the other hand, were caught between missing the meetings (which meant losing goodwill, not to mention the opportunity to forward their particular interests), and paying a dollar a minute for late pick-up at daycare, or a higher price in spousal relations...One probably learned all about these combats in seminars for boardroom gladiators.

Ham Ridgeway was complaining about some missing journals in the departmental library. Gillian's attention wandered. She thought about her promise to Rita. Had it been the right decision? She could make a shambles of this meeting by bringing it up right now. She looked around the long table in the seminar room. Fifteen of the twenty-three members of the history faculty were there—pretty fair attendance. Carole Stein was the only other woman in the room. Everyone was white. Fred Wong, who taught a course in Chinese history for the department, wasn't there. He was in

Asian Studies and only attended history meetings when they directly concerned his course. Any sociologist, for that matter, any moderately observant person, Gillian thought, would be able to identify this group as academic without hearing a word they said. The beards and the sweaters would be enough. In the past, pipes would have been the third clue, but few academics smoked now. Most of the men were in their fifties; two were nearing retirement, and two, plus Carole, were in their thirties: assistant professors hoping to get tenure. Thank God for Carole; it hadn't been comfortable being the only woman, department head or not. They weren't destined to be close friends; the mysterious alchemy of attraction was missing, in spite of their compatible historical interests and shared view of the university, but they were good colleagues.

Department head. How odd, she still thought sometimes, even after several years in the position. She knew perfectly well that she hadn't been chosen for the pure shining light of her intellect. Her respectable standing as a scholar had made her a plausible choice, but had the department not been cloven to the root by the rival candidacies of Ham Ridgeway and Jim Jacobsen, she would never have been considered. She had remained on the edge of the fray, partly owing to a term's leave of absence to teach at the London School of Economics, and as reputable scholar and outsider had been somebody both sides could accept because she represented victory for neither. With some reluctance, but hoping to pursue certain aims such as hiring more women, she had accepted a five-year term. She had been concerned that her research would suffer—it had, but not as much as she had feared—and she had suspected that the job would require more diplomatic skill than she possessed. But it had worked out. The tensions were there, but they lay under the surface most of the time. They would erupt again, Gillian knew, if anyone left or took early retirement, leaving a place to be filled.

The department hadn't altered much for some years; most of the members were full professors a decade or so away from retirement, and until recently the university budget hadn't allowed them to hire new people. Now they had several, but the numbers of new students had outstripped this expansion, and classes were far larger than anyone wanted them to be. This was what they were discussing now, not for the first time, and not for the last.

'I have sixty students in my introductory course, and I had to turn away thirty more.'

Kray, Gillian noted, managed to point to his own popularity while complaining. In two years, registration in his course on Japan and the West had tripled. Well, Japan was news.

Kittredge was asking, 'Why don't we let them all in? Maybe if they have to sit on the floor, and they complain to the Dean that a seminar with twenty-eight people in it is a farce, it will pressure the administration into giving us more money.'

'We've tried that,' Jim Jacobsen said. 'So did other departments. It made a big impression at first, but nothing was done, and after several years the administration got used to overcrowding; they began to regard it as normal. So now we do the opposite. We use the fire regulations to cut off enrolments and hope the students will complain about not being able to take the courses they want.'

Jacobsen, a Canadian political historian, was a heavyset, grizzled man. His broad nose was marked with the spidery red veins of a drinker. He wore a gown when lecturing, not a common practice at UPNW. His rival, Ridgeway, was tall and bony and concave, with an almost waxen cast to his complexion. He walked with a slight limp. They were hardly older than Daniel Kray and Rankin, but they seemed of a different generation. Kray and Rankin were fit. They played racquet ball and tennis and fought to hold middle age at bay. Verne Palmer, on the other hand, seemed to have been born middle-aged. Gillian glanced down the table at him. He was blinking rapidly and twisting a small corkscrew of paper between his right thumb and forefinger. In a moment or two he would polish his glasses.

'How are we doing compared to other departments?' Carole asked.

'About the same as Modern Languages, I believe,' replied Ridgeway. 'Rather worse than English. It's such a big department, they throw their weight around.'

'They also hire a lot more sessionals—there's a veritable army of them teaching English 100,' Palmer said in a complaining tone. 'That way, they up their enrolment and keep an iron grip on all their classrooms.'

'Stanley was head of the English Department. As long as he's dean, they'll get preferential treatment,' Jacobsen said. 'Political Science does all right without sessionals, and it's a smaller department—but Caldwell's a good politician.'

Caldwell being the department head, this was a not especially covert jab at Gillian.

Rankin leaned back in his chair. 'I'm all in favour of hiring more sessionals—preferably young and pretty ones.' He snickered, and Gillian's eyes met Carole's across the table.

'Oops, pardon me, ladies. No offence to present company.'

'We could consider putting another couple of sessionals in the budget,' said Kray. 'They don't cost much, after all.'

'And where would these *gastarbeiters* teach? In portable classrooms?' Ridgeway inquired impatiently.

The university was short of space as well as money. The women's studies programme, Gillian thought, will be competing for the same rooms we use. Palmer had started to polish his glasses. She watched a fly buzzing clumsily against the window and felt an irritable impulse to swat it.

'I've had students phone me at home, trying to get into my second-year course. I wouldn't mind a larger class if I could get another T.A.,' Carole remarked. 'But I can't mark papers for seventy-five or eighty students on my own.'

Ridgeway laughed grimly. 'Just be glad you aren't in Anthropology. You'd have to have one hundred students to get a T.A.'

'The fact is,' Jacobsen said, 'we need at least three more faculty members in this department, and then we need the space for their offices.'

'If one of our candidates gets the Carver this year, we'll have one more person on staff,' Gillian put in.

'Who'll teach only one course—' Jacobsen shrugged.

'And who's going to share an office with Rita?' chortled Rankin, looking across at Palmer, whose suddenly apprehensive expression revealed that this was a new and unwelcome thought. Jacobsen and Ridgeway looked undisturbed—no one imagined that their turf would be invaded—but most of the others were obviously imagining having to share and not liking the thought. John

Honeycutt, Rita's adviser, was among those who hadn't shown up for the meeting.

'As we don't know yet who the Carver Fellow will be,' Ridgeway said calmly, 'there's no point in worrying about that now.'

They went on talking about classrooms and office space. Gillian listened. Let them go on for a few minutes, she thought. The subject had to be aired. Rankin and Ridgeway argued. They had to turn away the largest numbers of students. They were both fine lecturers; their subjects were popular, but their classes were crowded because they could teach. Women students complained sometimes about Rankin's jokes. Too bad about his sexist tic, Gillian thought, he hasn't listened to anything I've said about it. I'd fire him— good lectures and all—if it were up to me. She glanced at her watch. It was time to pull the meeting together and get to the next item on the agenda.

When she returned to her office, Jane and Allie had gone home. She gathered up her coat and checked her mailbox for late essays. There was one, in a blue binder. Underneath was a note from Allie about a call from London. Edward? No, of course not. Just something about the conference. There was another envelope, addressed by hand. Gillian tucked it into her briefcase along with the essays. An excuse from a dilatory student, no doubt. She went along to the faculty club to meet Murray Kopf for a drink.

He was already there, sitting in the comfortable bar. The faculty club was an unremarkable example of west coast design, cedar and glass Frank-Lloyd-Wright-meets-Japan. It was long and low, tucked into a green square between the English and Chemistry buildings. Big windows looked out at young groves of pine trees. The interior was a large, open space, divided by levels rather than walls. The acoustics were abominable.

Gillian sank into a leather chair and ordered a Scotch. 'Oh God, Murray. Meetings.'

'The curse of working life,' Murray agreed. He took a pack of cigarettes from his jacket pocket and fumbled for a match.

'Murray! I thought you quit.'

'Shhh! The tobacco police are everywhere.' He exhaled a cloud of smoke and guilty pleasure. 'Want one?'

'Have you made a Faustian pact with Philip Morris? Don't tempt me.'

Murray was an old friend. He had come to UPNW at the same time as Gillian, and they had run into each other repeatedly at parties and in the faculty club bar. One evening, they had found themselves on the same side of a violent argument about American foreign policy in Latin America, and it had occurred to them to go out for dinner and see what they didn't agree about. For a while, they went nearly every Friday to a cheap Greek restaurant close to the campus. When they met, Gillian was still smarting from her last love-affair, which had ended in tears and acrimony when she moved west. She was not ready for another, and later, when she was, Murray had already met the woman he soon married. Neither of them saw this as a matter for regret; they were used to being friends. But the Friday nights lapsed, and, as time passed, the demands of teaching and research swelled to monstrous proportions in their lives. They leapt the hurdles of tenure and promotion and they saw each other less and less, except during the crisis weeks of Murray's divorce. Then one fall term, Murray had telephoned Gillian at home.

'You know what I'm thinking?' he said. 'I'm thinking that I've been working too hard for too many years. What am I doing in the lab Friday nights when I could be having dinner with you?'

So they had begun a new pattern. The old Greek restaurant was gone now, replaced by a fancy Italian place with starched pink linen napkins, and they didn't meet once a week, but they saw each other every month, if not for dinner, at least for a drink. Murray bought tickets to a concert in the chamber music series they had once attended regularly, and Gillian, reminded of a pleasure she had quite forgotten, wrote four more into her calendar. This year, Gillian had suggested they go to the opera as well, when *Salome* was performed in the spring.

Murray was a chemist. When he and another chemist spoke to each other, it was about as interesting to Gillian as listening to her nephew trying to count by ones to a million. When she asked Murray to explain what he did, he sighed and said he couldn't explain it to anybody who wasn't a chemist. Gillian retorted that specialists ought to be able to explain their work in English, but Murray insisted that if he were synthesizing pheromones he might be able to tell her in English about the sex lives of insects, but since what he was doing had no immediate practical application, there were no common English words to employ in describing it. Gillian gave up asking. He wasn't unwilling to answer, he simply hadn't the first idea of how to do it. So they never talked about his work. The closest they got was when he mentioned the politics of the Chemistry Department. Not that he was passionately absorbed by the turf wars—he kept clear of other chemists as a rule. 'They're a dull bunch. I can't think of anything to talk to them about except chemistry,' he explained mournfully. Murray had other interests—he read unusual biographies and regaled her with gossipy accounts of the lives of the near-famous; he was also a passionate fan of English composers—particularly Delius and Elgar, to whose music he had introduced her, and whose televised life-stories he had vainly urged her to watch. In the summers he sailed. He had navigated the Pacific coast from the Charlottes to the Baja Peninsula, but he was also content to take the *New York Times* for ballast on a warm sunny Sunday and anchor in the nearest cove. Then he would open a beer and rage through the crossword puzzle while Gillian grumbled over the editorials. He had grown up on Long Island, where he had suffered from acute envy as he watched the sailboats skimming across the Sound. Now he had his own. He was not entirely satisfied, but Gillian had never met anyone who owned a boat that was just right. Boats always needed some little improvement or weren't quite big enough. And water was very bad for them.

'You're off to London soon, aren't you?' Murray said now. 'Staying with Dick Tracy?'

'Yes, but we won't have much time together.'

'Can't you just give your paper and bag the rest of the conference?'

'Not really. You know how it is.'

'So how come Dickie never visits you here?'

'He's not tired of life.'

'What do you mean?'

'I mean he's a Londoner and doesn't see any point to being elsewhere. He was out here once, but it was just like having Dr Johnson—the main effect of travelling was to reinforce his conviction that he belonged at home. Frankly, I was so tense after the first week I *wanted* him to go home. We get on much better in London.'

'I'll say this much for your trans-oceanic romance, it's an improvement on adultery.'

'Trouble with Marilyn?'

'I can't say that—it's the same as it's been. I get tired of sneaking around, that's all. I'm not so sure I'd like to be married—it wasn't a big success the last time, but I wish we could just do some normal things together. Go to a movie, eat out. Like that.'

'When did that start?'

'What? Me and Marilyn? Five years ago.'

'No. Your desire for normal things.'

'I don't know. It's been creeping up on me. Work used to be enough. Every night in the lab—hey, fine. That's how you get to be a big noise. So I live in the lab, I listen to some music and read a few books, and all of a sudden I look up and I'm forty-seven and lonely as hell.'

Murray ordered another round of drinks and lit a cigarette.

'What are you going to do?'

'I don't know. What we were doing, it suited us both, you know. So I can't get mad at her now because it isn't what I want any more. But I catch myself looking at female students—not my own, I don't have many—but I'm feeling like a dirty old man.'

'Jesus, Murray, not a student. Please.'

'I know, I know. I'm just telling you what a weird state of mind I'm in.'

Murray slumped in his chair and ran his hand through his thinning curls. He had a rosy, somewhat fleshy face that had aged well, and a stocky body that hadn't. He had back trouble, and too much belly.

'Do you think I should run one of those ads? "Divorced Jewish male seeks candlelit dinners"? I won't say I'm a chemist.'

'No, don't. Just say you'll cook the dinners, and there'll be mobs of women after you.'

'I see. And what if I say I want someone who'll bring my slippers?'

'Some nice doggie will offer to marry you.'

Gillian looked up as the drinks came and saw the dean of engineering striding towards the dining-room with two other men whose faces she recognized but whose names she didn't know.

'Who are those guys with Dean Frost?' she asked Murray.

He turned his head. 'Department heads in engineering. Sacks and Berg.'

They sat down at the far end of the dining-room, well out of hearing range.

'What did you think of the Triumph Day affair?' Gillian asked Murray.

'I thought those women put themselves at risk. A drunken crowd has a highly unstable chemistry. It could have been very nasty.'

'They were aware of that possibility.'

'Well, I'm not sure it was politically wise. A lot of people resent them for getting UPNW a bad press and risking a worse one.'

'What are they supposed to do, then? Just let Triumph Day go on as is?'

'They could have picketed without blocking the parade.'

'Oh, come on, Murray. The slave wagon may be banned from now on—that's being seriously discussed for the first time. You're not going to tell me that this would have happened without the blockade? Who would stop the louts? Not the engineering faculty.'

'Don't be so sure. I know some of them, and they think the slave wagon is inexcusable. A lot of the students don't take part either.'

'But they don't *do* anything about it.'

'I think they will. Joe Wiegand in Civil Engineering told me Triumph Day makes him sick.'

'It doesn't make Dean Frost sick. He says the students have to let off steam.'

'Frost is old school. I know he sets the tone of public comment, but the others aren't all behind him. However, they don't like being collectively flayed by the media—that makes them go into a huddle. All I'm saying is that the women might have been better advised to use less aggressive tactics.'

'Murray, if there had been three Jewish slaves in that cart, would you say the same thing?'

There was a brief silence. 'No, I wouldn't,' he admitted.

When Gillian got home that night, she opened her briefcase and stacked the essays she was marking on her desk. She opened the envelope that had been in her mailbox. It was from Rita. The note was a brief scribble. The meeting with Jessie Rayne was set for the following Wednesday morning.

'Libby and I propose an addition to our list,' Rita had added. 'All male heads of faculties to perform janitorial duties in their departments.'

Gillian grinned. Rita was in high spirits.

CHAPTER 7

The weather was gloomy all weekend. Gillian finished her marking: twenty-two essays in fifteen hours. But the new Rioja she tried on Saturday evening gave her a headache, and the movie she wanted to see had left town, replaced by a rib-tickling comedy. On Sunday she read a tedious article on Gladstone and the franchise, turned out her bedroom closet and discovered a moth hole in a sweater she hadn't worn since the spring, and had a fight with Laura.

It was after Thanksgiving dinner, arranged for Sunday so they would have the holiday Monday to recover. Laura had fixed the traditional turkey with all the trimmings. The silver candlesticks Jack and Laura had received as a wedding present had been unearthed and polished, and the heavy, glistening bird, resplendent on its platter, would have provided a banquet for ten. The three of them were by turns jolly and nostalgic; they ate too much and drank two bottles of Beaune. Eventually, they collapsed by the fire in the living-room, sipping little glasses of the Calvados Jack had contributed to the occasion.

'We used to play "my grandmother's trunk" every Thanksgiving,' said Laura dreamily. 'And I won. I always remembered the list. "And in my grandmother's trunk I put an anchor, a balalaika, a chesterfield—"'

'Stop. Please. I'm feeling like your grandmother's trunk,' groaned Gillian.

Jack poured more Calvados. 'I have the remedy—*le trou Normand*. Astonishing apples they must have in Normandy—BC apples never taste like this. I'm going to write to Ottawa tomorrow demanding funds for a French apple project. My contribution to bi-culturalism.'

'I thought we were multi-cultural now,' Gillian murmured. 'You'll have to include apples from the Pacific Rim.'

'And where will you plant them?' Laura chimed in from her cushion near the hearth. 'The whole Okanagan will be suburbs before your grant comes through. There'll be one apple tree left that the farmers' grandchildren will be taken to see every Thanksgiving. California will be a desert. We'll all be eating algae and mangel-wurzels.'

'Persongel-wurzels,' said Gillian, draining her glass.

Laura leaned on her elbow and stirred the embers with a poker. 'That reminds me,' she said, 'I wanted to ask you—have you told your department about your decision?'

'There's not much to tell them yet. The meeting with Jessie Rayne is all I'm participating in right now, and it's confidential.'

'What about affirmative action? Didn't you tell me the Feminist Union might sue the university?'

'I said they were going to consult a lawyer. Can the university be legally compelled to hire more women? What do you think, Jack?'

'I don't know. Unlikely, I'd say. But I did hear recently of a case, in the mid-west, I think, in which an all-male chemistry department was taken to court on that issue and lost. They had to appoint a woman. I wonder what sort of time she's having.'

'Perfectly dreadful, of course,' said Laura. 'Can you imagine how nasty they'd be to her? And how patronizing? I couldn't bear to occupy a position that people didn't think I'd gotten on my own merit.'

'Even if you knew you did merit it, and it was only prejudice that kept you out?' Gillian asked.

'No. I don't have that kind of iconoclastic courage.'

'Well, those who do will be the pioneers for the rest of us.'

'The women at our firm have been hired on their merits,' put in Jack. 'We've got six, and we think the world of them. And they're not all in family law, either.'

'Six out of how many?'

'Twenty-six.'

'Over twenty-five per cent,' said Gillian. 'You're way ahead of the university.'

'You see,' said Laura. 'They hire the best, and they hire women. It works. Jack, would you ever bring in someone who wasn't as good, to promote equality?'

'Would I personally? It's not even worth thinking about because I'd never get it past the partners. Everybody's income depends on the money each member brings in. How many people do you know who're willing to pay out of their own pockets for equality?'

'But we do already,' said Gillian. 'In taxes. What's more, we pay for inequality, which is a lot more expensive.'

'Hard to prove that,' Jack replied.

'Anyway,' Laura argued, 'it's a spurious equality. The university will suffer academically if we hire on the basis of sex only.'

'The trouble with you, Laura,' said Gillian, 'is that you're still looking through male spectacles. You think what's happened so far has been just fair competition. Well, it hasn't. It's been affirmative action for *men*. You might ask yourself how much academic standards have suffered because of that.'

'No!' said Laura angrily. 'The trouble with me is I don't want charity, I want respect. Where am I going to get it if women don't advance through genuine achievement? I don't want women to be devalued. You and I are coin of the realm, Gillian, and I don't want us lumped with a lot counterfeit currency.'

'Why should you think we would be? Half the new Ph.D's in the arts are women now—nearer sixty per cent in English, I've heard. Do you think those are counterfeit degrees?'

'No, but I think that if women get special treatment it will reflect badly on all of us.'

'So in fact you won't risk a little bit of prestige for other women, will you?'

'And you'll bend rules for women and nobody else!'

Gillian went home feeling sore. She and Laura couldn't agree on the principles, and it mattered too much to set aside.

⬦

On Tuesday the clouds were denser than ever, a flat grey roof miles thick. Just before lunch Gillian ran into Denise, and they crossed the Green together. Denise was full of her latest discovery.

'Elizabeth Maconchey—her quartets are incredible. Have you ever heard them?'

Gillian admitted she hadn't.

'They're really great,' Denise began. 'Like Bartok, only better. She's written thirteen, and all kinds of other stuff. Even some operas. There's one called *The Sofa* I'm dying to hear, but I don't know if I can get hold of a recording. I'm thinking of writing my thesis on her work. You know, music history's so far behind—lots of women are being discovered now, and that's incredibly exciting, but there isn't any analysis—'

'Just add women and stir?'

'Exactly. You know, Maconchey—'

She broke off. Ahead of them, eddying along the path in their direction, was a raucous knot of youths, two of whom were dressed as mock women, with balloon-stuffed sweatshirts, miniskirts, and clownish lipstick. Their clothing was crudely lettered with invitations: FEEL MY TITS, Gillian read in distorted capitals stretched obscenely across a bulging sweatshirt. She looked away, and, with Denise, stepped off the walkway and walked across the squelching grass, giving the group a wide berth.

'We should *say* something. They shouldn't get away with it,' Denise hissed when they were safely past.

'I know,' Gillian said. 'But it's hard to face a mob, even a small one.' It was instinctive to avoid them, in fact. It was the survival tactic of a lifetime. She could hear the men behind her, joking lewdly and laughing.

'I'll face them if you will,' said Denise. 'I've seen this act one too many times.'

Gillian felt a surge of panic. To confront a rowdy crowd of men was the stuff of nightmares. She took a couple of deep breaths.

'All right,' she said. 'I'll try.' As a faculty member, she was armoured with authority. Her heart hammering, she turned back and approached the group. They fell silent and looked at her, hostile but wary. Her mouth was dry. Denise stood beside her.

'Do you know,' Gillian said quietly, 'that you're insulting every woman on this campus? Women belong here, and this sort of thing is intolerable.'

Sullen stares.

'It's just a joke,' one of the ersatz women said aggressively.

'It's not a joke to us. It's an assault. Please leave right now. And don't do this again.'

She folded her arms and stood on the path, blocking their way. How ridiculous, she thought. They can just walk around me. But I am a faculty member. One of them had the grace to look a little embarrassed. Another shrugged and turned back the way they had come. The others followed. They moved off slowly, as if to show they refused to be hurried.

'Fuckin' tight-ass bitch,' Gillian heard. Her heart was still beating hard.

'Why doesn't the administration stop them?' Denise asked bitterly. 'Why is it left up to us?'

In the cafeteria Gillian saw Murray eating a hamburger. She sank into the seat across from him, and related what had happened.

'You could practically smell the testosterone,' she grimaced. 'Like Lucifer's odour of sulphur.' She spooned up some warm soup, still feeling slightly shaken. 'Christ, it was hard to say something. I felt utterly panic-stricken.'

'Why?' asked Murray. 'I can see it was unpleasant, but you must have known they wouldn't actually hurt you.'

'Yes, that's why I could speak, but hostile groups of men are frightening—one learns it early and doesn't forget it. They're bigger and stronger than we are. They know it and we know it. There's a visceral fear most women have—we've heard too many stories. Or lived them. All that history wells up when we confront a group of men or even think about it.'

'It's frightening for us, too—don't forget that. Mobs are dangerous to everyone. Some men all by themselves scare me.'

'OK, but you don't grow up being told not to go out at night because your mere *existence* is a provocation. It's not the same for you, Murray. How many men you know have been raped? The sexual fear we have is learned in childhood, and it keeps its grip because as soon as we're teenagers, or even sooner, we find out about the way some men gang together to humiliate and frighten us. I *still* remember when I was only fourteen, walking past a construction site and having a whole bunch of men, all twice my size, start hollering obscenities at me…Those things don't happen to you.'

That afternoon Gillian spent hours with Rita, Frances Romano and a committee of the Feminist Union, considering how best to present their proposal to Jessie Rayne. They would have little control over the unfolding of events subsequent to the meeting. Provided their proposal attracted Ms Rayne, she would have discussions with the administration and cagey financial negotiations, and then there would be announcements orchestrated by the established powers. If the Feminist Union muffed this first meeting, there would be no second chance. Their time was now.

On Wednesday morning the delegation met in the lobby of the arts building and marched through the drizzle to the faculty parking lot. They were going downtown in Gillian's car, an ageing, nondescript Ford with room for all five of them. Frances opened one of the rear doors of the car only to be politely shooed to the front by Libby, observant of the conventions. Rita, in the background, raised a sardonic eyebrow but said nothing. This boded well, Gillian thought. If Rita refrained from hindering their progress with a comment on the politics of the front and back seat, she would probably not be difficult at the meeting. At their own strategy session, two days earlier, she had twice diverted them from the signposted road of practical matters down some unpaved political by-way. The second time, Gillian had said, 'I don't have all day. We must stick to the task at hand or I'll have to resign.' Libby and Denise had looked a little shocked, but Frances had thanked her afterwards. Even so, the meeting had had to resume in the evening, and it was very late before they reached a consensus. Rita had been very strung up, Gillian thought, but this morning she was buoyant, as though now, when the moment came, she could transform her anxieties into energy. She was the same with exams, Gillian thought, remembering her orals. She had been in shreds the week before the examination, but when the day came, she had performed without a tremor.

The third occupant of the back seat was a 'mature student' in the English Department. Gillian didn't know her very well, and neither did Laura, it had turned out, when Gillian asked her the night she had come to dinner and discussed the Rayne committee. The English faculty was large, and Laura's field—the English novel from Austen to the Brontës ('I run the gamut of literature from A to B,' she'd said when Gillian first met her) was not of great interest to Marnie Borowski, who was writing an MA thesis on Aphra Behn. She was thirty-five, Gillian guessed. Frances had told her that Marnie had two children in school and a bank loan, and had moved back to her parents' house for a year while she finished her degree. No wonder she looked so tired.

They had been instructed to park in one of several reserved spaces in the lot beneath the Rayne Tower and take the elevator to the twenty-fourth floor, where Jessie Rayne had her office. The tower was quite new, part of the forest of new office buildings that had sprung up in the downtown core during the 'eighties. Its mirrored exterior reflected the clouds scudding overhead, and the big glass doors leading to the lobby were surmounted by an elaborate frieze, executed in brass, dignifying the history of mining. Across the street, a grey stone church huddled in the shadows of the surrounding towers.

The elevator, likewise decorated in polished brass, whizzed upward in efficient silence. At the twenty-fourth floor the doors opened to reveal acres of grey-blue carpet and miles of sky outside the huge windows. The receptionist looked up, and Gillian was suddenly uncomfortably conscious of their appearance. Rita was tidier than usual, but in this opulent setting she looked like a refugee. Frances, in a carmine wool suit, was assertively elegant, as usual. But the rest of us, she thought, need fresh haircuts and new clothes. Our shoes are polished, our hands are clean—like the deserving poor. Well, perhaps that was the right way to look when you were asking for money, but Gillian suspected that it would be better to look like people who gave wads of cash to the symphony.

The receptionist was sleek and silky. Short, ultra-smooth hair (a cut every three weeks, at least, Gillian estimated), a slithery aubergine wool dress, heels, a subtle mask of make-up. Her eyes revealed no thoughts about them. She smiled, she offered them chairs, she buzzed her employer and murmured their arrival into an intercom. At the far end of the room, a silent secretary sat behind a computer terminal. The space was very quiet, except for the clicking of her keyboard and the muted hum of the city below.

Jessie Rayne did not keep them waiting. She came out to meet them. Rather nice of her, Gillian thought, she could have stayed behind her no doubt enormous desk. That was her last thought about Jessie Rayne that was not impressed with the weight of Jessie Rayne's commanding personality.

She was about sixty, a woman of medium height, shorter than Gillian and broader through the ribcage. Her hair was wiry, pepper turning to salt, and immaculately cut. She wore a Chanel suit and discreet diamonds, and low-heeled shoes that did not impede her rapid stride. She shook hands as they introduced themselves, with a friendly if appraising glance. Gillian suspected she knew quite a lot about them already. Her face was leathery, with deep crow's feet at the corners of the eyes. (Hawaii every winter? Gillian wondered, and then thought: No. Summers on the ranch. I'm sure she has a ranch somewhere. She probably rounds up the cattle in her spare time.)

'I'm very glad you've come to see me,' she said, sounding as if she meant it. She had an unexpectedly light voice, at odds with her appearance. She swept them into her office and asked the receptionist to bring coffee. Her office was large and flooded with light from the floor-to-ceiling windows on the north side. A vast desk occupied one end of the room, but she led them to the other end, where a comfortable sofa and chairs were grouped about a low table.

'While we wait for Elke to bring the coffee, let me tell you a little story,' she said as they sat down. 'Last year I went back to Cambridge for the first time since I was an undergraduate there, many years ago. Naturally, I was delighted to see it again—the old buildings, and the Backs, and especially the chapel at King's, which has been cleaned, so the stonework looks marvellous. The town has changed a great deal, of course. But the change that really struck me was in the colleges. There were girls *everywhere*. They were going in and out of places where I wasn't allowed when I was a student. Each time I saw a girl in one of those places where I couldn't go, it was like a little electric shock. I think I didn't quite realize how penned in I'd been until I saw the freedom that girls have now. The moral of my story, of course, is that your proposal interests me...Ah, here's the coffee.'

Elke wheeled in a Victorian trolley, with a silver pot, flowered china cups, sugar tongs and little cakes.

'An indulgence of mine,' said Jessie Rayne, in the tone of one who has few but expects them to be pandered to. When everyone had a cup, she suggested they get straight to the point. 'My father and my father's father were happy to pay their debt to society with gifts of expensive machinery, and buildings,' she said. 'It would be easy for me to do likewise, especially since that is what is expected of me. Geology and mining technology gave my family everything we have, and it has seemed appropriate to give something back. Why should I alter this admirable pattern?'

Rita took a deep breath. 'Ms Rayne, you are the head of a powerful company. This is partly because your family owns it, but it's also because you're good at running it. You wouldn't be in this office if you weren't.' Jessie Rayne inclined her head in acknowledgement. 'Well then,' Rita went on, 'you know what women are able to do. Doesn't it strike you as odd that in a university community of twelve thousand, half of whom are women, there is not one woman in the president's office? That the president and all the vice-presidents and the deans are men, that all the heads of departments are men, except Gillian Adams here, and that nearly all tenured faculty are men? That the women who teach are often underpaid sessional lecturers with no job security? That this perpetuates itself in an institution that is supposedly a standard-bearer for progressive values? Why is this?'

Rita paused and looked at them all. So far so good, thought Gillian.

'There are various causes, linked in various ways, but we think that a primary cause, which we can tackle directly, is the way women are taught. Everything is taught from a male perspective, which women absorb. They don't learn about what women have done, or why, and they don't learn to consider these things important. On top of that, they see no—or few—rôle models to suggest that things could be different.'

'There are two in this room, surely,' said Jessie Rayne.

Frances answered, 'You might think so, but I, as Dean of Women, have little power to alter their circumstances on campus. I'm not really in the pyramid at the president's office, but somewhere off to the side. The students see me as a glorified counsellor, and they're right.'

'It's a ghettoized position,' added Libby.

Jessie looked at Gillian.

'You could call me a rôle model, perhaps,' said Gillian 'except that I'm such a rarity that I'm more likely regarded as a special case. Someone with extremely unusual abilities or luck. A freak, you might say.'

Jessie Rayne smiled. 'Point taken.' Gillian thought that at that moment a bond began to form between the coal queen and the Feminist Union.

Rita went on with her speech. 'It's our conviction that this state of affairs will not be altered within the conventional structures, because, in words of one syllable, men will continue to hire men, who will continue to teach like men. Therefore, we propose to establish a department that will teach differently. History, literature, art, anthropology, economics, even the sciences, all these subjects will be changed when women are no longer relegated to a minor rôle. Not only that, but women will be hired to do this, and will begin to rectify the imbalance in the faculty. In a women's studies department, women will teach women to reconsider the world from their own point of view.'

Well done, thought Gillian. Concise, and no political jargon. (Vocabulary had been thoroughly thrashed out on Monday, as had the spelling of 'women' on the documentation for Jessie Rayne.) It had been at Frances's insistence that they had proposed a department, not only a programme of study. 'A women's studies programme is a good start,' Frances had said, 'but the way the university is structured makes it difficult to fight for the interests of a programme. A department gives you a power base. As long as we're doing this, let's go for broke.'

It was Frances's turn to speak now.

'It's important to point out that these arguments have been accepted by top-flight institutions all over the country and all over the continent: *we* are the anachronism. Women's studies programmes have been going now for a quarter of a century, and the literature is growing all the time. It's ridiculous that we have almost nothing to offer in this area. A few undergraduate courses don't fill the bill. Right now, we're very backward. We could compensate for our late entry by giving women's studies full status as a department: that would put us in the vanguard and position us for the future.'

Jessie Rayne had a good poker face, but Gillian was sure she wasn't bored. If she gives us the money, why will she give it, Gillian suddenly wondered. Our cogent reasoning, or some door slammed in her face at Cambridge? Maybe some perfectly irrational impulse, like pissing off her brother. We might never know.

'Whatever my intentions,' Jessie Rayne said, 'I can't endow an entire department. You're aware of that. You propose a chair and a library fund, I see. Why?'

Frances answered her questions about money and administration. Marnie and Libby talked about a library of feminist criticism and history, subjects in which the holdings in the main library were sadly deficient. Each department had its own library to supplement the more general fare in the main stacks; women's studies should have one, too. Scholarships were brought up, and money for visiting lecturers. Jessie Rayne's questions were good ones. Gillian was put in mind of her Ph.D. orals.

Abruptly, this phase of the interview was over. 'That's enough detail,' Jessie Rayne said. She leaned on her elbow and looked at them. 'Now I'd like to ask you what sort of response to your project you've had from the administration and the faculty.'

This was a question they'd been expecting. Jessie Rayne was no fool and wouldn't relish being treated as one. She would have her own sources of information. They'd agreed to be candid, even at the risk of outright refusal. Gillian answered her.

'As head of the History Department, I can tell you that faculty opinion is divided about the worth of women's studies,' Gillian began. 'Many, particularly the older men who fill the senior positions, but even some women, will argue that women aren't a subject, but are part of other, recognized subjects.'

'Everywhere and nowhere, like God?' Jessie Rayne asked, to a ripple of laughter. Her little joke released the tension.

'Come to think of it, God doesn't have a department either. But a chair in theology is not what we're here for. We believe that women must be a separate subject or there will be no conceptual change, merely little paragraphs about women appended to tomes about men. We need women's studies to develop the tools and the ideas, to gain recognition, and to offer female students a kind of nourishment that may make up for the deficiencies they experience elsewhere. Integration with other subjects will follow—quite naturally, we will hope. As for the administration, they'll worry about finding the rest of the money that's needed, but as I'm sure you realize, if a substantial endowment is offered, many a doubter will turn advocate.'

'Have you been a longtime advocate?'

'Is five years a long time? Before then, I thought that forging my own path was all I had to do. But it's since dawned on me that if I don't use my position to open the way for more women, then I'm not using it well.'

'I see.' Jessie Rayne's eyebrows lifted just a fraction.

Soon afterward the meeting ended. Before she stood up to usher them out, Jessie Rayne said, 'I'll give your proposal some thought. One thing I will tell you: it is my own decision, no one else's, so far as the company is concerned. But of course, if I choose to pursue this, I'll have to consult with your administration before I reach a final decision. Cooperation and financial support from the university will be essential to the project's success.'

⟜Ⱦ⟞

They were silent all the way down to the parking lot. There, Libby let out a whoop of excitement.

'She's going to go for it!'

'There's a chance,' said Gillian. What enormous vitality Jessie Rayne had, she was thinking. She reminds me of Edward. How funny.

CHAPTER 8

It rained for a week, almost without stopping, it seemed to Gillian. When she drove to work in the mornings and home again in the dark evenings, the rain streamed over the windows, and the puddles in the parking lot were ankledeep. There was no word from Jessie Rayne, but Rita and Libby and Denise were full of hope. They glittered with their secret like phosphorescent seas. Gillian was more cautious. She assumed that Jessie Rayne would talk to a lot of people before making up her mind, and most of them would advise her to forget the proposal and stick to the tried and true. Still, the Feminist Union's excitement was infectious; she knew that Rita and Libby had seen a conspiratorial sparkle once or twice when they had caught her eye in the history office.

Charlie Rankin, watching Rita shrug into her raincoat one afternoon and noting the absence of her helmet, cocked an eyebrow and said, 'She's leaving on foot. She must have left her broom at home.' As she disappeared, he added, 'Good God! She's smiling. What's the occasion? Lucrezia Borgia's birthday?'

John Honeycutt, Rita's adviser, riffled through the papers in his pigeonhole and thrust them back. He looked at Rankin with irritation. 'The Carver committee announces its decision next week,' he snapped.

Rankin raised his brows. 'You're so sure she'll get it?'

'She should,' Honeycutt answered. 'Provided common sense prevails over bigotry,' he added with a flicker of contempt. He moved off towards the elevators, passing Palmer, who was shuffling through the outgoing mail.

'Snooping?' asked Rankin blithely, seizing on a fresh victim.

'Forgot an enclosure,' Palmer answered, peevish.

Past the mail tray, on the floor adjacent to the counter, was a deep bin half full of paper—discarded memos, envelopes, letters, computer print-outs. Honeycutt glanced into it.

'Your recycling project seems to be catching on,' he said to Allie.

'It's doing OK. About half the department remembers now. But it's small potatoes. The university *has* to get into serious recycling. We're only saving about ten per cent of the paper right now. The rest is wasted—tons of it. It's a crime.'

'I know, I know. I feel guilty every time I use the Xerox machine now.'

'Who's not remembering?' asked Rankin. 'Charge them with criminal negligence.'

Allie's eyes slid along the counter to Palmer who was walking absently away, crumpling the envelope he had retrieved.

'Caught in the act,' Rankin shouted gleefully. 'Verne, where are you going with that envelope?'

Palmer started. 'What?'

'The envelope, man, the envelope. Miss Moore requires it for her recycling depot.'

Palmer came back, pink and cross. Ostentatiously, he smoothed the crumples and dropped it into the bin. He took his papers to a side table and turned his back on them. Gillian tightened her lips. Rankin never passed up a chance of twitting Palmer.

Rankin skewered the air with his furled umbrella. 'Any more villains I can dispatch for you, fair maid?'

Allie laughed. 'Sure. If you're Sir Charlie the Chivalrous, try duelling with Ridgeway.'

'At your service. But I thought he never threw anything out. He's got jars full of old pencil stubs and rubber bands.'

Palmer slewed around. 'How do you know? Snooping?'

Rankin laughed. 'Not necessary, old buddy. They're in plain view.'

As Palmer was extremely near-sighted, this was unkind.

Jane shut the drawer of her desk with a bang. 'Time to go home,' she announced. Gillian fetched her letters and dropped them into the mail tray. Palmer, shoulders stiff with resentment, walked smartly to the elevator and stabbed the button. Rankin returned to his office. Gillian looked out at the wet, gloomy sky and invited Jane and Allie for a restorative glass of sherry.

'Jesus, Charlie's a bugger sometimes,' said Allie behind the closed door. 'He's always crapping on poor old Verne. And this morning he was needling Jacobsen about Rita getting the Carver. Jacobsen didn't say anything, but you know how red his face gets when he's mad. He looked like a lobster with the mumps.'

⋅⊰⊱⋅

On Friday morning Rita bounded into Gillian's office. She waved a letter at Gillian. 'We did it! Jessie Rayne's going to see President Bingham this afternoon!'

Rita's eyes shone, her skin glowed. Her boots did a jubilant dance on the carpet. Gillian looked at the letter.

'Poor old Bingham,' she said. 'Tsk, tsk. The golden goose is a wayward bird.'

'I wonder if Frost has twigged.'

'Only if she's told him.'

Rita grinned. 'I've been thinking about space for our classes. We haven't got much room in this building, but Bingham's office is way too big…'

'And don't forget his janitorial duties.'

Rita's rare laugh bubbled up. 'Right. We'll present him with a presidential mop.'

⋅⊰⊱⋅

By Monday the secret was no longer secret. Rumours about Jessie Rayne's confidential discussions with the president and the prospect that Engineering and Geology could lose a million dollars to a new women's studies department seeped quickly from the administrators most concerned along devious channels to other departments and lower levels. The hum of speculation was mingled with the buzz and whine of outrage. Gillian found some well-wishers in unexpected places, but not many in her own department.

The faculty of arts, she remarked to Carole Stein, could be said to be anæmic supporters, while the engineers and some of the scientists were red-blooded foes. The engineers' comeuppance, as the arts departments tended to see it, was delightful. On the other hand, money that could have fattened their own comparatively skeletal budgets was going to be devoured by a new rival. A chilly current of unease ran beneath the voiced commentary: if the engineers and their sidekicks, the geologists, had wielded a disproportionate share of power on campus owing to their money from the Raynes, what did that imply about the Eff Yous? A women's studies programme might not be much to worry about, they were common enough nowadays, but a department? And what else might they go after, with Jessie Rayne's money flashing around in the president's office?

Several of Gillian's colleagues were quick to announce their disapproval of her participation.

'It won't do the department any good,' Jacobsen said bluntly.

For once, Ridgeway agreed with him. Looking even more sallow and dyspeptic than usual, he sat down in her office and favoured her with a lecture on the dangers posed by the Feminist Union. 'Stanley may indeed want the money, but you Eff Yous have bypassed the administration, which causes offence, and their wild and woolly tactics make him nervous. The next thing they do may well offend the Raynes, and UPNW could be out in the cold. They seem to have a habit of going too far. If UPNW loses the Raynes, the results will be extremely unpleasant for all of us.'

Vernon Palmer went so far as to suggest that she resign the headship.

'On what grounds?' Gillian asked coolly.

'On the grounds that the narrow views held by your group are not suited to your position. It's causing considerable talk.'

'What talk?'

But Palmer was vague. Gillian heard later that 'the talk' was that the Feminist Union were lesbians, and her own unmarried state, always the target of an occasional joke, was now cause for speculation.

Gillian saw Frances Romano for lunch and gave her a caustic report of these experiences.

'Yes. The fox is definitely in the hen house,' said Frances, 'or is it the hen who has invaded the fox's den?'

'Jessie Rayne isn't a hen—or a fox. She's a panther.'

'I wonder what the Dean of Engineering thinks we are.'

'Spiders, my dear. Spinning little webs of intrigue and eating our mates.'

Gillian asked Murray what he'd heard in the Chemistry Department. He laughed.

'Let's say they're cheering your end run around Dean Frost, but they're not so thrilled about the Geology Department. It might mean Geology will try to compensate by taking a bigger bite of the science faculty budget. And if the truth be told, it's aggravating for guys like my department head, who prides himself on his political savvy, to be beaten to the trough by uppity young women.'

They were standing at the edge of the green. On the far side, a swirl of hot pink descended the steps of the administration building. It could only be the Dean of Women in her iridescent raincoat.

'Nobody seems to be mad at Frances,' Murray added. 'Not even the engineers I've talked to. I guess they think she was doing her job. But Rita's been labelled chief witch of the coven.'

It was an uncomfortable week for Gillian. There were no further leaks, no information about the administration's response, or the progress—if any—of the negotiations. A rumour was floated that the president's office had turned Jessie Rayne down flat, and the idea was dead.

Gillian saw Marnie at the inter-library loan desk and asked her what she thought.

'I don't know,' Marnie said gloomily. 'Frost must be coming down pretty heavy. He'd do anything to keep that money. And Jessie Rayne might like the idea, but how does it really look to her when she goes into the president's bunker and all these big grey-heads in leather chairs are telling her it's a mistake and we're just a bunch of noisy extremists?'

'I wouldn't worry—she's a CEO, she's used to suits.'

'True,' Marnie said, brightening up. She handed in her request slip. 'See you. I'm off to another lecture in the land of the BDWMs.'

'BDWMs?'

'You know. The literary canon. Boring Dead White Males.'

Gillian and Laura had a stilted conversation on the telephone that didn't clear the air.

'How's your department reacting?' Laura wanted to know.

'They're all stirred up. They're worried about money, and where my loyalties lie, and will the administration punish them for my sins.'

'What're you going to do about it?'

'Leave town.'

On Wednesday afternoon Gillian left the campus early. She was giving a lecture in Portland at five, flying down and back the same evening. She was glad to get away.

But in the evening, having given her talk and been fed, she found that her return flight was delayed in San Francisco. Her host, who had kindly driven her to the airport, took her to the bar, where they ordered drinks and waited for the flight's arrival at eleven. They were both weary, and Gillian suggested that he go home to bed, but he courteously insisted on keeping her company. At twenty minutes to eleven the arrivals screen adjusted the estimated time to eleven-thirty. By now they were both oppressed by the obligation to go on chatting, and so Gillian was able to persuade him to leave her to her own devices. She decided that talking to Edward would cheer her up, extracted her telephone card and called London. There was no answer. She looked at her watch. Six-fifty a.m. and he was out. A case. Well, she wasn't going to telephone the Yard to see if she could catch him. No romance in that, she'd learned.

At midnight the supervisor confessed that the flight was cancelled, and Gillian stumbled off to a cheap hotel close to the airport. She ordered a wake-up call for six and went to bed.

When she woke, grey light was leaking through the curtains. She was confused for a moment, then she sat up abruptly and looked at her watch. It was after seven. The early morning plane was taking off in ten minutes. She had missed it. She leapt out of bed, threw on her clothes and stormed downstairs to the lobby, where a yawning clerk was drinking coffee from a styrofoam cup.

'I asked for a wake-up call at six!' Gillian said furiously. 'Why didn't I get one?'

'What room?' the clerk asked.

'Two-twelve.'

The clerk looked vaguely about.

'There's nothing here about a wake-up call.'

'But I asked for one, and now I've missed my plane!'

'Sorry.' The clerk, a heavy-eyed lad of twenty or thereabouts, was barely interested.

'Where's the manager?' Gillian demanded.

'Having breakfast.'

'Get him for me, please.'

The clerk slid off his chair and shambled to a door behind the counter. He opened it and poked his head through.

'Customer wants ya.'

The manager came out. He was a stubby, balding man with bad skin. A fragment of egg glistened at the corner of his mouth.

'Can I help you?'

'I asked for a wake-up call at six. I didn't get one. I've missed my plane.'

The manager was irritated. 'When did you ask?'

'Last night, of course.'

He turned on the clerk. 'Why didn't you call her?' he rasped.

The clerk shrugged. 'No message.'

The manager looked about the counter area. 'Who was on duty last night? Dave, right? That's the second problem with Dave this week. Why do I have to put up with this?' he sputtered. 'I don't pay you guys to sit on your ass and drink coffee.' He grabbed the styrofoam cup. 'Sorry for the inconvenience,' he grunted at Gillian. He seemed about to return to his breakfast.

'I'm not paying for my room,' she said loudly.

The manager started, slopping coffee on the carpet. 'What do you mean you're not paying? Of course you're paying. Forty dollars. You slept there last night.'

Gillian was now very cross.

'The sole function of your wretched hotel is to help air travellers catch airplanes. I've missed mine,' she said haughtily. She turned to the clerk, who had perked up and was enjoying the rumpus. 'Call me a cab, please.'

He put his hand on the telephone, but didn't pick up the receiver, waiting for the manager's OK.

The manager ignored him. 'What are you looking at?' he said aggressively to Gillian.

She was staring at his tie. A shiny blob of strawberry was slowly detaching itself from a surrounding ring of jam. The manager looked down just as the red blob slid silently to the carpet. He avoided Gillian's eye. He dumped the coffee cup on the counter and turned away, thrusting his palms outward in rejection. 'Call the dame a cab, and the both of you can go to hell in it,' he said and walked out. The door banged.

'A day in the life,' the clerk giggled and picked up the phone.

Gillian rode the mile to the airport in a fume. Her small financial victory gave her no pleasure and left her stomach in a knot. At the airport she checked flights and learned that she would not arrive at her office before eleven-thirty. At eight-thirty she telephoned the department and told Jane what had happened. Then she went to find some breakfast. While she was drinking her coffee, she began to laugh quietly. What a ridiculous scene, and how absurd she had been, carrying on like Lady Bracknell. She hadn't been intimidated, though, the way she'd been on campus that day. Why was that? Because they were too busy being each other's enemy to threaten her, she supposed. And the manager was a fool. Plus it helped that he was about six inches shorter than she was. By the time she took off, she was in quite a good humour again, though tired.

She flew home without further incident and drove straight to the university. The weather had partly cleared, and the sky was a deep blue above the evergreens massed on the distant hills. Off to the west, however, she could see another heavy bank of clouds rolling in over the water.

She went straight into her own office, barely pausing to say hello to Jane and Allie. Jane followed her in. There was a stack of mail on her desk, but she had no time to look at it before Jane said:

'The Carver was announced this morning.'

Gillian was caught off guard. 'I thought it wouldn't be out before noon.'

'It's out.'

Gillian looked at her. The news wasn't good. 'And?'

'Paul got it.'

'Paul!'

'That's right.'

'I don't believe it!' Gillian said. Her cheeks felt hot. The room turned a hazy scarlet for a moment, and a part of her mind noted with surprise that she had seen red—something she had hitherto taken for a mere metaphor. She swore under her breath. Jane shook her head. She knew all about the grad students. Paul Smith was a fine student who would doubtless make his way to full professor at a respectable university. He would have been a perfectly decent choice for the Carver if Rita hadn't applied.

'Have you seen Rita?' Gillian asked.

'Not today.'

'Would you find her number for me?'

Jane went out without a word. Gillian sat with her hands in her lap, doing nothing. Jane came back with the number, and Gillian dialled. There was no answer. She tried again an hour later with no better success. There was no further chance to call during the afternoon.

CHAPTER 9

She left the campus at about six, going straight from a seminar in another building to her car. It wasn't until she got home that she realized that she hadn't taken Rita's number with her. Cursing, she yanked open the drawer of the telephone table. She riffled through the book. Gomez, Goodwin, Gordon. There were five or six columns of Gordons. But no R. Gordon that corresponded to her imprecise notion of where Rita lived. Balked, she decided to telephone Laura. Life without Laura was too dismal.

Unexpectedly, it was Jack who answered.

'Hello, Jack,' Gillian said, a little nervously. 'May I speak to Laura?'

'Hi, Gillian. I'm sorry. She's out.'

'Oh,' Gillian said, at a loss.

'Anything I can do?'

'Well, no. It's about a student in my department who applied for an important grant—I've just found out she didn't get it. It wouldn't matter to anyone outside the university, but inside, it matters enormously.'

'Is this to do with the Carver Fellowship? Laura told me about your bet.'

'Yes. May I bend your ear?' Without waiting for his answer, she plunged into her story. At the end, she apologized— insincerely—for blistering his ears with her rage about a matter that didn't concern him.

Surprisingly, he said, 'But it does concern me. Laura cares about it, and besides, it sounds too much like a kangaroo court.' Then his lawyerly caution asserted itself. 'Mind, we don't *know* that there has been an injustice. We don't know why they didn't give it to her, do we?'

'But I know the quality of the short list, and no one was good enough to take it away from her.'

'Maybe your informant was mistaken about the list.'

'My informant, dear Jack, was Laura,' Gillian replied with a ghost of a laugh. 'You ask her about that.'

'I will. And I'll have her call you as soon as she gets home.'

Gillian paced savagely about her house, then poured herself some Scotch and sat morosely by the cold ashes of last night's fire. The clock on the wall behind her ticked loudly in the silence. A little wind came up and moved the branches on the trees, and rain began to patter against the library windows. Restless, Gillian thought of driving to the university and finding Rita's number, but she didn't want to miss Laura's call. She was getting up, uncertain whether she was going to pour another drink or scavenge for something to eat, when the doorbell rang.

It was Laura.

'I called Jack because I was late, and he gave me your message.'

She held up a bottle, flashing a tense little smile. 'I brought the champagne, but we don't have to drink it tonight.'

Gillian shook her head. 'You were right about that too. Even Krug would taste of ashes.'

'I'm really sorry about the Carver,' Laura said quickly, not quite meeting her eyes. Their recent dispute stood between them like an invisible fence. They could see through it, but they couldn't step across. 'I'll put this away.' She moved towards the kitchen, taking the champagne with her.

Gillian returned to the library. She heaped some wood on the grate and lifted the Cape Cod lighter from its kerosene bath. Laura came in with some ice in a glass. 'I'll pour, OK?' she said, seeing Gillian busy with the fire. She poured neat whisky into Gillian's empty glass. 'Have you talked to Rita?' The ice cubes crackled as she filled her own.

'No. I've been trying to call her all day.' Gillian struck a match and twirled the lighter gently over the flame, watching it catch.

'How will she take it?'

'She doesn't take anything lightly, and a lot was riding on this grant.' The lighter burned blue and gold, a fiery egg.

'Did she expect to get it?'

'She had doubts,' Gillian said bitterly, 'but I told her she was too good to be passed up.'

'Wasn't that a little unwise?'

'Obviously it was unwise.' She thrust the lighter under the grate and stood up. 'But the Carver was made for people like her. She could have had two years here with only one course to teach, she would have produced a book, and articles, and been invited to conferences where she would have impressed the ass off everybody. Even with her politics she would have her choice of jobs afterwards. Her career would have been made.'

'I know.'

'Now what will happen? She deserved the Carver. How many jobs will she be denied in the same way? Being the best isn't good enough, apparently.'

'It's disturbing, I agree.'

'When did you hear?'

'Earlier today. I tried to call you at your office, but you weren't back yet. I heard at the faculty club.'

'Our friends, the enemy.' The whisky burned in Gillian's throat.

'Don't overreact, Gillian. They didn't all vote against Rita. Can't you be a little bit philosophical about this?'

'No! I can't be bloody philosophical about it. Shit, Laura, why aren't you mad? You're the one who says we have to hire the best. Well, they didn't.'

'I am mad. I'm just not as mad as you, because I never expected anything different, and I don't know Rita. If she's as good as you say, she'll find a job sooner or later.'

'Later. Without the edge the Carver would give her, it'll be harder. Anyway, what happened is plain wrong.'

'We don't know that. We don't know why she didn't get it.'

'Is that your opinion, or do I hear Jack talking?'

'There could be—'

'Intangibles?' Gillian interrupted sarcastically.

'All right. Say it was pure sexism. There's nothing you can do about it.'

'I've got to try. I'm going to demand to know their reasons.'

'You won't get anywhere. That committee's like the Freemasons. It wouldn't surprise me if they wore funny hats and had a secret handshake. They never give reasons. They announce, period. People have complained before—remember the fuss about Bron because he was a structuralist? I thought my department would tear itself in two. But the committee sat back and let people rage. They never even bothered to defend themselves.'

Gillian said stubbornly, 'That was a long time ago, and the issue was absurd. Anyway, I have to ask. It's the least I can do.'

'Yes, I see that.'

There was a short silence. Laura set down her empty glass. 'I'm sorry we quarrelled the other night.'

'So am I.'

'And I do wish you luck with the Carver committee. It's a disgrace that they aren't publicly accountable.'

'If I need your help…?'

'I don't know what I could do, but yes, of course.'

At the door, they hugged each other, a trifle stiffly. 'I feel so bad for Rita,' Gillian said mournfully into Laura's shoulder.

'Don't sit up all night berating yourself.'

⊰⊱

After she left, Gillian stared at the fire for a while. The rift was still there; they had papered it over, that was all. She looked up Libby's number in the telephone book and dialled.

'Libby, this is Gillian Adams. I'm worried about Rita. I've been trying to reach her all day.'

'She's been out on her bike. She went up to Cypress Bowl, she told me. I saw her a little while ago.'

'Was she all right?'

'Well, she's pretty upset.'

'I'd like to talk to her as soon as I can.'

'She's coming over in the morning; I'll tell her.'

Gillian left it at that. Of course Rita had gone off on her motorcycle. It was the obvious thing for her to do. Get out of the city, go to the mountains, to the clear air above the smog, to the clean smell of evergreens and the immense quiet.

Gillian carried the glasses to the kitchen. The bottle of Krug still stood in lonely splendour on the counter. She put it in the fridge and went to bed.

CHAPTER 10

She slept for an hour and woke, sweating, from a responsibility dream. She'd lost something. All the grant applications, that was it. They were somewhere in the stacks, but she couldn't even find out what floor she was on. She fought her way out of the dream. For months after she had become department head she been plagued with such dreams—of missing briefcases and enigmatic road maps—but they had gradually faded as she became accustomed to her new position. She lay in the dark, appalled, remembering the repetitious torment of those old dreams and the exhaustion that followed many broken nights. This recurrence was a bad sign.

She woke again and got up at five, drank two cups of scalding black coffee and drove to the university while it was still dark. In the arts building lobby the fluorescent lighting buzzed behind its so-called 'daylight' panels, unpleasantly audible in the absence of other noises. The elevator clunked loudly as it began to ascend. The building was scarcely ten years old, but already it was frayed by use: the carpets worn and discoloured, the elevator doors scarred, the walls dented and smudged. There had been trouble with the plumbing, and there were rusty water stains on several ceilings to prove it. Some of the pipes were supposedly being fixed this week. Physical plant had sent a man to take down a section of ceiling tiles in the history office after they had become waterlogged—Jane had found two on the floor one morning. The hole in the ceiling and the bare pipes had now been there for days.

The lights in the corridors were left on all night, and the dim glow that reached part of the history office was enough for her to see her way. She glanced automatically at her mailbox; it was empty. The windows were huge black squares, faintly reflecting the dumb, shrouded shapes of the computers. She remembered a phrase from Thurber relished by her father: 'The doom-shaped thing in the kitchen', he'd called their squat, round-shouldered old refrigerator. Under their dust-covers, the monitors stood up like tombstones. She went into her own office and closed the door, shutting out the dark emptiness of the building, and turned on her reading lamp. She picked a couple of journals from a pile on the carpet and then slumped in her chair, suddenly overcome with sadness and distaste. She disliked this building, its blandness and shoddy materials. In this mood, she disliked her life, seeing herself entombed among books and papers, sentenced to read a thousand illiterate essays, to waste away her days in meetings. And Rita felt confined. Wait till she had a job. The journals lay unopened in her lap. She kicked off her boots and stared out at the black windows until the first faint light came into the sky. Then she turned off the lamp and fell asleep.

She was awakened by a noise in the outer office. Jane, she thought groggily. It seemed as if she had only been asleep for a few minutes, but if Jane had arrived, it was time to pull herself together. It was still awfully dark, though. The sun rose late at this time of year, but surely it wasn't this dark at eight-thirty. She heard a faint thump and a whispery sound. Jane taking the cover off her computer. She must have come in early. That, or it was one of those twilit mornings when the clouds piled up over the coast and daylight barely struggled through. She heaved herself to her feet and padded softly to the window. The dim, mist-shrouded delta lay below, dark patches of farmland and glowing strings of street lights. To the west, the water was a dull grey. I wonder what Jane had to do this morning, she thought vaguely. She heard the elevator's muffled thunk. More arrivals. She'd better wash her face before she had to confront battalions of colleagues. She went to the door and opened it. The history office was dark.

'Jane?' she said, puzzled.

She stepped out into the office and felt for a switch. The sudden brightness made her flinch. Then she saw it. A body—hanging by the neck from the ceiling pipes. A woman. Her back was to Gillian, she wore boots and jeans and a rough sweater. On her head, which flopped sickeningly sideways, was a witch's hat. Gillian's breath rasped inward, and she stepped backward with a choked scream. For a moment she was paralysed. Then she thought: Oh God, Rita! and ran around the counter towards the corpse. Maybe she was in time to save her. Chair, she thought; stand it up. But she had heard no noise of a chair falling over. There was no chair. Then she saw the woman's face. It was a Hallowe'en mask, a grinning, rubbery witch's face with a big nose and rough black hair. Gillian stopped dead with a little mew of fright, reacting to the shock before she had time to take it in. It wasn't a real body. It was a dummy. She stepped up to it, touched it with her finger. It swung gently away, almost weightless. It was an inflatable doll, lifesize, woman-shaped. The jeans hung baggily about the buttocks, the long sleeves of the sweater drooped over the plump plastic hands. Gillian's heart, which had been pounding against her ribs, began to thump more slowly. She wiped her clammy palms on her pants. The witch's hat was jammed on the dummy's head. She ought to have realized before that it wouldn't have clung to a real head that way. Now that she was a little calmer, she could see that the pipe wouldn't have supported a real person's weight. She didn't recognize the clothes; they were worn, cheap, unremarkable student garb. But the sweater was dark and rough, in Rita's style. And there was the hat. 'Chief witch of the coven,' Murray had said. The dummy was Rita, she was sure of that. Someone—or ones—had hanged Rita in effigy.

'Jesus, the elevator,' she said aloud. It was too late to chase him—or them. They would be at the bottom now. She rushed towards the windows, but she could see nothing except the reflection of the room. The dummy swayed, a grotesque shadow in the pallid glare of the fluorescent lights. Cursing, she turned off the switch. It was useless. Her eyes weren't adjusted to the comparative darkness outside, and anyway the windows didn't overlook the entrance, which was on the north side of the building. She should cut the dummy down. She paused in the act of reaching for the switch. What if he came round the building and hid in the darkness under the trees? He would see the lights go on. What if he could see her? The thought of someone out there was most unpleasant. Besides, she said to herself, why give him any hint about what happened. Obviously, he—or they—didn't know I was here; if he didn't see me turn the lights on the first time, and I don't think he had time, he'll be waiting for the mob to get here at eight-thirty. They probably thought the secretaries would get here first and scream their heads off. Or maybe they know Jacobsen often comes in first. This kind of thing could put Jessie Rayne right off, and Jacobsen would use it. So would Dean Frost, come to that.

Leaving the lights off, Gillian found a chair in the near-darkness and carried it gingerly around the counter. She placed it under the dummy and stood on it. The dummy swung and bumped her softly in the stomach. She fumbled with the knot around its neck. The rubbery texture of the witch's mask was revolting. The knot was tight, strangling the plastic neck. She could just see; her light-blinded eyes were adjusting. She glanced at the windows. The sky wasn't so dark now, the outlines of the trees were sharp against a brightening grey. The knot came loose and the dummy slid into her arms. She stepped down off the chair and carried the weightless body into her office. Then she looked at her watch. It was barely seven o'clock.

She laid the Rita dummy in a chair and contemplated it. Who had put it there in the history office? Most likely, some engineering students. It was their sort of joke, if it was a joke. Only the arts faculty and the physical plant people were supposed to have keys to the building, but a little matter of locked doors would hardly challenge the engineers, whose stunts of the past decade included the sudden appearance of an entire Volkswagen on the roof of the administration building, not to mention the fifteen-foot-high replica of Mickey Mouse they had attached to the arts building one night, to express their opinion of the 'artsy-fartsies'. What was the purpose of the dummy? To shock? To frighten Rita and the Feminist Union? Perhaps to taint the women's studies issue with scandal, so that Jessie Rayne wouldn't want her name associated with it? In that case, a single incident might not be sufficient, and others would follow. And what was the best thing for her to do? She could simply dispose of the dummy, or she could hide it. She could complain to the administration; she could call in the press, she could consult with the Feminist Union. On the whole, Gillian thought the best thing was to conceal the dummy for the time being. No one but the perpetrators would know it had been there. Let them—whoever they were—stew.

Gillian ran her hands over the body, feeling for the nozzle she knew must be there. It was on the left buttock. a little lump under the blue jeans. She slid her hand in and pulled the plug. Air rushed out, obscene and ludicrous. She gave a hiccup of nervous laughter. The dummy slowly flattened, and the clothing drooped on the chair. The grimy tennis shoes fell off, and the hat tilted down over the face. Gillian felt like Dorothy throwing water on the wicked witch.

The mask slid down towards the neck. Underneath it was a doll-like countenance, blank-eyed, with vermilion lips. Gillian picked up the legs and tried to fold them, but they resisted, ballooning between the creases. Odd parts of the body bulged at her like fat brimming over a girdle. Her hiding-places were small: she had to fold the dummy or roll it up. She sat on it. The air hissed out again, and she sank into its flaccid vinyl lap. She folded the body as flat as she could in its clothes and stuffed it into the back of the bottom drawer in her filing cabinet.

I need a drink, she said to herself, and opened the cupboard where she kept a social bottle of sherry and an emergency supply of Scotch. She poured a shot of whisky and drank it off, feeling the welcome heat travel down her throat to the knot of tension at her solar plexus. She almost had a second, thought the better of it, and decided to make some coffee. She went back to the outer office to fetch the pot. On the floor was the black, conical hat which had rolled off the witch's head. It was one of Jane's. She dusted it off and set it on Jane's desk. Only then did she remember the rope. It was still dangling from the pipe in the ceiling.

'Jesus Christ!' she muttered. 'I can't leave that there.'

The pipe was too high for her to reach, even standing on the chair. She would have to stand on a desk, and the desks were too big for her to move. Ladder? There was probably one somewhere in the building, but she didn't know where to look, and it was likely to be locked in a closet to which only the maintenance personnel had the keys. She tugged hard at the rope end. The knot was secure. She looked about the office. The two secretaries' chairs were useless; they had castors and wouldn't stack. Neither would the upholstered chairs in her own office. The library. She got her keys and hurried down the corridor to the history library, where there were twenty or so plain wooden chairs. She carried four of them, one by one, back to the office and arranged them in a square; then she lifted the visitor's chair she had already used and placed it on top. She climbed up. Her pyramid felt stable. She began to work at the knot, which was tight, perhaps partly because she had pulled at it. They had used clothesline. It was stiff, and her fingers hurt before the first twist loosened. She worked feverishly at the next loop. Time was going by. As she was tugging at the final twist, the elevator came to life. It creaked upward.

What if they come back? she thought. She pulled the end of the rope over the pipe, coiled it up and threw it behind a desk. There was no time to do anything about her improvised ladder. The elevator door opened as she was lifting down the upper chair. She stood still, breathing quietly. Someone stepped into the corridor. I'll confront him, she thought, suddenly more angry than scared. She set down the chair with a bang and started forward. Footsteps came down the hall towards the office.

It was Jim Jacobsen. He paused in the doorway, staring.

'What are you doing?'

'There was water on the floor when I arrived. I was having a look at the pipe.'

He came further into the office. 'In the dark?' He switched on the lights and looked around the office and then down at the dry floor. 'You'd do better to call maintenance,' he said, and turned away. He stumped down the hallway to his own office.

Gillian watched his retreat. He had been startled to see her. Too startled? And what was he doing here so early on this particular day?

CHAPTER 11

When Jane arrived at eight, Gillian had made a fresh pot of coffee and was quietly working in her office. Jane moved energetically about, humming to herself. She tapped at Gillian's open door. Gillian looked up, and her heart jumped. Jane was wearing the witch's hat.

'A cup of toads' blood? I brought some muffins.'

'Muffins! Please,' Gillian said greedily, realizing she needed breakfast.

Jane brought her own coffee and the muffins. She sat on the corner of the desk and inspected Gillian.

'You look tired.'

'I didn't sleep much. Jane, would you get me an appointment with Dean Stanley? Today if possible? I want to find out why Rita didn't get that fellowship, and the Dean chairs the committee. I haven't much hope, but he's more likely to spill a bean or two than my honourable colleagues.'

'OK...Paul was in yesterday afternoon. It was weird. Everybody was congratulating him, but it was like you could hear them thinking why didn't Rita get it. He acted a little embarrassed.'

'It's an awkward situation—and he's no diplomat.'

'No, he's stuck up,' Jane said, with disdain.

Gillian stopped nibbling at her muffin and looked at Jane with mild surprise. Jane rarely criticized people.

'I've heard him. He thinks he's got all the brilliant ideas and everybody else is just a bricklayer.' She stopped, looking guilty. 'Oh well, he's just insecure, I guess. He'll grow out of it.' She took off her black hat and examined the brim. 'This looks good, doesn't it? I'm going to wear it on Hallowe'en when I give out the candies.'

'Did you leave it here last night?'

'I was working on it yesterday at lunch—sewing the crown to the brim. I forgot to take it home.'

'Did you ever read about the witch-craze, Jane?'

'When they used to burn them at the stake?'

'Thousands and thousands of them. Women like us.'

Gillian had a ten-thirty lecture. She was obliged to teach only one course, owing to her duties as head of the department. Once a week she met her fourth-year seminar in British imperial history. But she also shared responsibility for a first-year survey course, participated in a graduate seminar and supervised several graduate students. If she stepped down as head, she thought, feeling a little fuzzy, she would teach more courses, but more of her time would be free for research—if days interrupted by meetings, office hours for students, and marking papers could be called free. Today, she would gladly trade an hour of Dean Stanley's company for a class full of eighteen-year-olds. On the other hand, she was in a better position as head to tackle issues like the Carver Fellowship.

In class, she didn't think about Stanley. Lecturing, like hanging, concentrates the mind wonderfully.

When the bell rang at the end of class, she went straight to the Dean's office, to catch him before lunch.

Dean Stanley was bald and affable. He had been head of the English Department before he was Dean, where his appetite for administrative detail and his unusual skill at watching his own back while he manœuvred among the factions had been regarded with a mixture of awe and contempt. It had been good practice for the job of dean, in which he had to manipulate the rivalries among the departments within his own faculty of arts, while defending them collectively against the other faculties, such as science and engineering, all of which were engaged in a perpetual struggle to claim the largest possible share of the university budget.

Gillian had sat in many meetings with Dean Stanley, and she was not hopeful of acquiring the information she sought. She didn't have the leverage.

'Well, Gillian,' he said, leaning back in his padded swivel chair, 'I understand you're here about the Carver Fellowship.'

'I'll come straight to the point. The best student didn't get it, and I want to know why.'

The Dean sighed. 'Gillian, you've been in academic life a long time. There is an element of subjectivity in these matters—surely you've recognized it often enough. Your best isn't always mine, mine isn't always yours—these things aren't cut and dried. Paul Smith is a wonderful student.'

'He's a very good student, yes. But it would have been plain to any experienced judge that Rita's work is at another level entirely. And publishing an article in *Signs* is hardly material for a subjective comparison.'

'Perhaps not, but the committee felt that Paul Smith was the most suitable candidate.'

'Why?'

'The committee's deliberations are confidential. They always are, and for sound reasons.'

'Maybe so, but justice must be seen to be done—which it isn't when you exclude the best candidate without an explanation.'

'I can see how it looks to you, my dear Gillian,' said Stanley, with a credible imitation of friendliness, 'but that simply is not how it looked to us. We chose the best candidate, and you'll have to take my word for it.'

'I'm sorry. I can't let it go at that.'

The Dean leaned forward. 'Let me assure you, though it shouldn't be necessary: Rita Gordon was not passed over because of her sex. I could not have supported such a decision.'

'And what about the Rayne money?'

Stanley raised his eyebrows. 'What about it?'

'Did Bingham veto Rita?'

'The Rayne money had nothing to do with the decision,' he answered with cold finality. Then he produced a smile. 'Personally, I give her high marks for initiative. You and Frances, too. It's about time some Acid Rayne came our way.'

⎯⊤⎯

Gillian left the interview in a puzzled frame of mind. Dean Stanley was a politician, but not, she thought, a man to tell an unnecessary lie. She would swear he was telling the truth as he saw it when he said they hadn't ruled Rita out because she wasn't a man. For one thing, he had looked pleased at his own virtue, and for another, if that *had* been the only reason, he wouldn't have told her anything. But what had gone on in the committee?

She strolled thoughtfully towards the central staircase. The deans' offices were on the second floor, the offices of the president and vice-presidents above. She glanced up. Two men were ascending side by side, their backs to her. She stared after them. Dean Frost and Ridgeway—on their way to see the President. Now that's a combination that bodes no good, she said to herself as they disappeared.

She grabbed a sandwich from the student cafeteria and made her way to a table that was just being vacated. A young man crumpled up a piece of pale green paper and walked away with a look of disgust. As Gillian sat down, the creases slowly unfolded themselves. Curious, she glanced at the paper, her mouth full of sandwich. It was a bulletin put out by one of the male residences. A list of events and other announcements. There would be a party the following weekend for the men in the residence and their dates. 'Come all ye faithful,' it said, 'When you feel skin, you know you're in. Don't forget: no small dicks, no fat chicks. And BYOB.' Below, at the very bottom of the sheet was a joke: 'What's the best thing about fucking a 12-year-old?' it asked. 'Killing her afterwards.'

Gillian's appetite was gone. She stuffed the paper and the remains of her sandwich in the waste-bin. Inwardly raging, she headed back to the History Department, where she found Rita waiting for her.

'Jane said you'd be back.'

They went into Gillian's office and shut the door. Gillian shoved the paper to the back of her mind: Rita had more important things to worry about just now.

'I've just been to see Dean Stanley,' she told Rita immediately.

'And what did he have to say?'

'That the reason you didn't get the Carver had nothing to do with your anatomy.'

'He'd have to say that, wouldn't he?'

'Well, no. He didn't have to tell me anything.'

Gillian saw that this meant nothing to Rita. And why should it, she thought.

'If it wasn't that I'm a woman, then it was the kind of woman I am: "a strident feminist", I know they said that. If I were in a traditional field and wore frilly clothes, they would have given it to me.'

'You're probably right.'

'Yeah.' Rita's stiffly upright body slumped suddenly. She sat down. 'I know it was stupid, but I believed I'd win. I actually believed it.'

'I blame myself,' Gillian said. 'I had no business to encourage you. I can't undo that; but what I can do is find out what happened, and if there are any grounds for challenging the decision.'

'How?'

'Poking and prying. There'll be plenty of gossip about this. Seven people—more, counting the secretaries—know. There's bound to be a leak. Look at the Rayne meeting.'

'But we know the answer already.'

'Not precisely. We don't know who said what, or how the decision was justified. We need to see the files, read the minutes, if I can get them. Then maybe we can challenge them. All right?'

Rita sat hunched in her chair, looking down, her dark hair falling unevenly over her face. It was an uncharacteristic posture of dejection. 'I guess,' she said dully, after a pause. 'If you think it's worth it, go ahead. But you won't change anything.'

Gillian waited, to see whether she would say more. She didn't. She continued to sit, heavy-limbed, like someone stunned.

'Any news on women's studies?' Gillian asked, looking for signs of life.

'An article's coming out in the *Drum* on Monday.'

'Do you know what it's going to say?'

'Not exactly, but I know the editors are supportive, and we've kept them fully informed.'

'I see. Well, let's hope Jessie Rayne enjoys a scrap.'

Rita looked up at that. 'The more fuss the better. Dean Frost will give her a load of rubbish about what a terrible mistake she's making, but she's the sort that would hate to back down in public.'

Gillian agreed, inattentively. Her real concern at the moment was Rita's state of mind, not Jessie's. She suspected Rita would hole up somewhere and eat her heart out. It would be a relief to see her angry.

'Has Paul said anything to you?'

'I haven't seen him. But he wouldn't talk to me about it—he's too busy practising his Important Young Mind expression.'

Gillian took this animosity as a sign that Rita's fire was not entirely out, and was glad.

'Do you have any plans for the weekend?' she asked.

'Getting on my bike, I hope. Speed is a terrific anæsthetic.'

'Off to the mountaintops?'

'If it's not pissing down again.'

'You live alone, don't you?' Gillian asked hesitantly. But Rita was unusually forthcoming.

'God, yes,' she said emphatically. 'After *my* family, anyone would. My sister—the one I speak to—lives with a man, but she's the only one of the five of us whose tolerance for human contact extends to the sharing of living quarters.' She grimaced. 'Voluntary sharing, I should say.'

'How do you mean?'

'One of my brothers is a nutter. He's lived a lot of his life in an institution. My other sister still lives at home, as an unpaid drudge—she thinks she doesn't have a choice.' She paused. 'That was supposed to be my job.'

'So that's why you came out here—to escape?'

'The other side of the earth wasn't far enough. But I came out here because of Mary Mayhew. A teacher I had. She took an interest in me, and she was, oh, a glimpse of another world. She was from Oregon, but she married an Englishman. A war bride—she showed me her wedding pictures once—she looked like Betty Grable in the old pinups. Blonde curls, the lot. Funny, I'd never thought of her as young. When she taught me, she had grey hair and varicose veins. She was my history teacher. She was brilliant. And kind. I used to visit her at home sometimes. She told me about the west coast, about the big trees, and the mountains and the clean air. She missed it, even after forty years.'

'Is she still teaching?'

'No, she retired. And then her husband died. She lives in Sussex now. She and her friend. They grow things.'

'So you're still in touch?'

'I think of her sometimes. I don't write much.'

Gillian glanced at Rita and away. She's really had the wind knocked out of her, she thought. She's told me more about herself in the last four minutes than she has in the last four years.

'What about money?' she asked aloud. 'Do you want me to try and find you some teaching in spring term?'

Rita shifted in her chair. 'I don't know. Could I stand to watch Paul swanning around with the Carver while I swell the ranks of the marginally employed? I can't deal with it now.' Her mouth twisted. 'I have to confess, the future's a bit of a blank.'

'Well, let me know as soon as you can. Somewhere else, if you'd rather. I can nose around, call people, see if there are any openings.'

'No. I have to see this Rayne thing through. I can't think about leaving yet.' She looked up at Gillian. 'Though I've got reason. Not just the Carver. I've had two obscene calls in the past two nights—I'd probably have had more if my number was in the book. Libby and Marnie have had them too.'

Gillian winced. 'I'm sorry. That's horrible.'

'It is. But I got the second charlie with my police whistle. He won't try again.'

'I hope the women's studies negotiations don't drag on all year. I must say, I wish I could have been a fly on the wall when Ms Rayne told Dean Frost,' Gillian said.

'I wonder if anyone rings Jessie Rayne in the middle of the night and shouts obscenities in her ear.'

'She undoubtedly has an answering service.'

CHAPTER 12

It was traditional for the two Carver committee members from the winner's department to invite him for a congratulatory drink at the faculty club. It was also traditional for the head of the department to join them, but absences had not been rare. Gillian, faced with the prospect of a social hour with Paul Smith, Ham Ridgeway and Jim Jacobsen, had made sure that she would be unable to attend on Friday afternoon.

'I wimped out,' she told Jane, departing for the meeting she had arranged.

When she got back, it was nearly dark. She gathered up the papers she needed for the weekend and went out again into the cold gusty evening. She crossed the road and passed behind the library. Ahead, on the steps of the English Department, she saw Rita, Libby and Marnie shivering in the wind, intent on their conversation. A large drop of rain hit her face, and she realized that she'd left her umbrella behind.

Alzheimer's strikes again, she thought, and turned back. When she re-emerged, it was darker, and the rain had begun in earnest. The little library parking lot was empty. Rita and the others were gone from the steps. Gillian thought she saw Marnie standing by the elevator inside the English building, but she wasn't sure. She hurried on under the trees, past the dark, heaped shapes of the rhododendrons. There were lights on in the engineering complex, but the path was hard to see. A sudden gust caught at her umbrella and wrenched it inside out. Swearing, Gillian turned around and held it the other way, trying to bend the ribs back to their proper position.

'Damn this weather.'

She had given up carrying any but the cheapest umbrellas to campus; too many were stolen to make having a decent one worthwhile. The wind had destroyed many of her bargains and other people's, too. Their skeletal remains littered the winter campus.

As she was struggling with the catch, Gillian heard a scream in the darkness behind her. She turned around again and stepped forward, peering through the rain, but she saw nothing. The parking lot she used was a short distance ahead, and the student lots were beyond. She splashed along the gravel path and burst into the open at the edge of her faculty parking lot. There were a few cars in it still. Rain like silver needles shone in the cloudy glow of the lamps.

'Hello!' she yelled. 'Does anyone need help?'

She heard running footsteps coming from the student lots. Then two figures shot towards her from between the cars. For a moment she was horribly frightened, then she realized they were women.

'Who's there?' a voice called. Then it said, 'It's Gillian Adams.' The two figures came to a halt, panting. Gillian recognized Rita's voice and hurried towards them.

'What happened?'

'Flashers in the parking lot. Guys in Hallowe'en masks,' Libby said, still gasping. 'I wouldn't have been so scared, but there were four of them.'

'They threatened us,' said Rita. 'They said if the Eff Yous didn't quit making trouble, we'd get what we were asking for.'

'Where'd they go?'

'Towards the main road. Into the bushes. We won't catch them.'

'You should tell the campus police anyway.'

'Yeah, I guess,' Libby said. 'But something's got to be done about more lights back here. It's so dark in the winter.'

The police sent a patrol car to the parking lot, but of course no one was there. Afterwards, Gillian, Libby and Rita went to the student union and Gillian bought them all a glass of wine. Gillian suggested to Rita that she consider moving in with Libby until the fury over the Rayne money died down.

'Someone's after you especially,' she warned Rita. 'You shouldn't be going about in the dark alone.'

'They just want to scare me off. I can't let them do that.'

Gillian reluctantly mentioned the effigy.

'What makes you think it was me?' Rita asked. 'It could have been any of us.'

'I'm just certain it was you,' Gillian said.

'Then why didn't you say anything today in your office?'

'You had enough on your plate, and I thought it was just theatre. But now you've been threatened.'

'We can't let them think they can intimidate us.'

Gillian had to be satisfied with Rita's promise to be wary. 'I'll be careful. I won't come and go from campus alone at night.'

⸙

It was another wet weekend, and the weather grew considerably colder. Curled up by the fire, Gillian thought of Rita and wondered if she should have pressed her invitation. Rita had declined her offer of dinner, saying only that she preferred to lick her wounds in private. She wanted to see the inflatable effigy, however, and she asked Gillian if she could stop by the office.

'Could I blow it up and photograph it?' she wanted to know.

'Come along after the office is closed one day next week,' Gillian suggested.

On Monday morning the roads were wet, but patches of cold blue appeared fleetingly among the clouds. The last leaves skirled in the racing wind and then were pasted to the pavement. Outside the arts building, Gillian stood still for a moment, breathing the fresh, wintry air and looking at the mountains. There was a faint dusting of snow on the heights.

The *Drum*, UPNW's student newspaper, came out Mondays and Thursdays at lunch-time. In the 'sixties, when it had been prone to bursts of ripsnorting counter-culturalism and Marxist arguments on the letters page, it had been called the *Jungle Drum*. But by the end of the 'seventies, it had been decided that 'Jungle' should be left behind with beads and other childish things, and the *Jungle Drum*, shorn of its crude comic strip and drug-culture slang, had become the *Drum*. The subject of tuition costs appeared more and more often on the front page, and where anti-war opinion had predominated, racism and then sexism took up more space. Now, in 1990, tuition increases and big classes were the old war horses of the editorial page, while parking and the bus service were the hot new topics. Anti-war editorials were making a comeback, owing to the situation in the Persian Gulf.

At noon, Gillian raced down to the main lobby for her copy and read it in the privacy of her office. There was a front-page article that carried over to cover half of page two, and there was an editorial. She skimmed rapidly through the article, which went over ground she knew. Then she turned to the editorial. Women's studies at UPNW were long overdue, Gillian read. The Feminist Union had come up with a proposal which had been presented to Jessie Rayne, whose family had donated generously to UPNW for several generations. Negotiations were currently under way with the administration. So much was straightforward. Then the article went on to address 'Acid Rayne'.

⊸⊤⊸

Some members of the engineering faculty and student body [Gillian read] are opposed to the continuation of these negotiations. They believe that any Rayne money should come to them, as in the past. A number of individuals in the Geology Department, which has also benefited, support this view. We see no reason why these two departments should have a monopoly. The Faculty of Arts appears to generally support the proposal, although some people are concerned about the costs and some question the validity of the concept of women's studies.

These issues can be and should be argued out in a democratic way. But there are people who oppose the women's studies department who are resorting to intimidation and harassment. Members of the Feminist Union have been bombarded with obscene phone calls and two of them were flashed by four men in the parking lot Friday night. Rita Gordon and Libby Hosmer say the men threatened them with 'what they were asking for'.

⊸⊤⊸

'Fully informed is right,' Gillian muttered to herself. But there was nothing about the effigy of Rita. Probably she and Libby had held that back until they could take photographs. There was more. A protest march from the library steps to the student parking lot was being held at noon on Tuesday. Anyone who disapproved of the violence and threats, whether or not they supported women's studies, was urged to take part. Gillian made a note in her diary. Then she read the next paragraph.

❦

In light of these events, it seems worthwhile to question the behaviour of the Carver committee. Once more they have avoided giving the award to a woman, and this time the woman is Rita Gordon. Without doubt, she was the outstandingly qualified candidate. This is widely acknowledged, even though Paul Smith, the winner, is certainly no disgrace to the Fellowship. We have heard that three of the committee members have taken stands against the proposal for a women's studies department. Are these events connected? In our opinion, the Carver committee owes Rita Gordon an explanation.

❦

'Jesus Christ!' Gillian said. Her telephone rang. She reached for it and paused, her hand on the receiver. It might be Ridgeway or Jacobsen, or the dean. If they'd seen the editorial, she didn't want to talk to them yet, until she'd had a little time to reflect.

'Yes?'

'It's Laura Byng,' said Jane.

Gillian was relieved. 'Thanks. Put her through.'

'Have you seen the *Drum*?' Laura asked.

'Yes, I'm practically cowering under the desk. There's going to be a major meltdown when Ridgeway and Jacobsen see it.'

'Is all that true? About the obscene calls and the flashing and the threats?'

'Rita told me on Friday she'd had two calls, and she's got an unlisted number, so the others may have had more. I found her and Libby running from the parking lot on Friday night, and I heard them scream.'

'This is disgusting.'

'It's worse than that.' Gillian told Laura about the effigy.

'It sounds like a campaign,' said Laura.

'I think so too.'

'But what about that last paragraph, about the Carver? That's pure speculation. They shouldn't have put it in.'

'Somebody's smelled a rat, I'll bet. They wouldn't print that kind of thing on Rita's say-so.'

'I have to go. I gave my lecture on *Sense and Sensibility* yesterday, and today we discuss it.' She sighed.

'What's the matter?'

'They won't like Elinor. They never do. They always fall for Marianne's histrionics. The only Austen that makes sense to them is *Pride*. I'll see you at the protest tomorrow, OK?'

⊥

Not long after this conversation, Jim Jacobsen strode into her office waving a copy of the *Drum*.

'Did you have anything to do with this?' he boomed.

Gillian, standing at her filing cabinet, could see Allie through the open doorway. She had stopped whatever she was doing, and the normal rustle and murmur of activity in the history office had ceased. A moment ago she had heard Palmer's querulous tones, but no one was speaking now. Everyone was listening.

'No, I did not.'

Jacobsen glared at her. He didn't believe her, or didn't want to; what he wanted was to give full rein to his temper. He waved the paper violently. 'This is outrageous. I will not sit by and be a target for innuendo and slander. There's not a shred of truth in it.'

'In what?'

Jacobsen's face was purple; the big veins stood out. His eyes were bloodshot. His worn herringbone tweed strained across his barrel-shaped body. It occurred to Gillian that he was a probable candidate for a heart attack. He smacked the newspaper on the desk. 'You know perfectly well. In the claim that the politics of the Rayne money had anything to do with our choice.'

'The editorial doesn't claim that it did. It says that certain facts are suggestive, and asks the committee to explain them.'

'Smear tactics. A standard technique in propaganda.'

'You can offer an explanation.'

'Why should we? We did our job. We shouldn't have to stoop.'

This was too high-handed. Gillian's temper flared up.

'Well, I for one, would like an explanation. In fact, I'd like to see the files and the minutes of the meeting.'

The atmosphere changed, as though a door had opened into outer space. Jacobsen stopped shouting.

'That's out of the question,' he said.

'Not with enough public pressure, which I shall do all I can to apply,' Gillian retorted with equal determination.

Jacobsen's voice rose again. 'You *did* have something to do with it!'

She was now thoroughly angry. 'No, I didn't. I was as surprised as you. But I hope it gets some results.'

'Not from me.' Jacobsen stalked out of the office.

'Oh hell,' Gillian thought. 'And the day's not half over yet.'

The committee issued no statement that day. The History Department buzzed; Charlie Rankin was overheard making jokes about the flashing incident; Vernon Palmer stopped into Gillian's office to tell her that it was her job to quell the hostilities and speculation that were so harmful to the department; Ham Ridgeway left Gillian severely alone, but when Jane praised the *Drum* for taking a strong stand, he barked at her so rudely that she burst into tears. Carole's usual cool professionalism deserted her; when Kray rashly suggested that the editorial was out of line, and the committee quite right to keep silent, she told him loudly to stuff it and slammed the door. This was heard and duly reported up and down the corridors.

Outside, the temperature dropped. The clocks had been moved back over the weekend, and now when Gillian drove home it was quite dark. Rita didn't come that evening to see the dummy.

By Wednesday, the last day of October, there were little patches of black ice on the side roads. Gillian drove slowly. Here and there, a jack o'lantern glowed on a front porch, and chattering goblins flittered up the walks, while their parents, muffled against the cold, stood waiting in the dark. There were few young children living in Gillian's immediate neighbourhood, so she wasn't expecting visitors. She had half-a-dozen chocolate bars just in case, but no carved pumpkin to signal her participation in this modern folk festival.

The porch light was out. She'd forgotten again. She put the car in the garage and singled out her house key in the reflected glare of the headlights. Gathering her briefcase, books and the bags of groceries and liquor she had acquired, she picked her way across the driveway and up the steps. On the third step her foot skidded on something soft and slimy. She pitched forward, flinging out a hand blindly. Her books slid away, and she dropped her briefcase. She landed prone, one hand stretched out to the porch, the other bent beneath her, between her sternum and what turned out to have been the bag of groceries.

She raised her head cautiously. She was lying slantwise on the steps between the house and the low stone parapet that protected the stairs and formed the base of the square stone columns supporting the porch roof. Her head had missed the projecting corner of the granite column by an inch.

Sore and shaken, she sat up and assessed the damage. An abraded palm, scraped and bruised knees and shins, a shock. Adults aren't used to falling down. Her books were splayed on the wet pavement. She looked at the flattened plastic bag from the market. Her groceries—bread, fish, pears, lettuce, a wedge of Brie—were *fottuto*, but they had saved her ribcage from the steps. She shut her eyes and felt her ribs. They were tender. What had she slipped on? Wet leaves? How stupid not to have raked them up. Even stupider to have forgotten the light again. She should never turn it off. But she could swear she'd remembered it this morning. Maybe the bulb had burnt out. She opened her eyes again and looked up into the roof of the porch, but it was too dark to see anything within the shadows of the projecting eaves. She looked at the steps. A fat yellow fragment of pumpkin lay at the bottom. She twisted round and inspected the porch. It was covered with strands and jagged lumps of pumpkin and fragments of broken glass. A smashed jack o'lantern, its gap-toothed grin cracked in two, lay on the doormat like a severed head.

Gillian got up carefully and collected her things. There was a narrow brown bag next to the head. She eyed it warily, then abruptly remembered her bottle of Scotch. Apparently it had landed on the mat when she flung out her hand. The bottle was unbroken. Gratefully, she picked it up and went in. This sort of thing, she decided, pouring herself a tot, is what David Hume meant when he defined a miracle as a transgression of a law of nature by a particular volition of the Deity. Thank you, David Hume, your cheque is in the mail.

She swallowed her drink and felt calmer. Nasty pranks on Hallowe'en were not unknown. The tradition went back a hundred years, at least. She herself had once soaped the screens of a pair of cantankerous neighbours. But on her porch, in this particular year? A coincidence? She doubted it. She carried a flashlight and the folding kitchen steps out to the porch and got a light bulb from the cupboard at the top of the cellar stairs. Climbing on to the first step, she pointed the beam of the flashlight up at the light fixture. The globe was gone, and there was no bulb in the socket.

She shone the flashlight on the driveway. Shards of thick, milky glass lay just beyond the edge of the porch.

CHAPTER 13

Thursday dawned cold and clear. A night wind had blown the clouds off the hills, and Gillian could see the spiky outlines of the distant fir trees. At the summits of the tallest hills there was now a thin blanket of snow.

Gillian cleaned up the mess on the porch before she left for work. She threw the pumpkin head, its menacing grin turned pathetic in the cold bright daylight, on to the compost heap. But she took a snapshot of the porch first. Just in case it's a campaign, she thought, and this is evidence.

She joined Laura at the library steps just before noon.

'They're beefing up security in the parking lots at night,' Laura reported. 'A patrol car will come through more often. That's a nice little Band-Aid isn't it?'

A throng was gathering around them. Laura began a rough count. Gillian looked the crowd over. She saw mostly young women, several hundred of them, she thought. But there were also older women, faculty members she knew by sight, and others, perhaps mature students or staff, whose faces she didn't recognize. A number of men had come, too, both faculty and students. Maybe twenty per cent, she guessed. She saw Murray threading his way towards her.

'So,' he said when he came up. 'How's the weather today in your department? Gale warnings up?'

'It feels like one of those neighbourhoods in Iceland—where people see the lava rolling down the hill and wonder whose house will be buried.'

Murray pointed to a knot of three or four young men on the far edge of the crowd. 'Those are engineering students.'

'Really? Where?' Gillian looked for the red jackets and saw none. 'I don't recognize them without their juvenile plumage.'

'I hope they're not here to make trouble,' Laura said sharply.

'I think they're here to join the march,' Murray replied.

'Really? That's brave of them,' Gillian said. 'I don't suppose they'll be very popular with their classmates.'

Murray was still watching the group. 'Yes, there's Joe Wiegand with them. I know him, he's on the civil engineering faculty.'

'I don't see President Bingham,' Laura said. 'Or any of the vice-presidents. And the only dean here is Frances.'

The crowd began to flow slowly down the steps and along the edge of the lawn at the heart of the campus. Their route would take them past the geology and engineering buildings and the parkade, through the student parking lot, and around the central administration building to the campus gate. The march was to end there, at the arch, under President Bingham's windows.

'I see most of the Feminist Union,' Gillian said, 'Libby and Marnie and Denise are all near the head of the line. But I don't see Rita.'

'Maybe she's had enough of the limelight,' Laura suggested.

Gillian looked up at the crisp blue sky. 'Maybe she just took a ride. It's been ages since we had a day like this.'

'It's cold.' Laura shivered. 'There was ice on the bridge this morning.'

'Cold?' Murray snorted. 'Hey, this is lotus-land. People go swimming on New Year's Day.'

'Only lunatics—of whom we have more than our fair share.'

'Never mind Murray,' Gillian said. 'He's never cold. He's always wearing a T-shirt out sailing when any normal human being needs a sweater.'

They strolled along the edge of the rectangular lawn, eating apples Murray had produced from his coat pocket. The trees were almost bare of leaves, the sun shone on the wet grass. The marchers were animated, and despite its serious intent, the parade had a holiday air compounded of youthful energy, group solidarity, and gaily coloured jackets in the bright sunshine. Hand-lettered signs and banners rode above the heads of the crowd. The protest had been interpreted broadly. A big red stop sign with white letters simply read SEXISM. END CAMPUS VIOLENCE, Gillian read. NO MEANS NO! STOP RAPE. GAY WOMEN AGAINST VIOLENCE. WOMEN'S STUDIES NOW. EXPEL SEXUAL TERRORISTS. Craning her neck to read the signs, Gillian caught sight of Jane, far back in the parade. She was walking with the Dean of Arts' secretary. Gillian waved and smiled to herself. Earlier in the day, Jane had said, 'Cynthia's coming to the march with me. I can't believe it—she'd call a cab before she'd walk to the corner store.' But there was Cynthia, teetering along in her high heels, her earrings bouncing and flashing in the sunshine. Another placard bobbed behind her, proclaiming, MISOGYN IS A MOR(T)AL ILLNESS.

They had passed the English building and the back corner of the geology building. Now they were marching past the front entrance. The steps were bare of students, but there were faces at the windows. Ahead stood the engineering complex, a massive structure in concrete and brown brick with high sheer walls like a fortress. A broad plaza with shallow steps led to the main entrance, which faced the campus's western gate. In another context, it might have been a pleasant gathering place for a sunny afternoon, but now it was empty. It looked bleak and outsized compared to the other buildings.

'All it needs is a statue of Mussolini,' Gillian said as they rounded the corner and began to traverse the long front face of the building.

Ahead, they saw the heads of the crowd turn towards the windows. People were pointing upward. The line of march straggled, as some paused and some moved determinedly onward. Gillian looked up. From the windows of the second floor hung four or five crude posters. DYKES OFF CAMPUS, she read. WOMEN'S STUDIES ARE IN THE KITCHEN. GANG RAPE IS A TEAM SPORT and FEMINISTS SUCK MY DICK.

'Jesus Christ,' Laura groaned. 'What a bunch of assholes.'

'Literally,' Gillian replied. Above each poster, fat pale shapes were pressed against the glass in rounded, symmetrical pairs.

'Good grief, a mass mooning,' Murray said. 'Quick, call the Anthropology Department! It may be their last chance to record this primitive tribal ritual.'

'It better be,' Laura said.

The march kept shuffling along; what else was there to do? Gillian thought, they couldn't storm the building. Then she noticed the video-camera.

'Look, someone *is* recording it,' she exclaimed, pointing to a woman who had stepped out of the line of march and was panning slowly across the face of the building. There was a slight commotion at the tail of the line, and the man Murray had pointed out earlier raced up the steps towards the main entrance to the building.

'That's Joe!' Murray said. 'What's he doing?'

Suddenly the flattened posteriors peeled away from the windows, one after another.

'Look!' Murray said. 'He must know which rooms they're in. But they've seen him coming, so they're scattering.'

The windows stared blankly down. There was no more to see. They marched through the parking lot where Rita and Libby had been threatened by the flashers, skirted the gym, and spilled over the green lawn that lay before the central administration building. A cold wind blew across the wide open space. Standing under the great arch of yellow cedar, Frances Romano made a brief speech, while the crowd shivered.

'I'm glad to see both men and women here,' she concluded. 'It's going to take all of us to solve this problem.'

Gillian's ebullient mood was dampened by the intransigence of the engineers—some engineers, as Murray kept reminding her—but the students around her were filled with a kind of exuberant scorn. If the posters had been vicious, the display of naked buttocks had been fatuous; the crowd was glad because it saw its enemies as fools. Gillian, thinking of the smashed face of the pumpkin, was not so sure. The bare-assed youths in the windows were foolish, but the intimidation of women who were perceived as threatening the hegemony of the Engineering Department was neither haphazard nor inane. And the two—the harassment of individuals and the mob displays—were interlocked.

Before the rally broke up, Gillian made her way over to where Libby stood in her boots and padded jean jacket, stamping her feet for warmth, her big brown eyes wide with excitement.

'Hi!' Libby said. 'This is Alice Rhodes. A friend of mine in biology. I had to perform surgery to part her from her computer terminal, but here she is.'

Gillian said hello to Alice, a short, sturdy woman in her mid-twenties with cropped black hair and a yellow parrot dangling from one ear. Her skin was beautiful, a silky brown like the inside of a shell. 'What did you think of that little display?' Gillian asked her.

Alice gave a little flick of her shoulders as if shaking something loose. 'The dinosaurs lasted a hundred and fifty million years,' she said—a smile lurked at the corners of her mouth—'but then there was a drastic change of climate.'

Libby, in high spirits, cackled loudly. 'Yeah. Can't you feel it?'

Anxiety was nagging at Gillian. 'Where's Rita? Didn't she come today?'

Libby looked puzzled. 'I don't know why she isn't here. She went for a ride this morning, but she said she'd be here for the rally.'

'Where did she go, do you know?'

'Her favourite ride, she said.'

'Let me know if you see her later, OK?'

'Sure. Maybe it's so beautiful up there she doesn't want to come down.'

Gillian lifted her gaze and looked at the craggy line of mountaintops above the city. It was often blotted out by the clouds, and even in clear weather a brown haze of pollution usually obscured its details. But today, after all the rain of the past weeks, the air was crystal clear. The frosted summits gleamed, and the dun-coloured scrape on Grouse where the trees had been cleared for a wide ski run was mottled with white. The road to the top of Mount Seymour was invisible, but the newer highway cut into the hillside below Cypress Bowl marked its face with a long zigzag scar. Gillian had driven up the road now and then with visitors. From the viewpoints on its upper stretches you could see miles of coastline, the city and the islands and the farms of the delta, and, ninety miles to the south, the huge white volcanic cone of Mount Baker. It was peaceful up there in the fall before the ski season began, and spacious, with a cool, resinous scent of evergreens in the air. Libby was probably right; Rita just didn't want to come down.

Murray had already returned to the chemistry building. Gillian walked back along the road with Frances and Laura. Less than a month back, the Triumph Day parade had travelled the same route. The last grey shreds of toilet paper clung here and there in the naked forks of the trees like empty cocoons.

Frances watched two students with signs disappear around the corner of the maths building. 'Well, that's over,' she said, pulling her fleecy scarf close about her neck. 'What to do now? Sixty per cent of women university students are afraid to walk around campus at night; we have a recent survey that says so. And what are we doing about it? I can tell you because I'm on the committee and I've just received the memo from the president's office. We're going to improve campus lighting and develop new parking policies. And we may get a minibus service to take women back to the residences at night. In a nutshell, more security. Don't get me wrong, I'm glad the administration is finally willing to spend money on this. But men's attitudes have to change, and sweet FA is being done about it. That goal just isn't taken seriously.'

'Aren't the men in one of the residences organizing a volunteer escort service?' Laura asked her. 'That's pretty admirable, don't you think?'

'Sure, but imagine calling up the residence and asking for a man to come and get you. Or always having to arrange an escort ahead of time. Think of waiting on the library steps at ten o'clock at night feeling ridiculous, asking a favour that might not be necessary. How often would you do that? Every night? Women shouldn't *need* escorts—this is their campus too.'

Gillian shivered in the cold wind. 'I hear that at Brown they post lists of campus rapists in the women's rooms. That's made the administration pay attention.'

'But some of the men say they've gotten on the list by mistake,' Laura protested. 'They're publicly branded and can't defend themselves.'

'The Scarlet R,' said Gillian. 'There's an idea.'

'But it's not fair.'

'Don't be so sure. Those men could be lying.'

Laura didn't answer. They kept walking, heads bent into the wind.

'I wish there had been more of us at the march. There must be six thousand women on this campus, and maybe five per cent of them came. I have trouble understanding why every woman wasn't there,' Gillian said. 'Do you know why, Frances? They come to you for counselling.'

'Various reasons. Some of them think all feminists are angry man-haters—they've heard it at home, or at school, and they haven't met anyone who's explained that you don't have to hate men to want to stand up for women. They haven't had to make their way in the world yet. Lots of them still think they'll get married and have children and live happily ever after. That *that* is the answer to the riddle of life, so there's no need to worry about equal opportunity, or child support after divorce, or wife-battering. It won't happen to them, they know that. And some of them have the idea that feminists are all lesbians—and lesbians are deviant and frightening.

'Think of how young they are, Gillian. Lots of them are from small towns. Feminism challenges all the orthodoxies they were brought up with. And they live in residences surrounded by men who are hostile to feminists and target anybody who acts like one. But these are the same men who are supposed to protect them from the dangerous ones they all know are lurking out there somewhere. To be a feminist would be to give up the illusion of protection.'

'But the young are brave, and they aren't worn out, like us. At least, I feel like a hollow husk sometimes. They're supposed to rebel—that's an orthodoxy itself.'

'They don't rebel against each other, Gillian.'

'Maybe feminism is the orthodoxy they're rebelling against,' Laura said drily. 'Do you think you and Gloria Steinem look like revolutionaries to them?'

Gillian laughed, conceding the point. 'No. Wrong outfits, for one thing.'

'I'll tell you what I hear in my classes, when we talk about Austen's view of marriage. I hear that old nostalgia for the absolute. What do the kids see when they look at their parents? A generation that tore its marriages apart over who does the dishes. They want to do better, and they think they can control the agenda. You know what they say? I've heard the women say they'll get married, but they'll only have babies after they've got enough money to stay home and look after them—of course, with all the comforts they're used to. They've no idea how unrealistic that plan is. And if you mention feminist analysis, they roll their eyes. They don't want to hear about it.'

'The high schools aren't any help,' Frances added. 'They don't tackle these issues at all.'

The wind was dying down. Twin black umbrellas flapped fitfully on the grass beside the road.

'They look like crippled bats,' Gillian remarked.

'Now, Gillian, mind your P's and Q's! They're not crippled, they're aerodynamically challenged,' Laura said severely.

Gillian chuckled with relief and pleasure. It had been weeks since they'd been easy enough to tease each other.

They all paused by the steps of the administration building before Frances went in.

'I was just thinking about *A Room of One's Own*,' said Laura. 'The opening scene, when Virginia Woolf walks on the college turf, and the Beadle shoos her away because she's not a Fellow, so she loses her train of thought. And then she's not allowed in the library either. It's really the same now, in a way. I mean, we're still having problems using the library,' she said half in jest.

'Absolutely,' said Frances. 'I should use that in a speech.'

Gillian thought of the lawns at Cambridge. Not many women could walk on the grass even now. There weren't many women Fellows. Even the word implied the masculine, although it wasn't exclusive. And she was certain that without affirmative action things would remain the same, here or there. She kept these thoughts to herself, rather than reopening the breach with Laura. What will become of us if affirmative action heats up here, she wondered, shooting a quick look at Laura. Almost twenty years of braided memories. Laura's eyes met hers, and Gillian thought she saw her question mirrored there.

The protest march was the top story on the six o'clock news that night. The media had found no engineering students willing to own up; the bare buttocks indistinctly visible on screen remained nameless. The posters had been taken down, the head of the ESS said: they had been 'out of line', he admitted, but the whole thing was being blown up out of proportion. Frances asserted the opposite; 'On the contrary, these incidents are being trivialized,' she said.

Gillian watched again at eleven, but there were no new developments. President Bingham couldn't be reached for comment.

⊰T⊱

It wasn't until the next day that she heard that Rita was dead. She had died on the Cypress Bowl highway, coming down the road on her BMW. Several people had seen the accident. The road climbed up the mountain in a series of steep switchbacks. Well up the slope, there was a huge curve, nearly a full circle, that took advantage of a jutting promontory of rock to widen the turn. Beside it was a parking lot where people stopped to enjoy the view. Rita had come very fast down the road leading into the curve and then leaned into it, the bike and her body canting sideways into the curve, using her weight to pull the heavy bike against its own momentum that would have carried it in a straight line off the road and out into space. Sparks flew up from the asphalt as she leaned further, then suddenly she seemed to lose control. The bike rocked, jerked around, flipped, and catapulted itself and its rider over the concrete barrier at the edge. Two horrified spectators saw Rita's body tumble through the air into the steep ravine nearly a hundred feet below. The bike crashed its way down through the brush for some thirty feet and then the gas tank blew up. The gasoline flamed wildly in the wet green jungly growth, and went out.

CHAPTER 14

The news came from Frances. She walked into Gillian's office at the end of the afternoon, after Jane and Allie and most of the department had gone home, shut the door and sat down.

'What's wrong?' Gillian asked, seeing her face.

'I'm sorry. The most dreadful news. Rita's had an accident.'

'On the motorcycle?'

Frances nodded. 'She's dead.' She burst into tears.

Gillian was too shocked to cry. Her hands went to her cheeks. 'When?' she said, after a little.

'Yesterday. Her name will be in the papers tonight; the police have told her family.'

'How did it happen?'

'It was on that big turn in the road up to Cypress. She was coming down too fast and lost control. She went right over the edge.'

'Jesus.' Gillian shut her eyes, fending off the image of Rita's body tumbling through space.

Frances was rummaging in her bag for a handkerchief.

Gillian remembered her anxiety at the march. 'Does Libby know?'

'Yes. She called the police last night; she was worried that Rita hadn't come to the rally and hadn't come home.' Frances blew her nose.

'Poor Libby.'

'Yes. I think she went down to identify the body today. Was Rita close to anyone else?'

'I don't know. I only know what she chose to tell me, and that wasn't much. She was reserved, and not only in the British way. She had to develop a protective shell early in life. The collectivity of feminism was hard for her, but she believed in it.' Tears began to gather behind Gillian's eyelids. She bent down to open the cupboard behind her desk, and got out the whisky. She passed Frances a glass, and then poured a shot for herself and drank it off.

'Have another,' said Frances. 'I'll drive you home.'

'That's all right. I just wanted one.'

After a minute or two, Frances pulled a newspaper out of her briefcase.

'Have you seen today's paper yet?'

'No.'

'The protest is on page one. With pictures.'

She handed it over. 'UPNW harassment protest,' Gillian read, beneath a photograph of the marchers strung out in front of the Applied Sciences Complex. EXPEL SEXUAL TERRORISTS was prominently displayed on a sign in the foreground. Behind the marchers, the windows of the building were visible, but the offending signs were too small and blurred to read.

'They've described the mooning and the signs—with decorous dashes—in the article,' said Frances, 'but I guess they thought a clear view of their bare bums wasn't suitable for the front page of a family newspaper.'

'I'll read it later, I guess.' Gillian handed the paper back. 'I just don't care right now.'

'No. I just thought you should know. The administration's in an uproar today.'

I want to call Edward, Gillian thought, when she was alone in her house. She looked at her watch. It was three a.m. in London. She wouldn't wake him. Laura and Jack were in Seattle; Laura had triumphantly announced at the protest march that Jack was taking time off so they could have a weekend away. Gillian telephoned Murray at his office.

'I'll be there in twenty minutes,' he said.

Gillian sat down to wait. The memory of Rita prancing round her office, brandishing the letter from Jessie Rayne, came back to her. That had been only ten days ago.

'This is a hell of a thing,' Murray said, walking in.

He stayed for most of the evening. At some point, they went into the kitchen. Murray fixed grilled cheese sandwiches and made Gillian eat one.

'There was probably black ice on the road,' he said. 'It was slippery even in town this morning.'

'I was just beginning to know her,' Gillian said sadly. 'As a person, I mean, not just as our star student.' She told him about her interview with Dean Stanley. 'I guess there's not much point in making a scene about the Carver now.'

'I suppose not,' Murray agreed, refilling her glass.

He left at ten-thirty. 'Are you sure you're all right?' he asked. 'I could stay the night.'

'I'll be OK. I'm going to call Edward and then go to bed.'

But as soon as Murray was gone she felt desolate. She telephoned Edward at eleven.

'Darling!' Edward's buoyant early morning voice said, as if he were right there and not ten thousand miles away. Gillian could never get used to how good the connections often were now. In her childhood telephoning across the ocean had been like talking to someone in a locked trunk fifty fathoms down. Nowadays, the satellite echoes sometimes interfered, and your own words came back to you instead of a reply, but at other times calling England was like calling the next-door neighbours. In a way, the better connections were more frustrating. In the old days, you felt you'd achieved something just by shouting a few words and being heard. Now, the voices were so real you felt cheated that the person wasn't right there with you. A voice that real should be able to put its arms around you.

'I was just thinking that you'd be here soon, sitting across the table from me at breakfast. Or dinner, more likely.'

'Edward,' Gillian interrupted, miserably.

'What's the matter? You *are* coming, aren't you?'

'Yes, I'm coming. But I can't even look forward to it right now. Something awful's happened.'

'Tell me.'

Gillian hurried through the story. 'And the worst thing is, I can't help wondering if she did it sort of on purpose.'

'Killed herself because she lost a grant?' Edward asked in disbelief.

'No, not deliberately, the way you mean. It was awfully important, and like a dummy I told her I was sure she'd get it. She was crushed, I'd never seen her like that. But no, I don't think she made up her mind to commit suicide. I know it could have been a simple accident. But what if she had bouts of depression? She was terrifically highly strung, and her brother's in an asylum; she just told me that a few days ago. What if she just let it happen?'

'Don't borrow trouble, Gilly. A motorcycle on an icy mountain road is explanation enough. How often had she been up there?'

'It was her favourite ride. She knew that road like the back of her hand.'

'So perhaps she went too fast for just that reason. Look. She's dead and you're alive. You feel rotten about it, that's all.'

'OK, Edward, I see what you mean. But listen, I think I'll go see the family while I'm there. It's the least I can do.'

'Shall I find them for you?'

'No, I can get the address from the university. They always have the next-of-kin on file.' Gillian's voice cracked. '...In case something happens. But there is something you can do. Would you find Mary Mayhew, in Sussex? A retired schoolteacher from London. She meant a lot to Rita. More than her parents, I think.'

'Of course. Shouldn't present too many difficulties. If you're going down to Sussex perhaps I'll go with you. Now, what time is it there? Eleven-thirty? Have a drink and go to bed. And I'll see you at Heathrow in a week.'

Gillian slept badly. She got up early when she would have preferred to doze comfortably until ten and made herself some coffee in the dim grey morning light. When she opened the refrigerator to get out the milk, the champagne was still there, lying coldly on its side. Like a corpse, she thought. I'll never drink it. She lingered in the kitchen, tidying away the glasses and plates from the night before, and then pulled all the crumpled napkins out of the clean laundry pile and ironed them. Then she lay on the sofa and read Emily Dickinson for a while. Then she did nothing. This was the Hour of Lead.

Eventually, she opened the newspaper. There was the crumpled motorcycle among the blackened bushes. Gillian looked away and then back, not wanting to see it, but unable not to look, not to search the image as if it might give her a clue to the unreason of Rita's death. Above the blurry shapes of wheels and branches was a photograph of Rita, taken several years earlier. A student ID picture, Gillian guessed. It wasn't much like Rita. There was the shaggy hair and the nose, but the intensity didn't show. Rita was wearing an open-necked shirt, not a sweater, so it must have been warm weather when the picture was taken. Gillian looked closely at it. There was something, a spot, in the V of the collar. A medallion? She couldn't make it out. Rita had never worn any jewellery, as far as Gillian could recall. She got up and went to her compact edition of the OED and fished out the magnifying glass. She put the newspaper under a strong light and stared through the glass. The grey dots resolved themselves into a medal with a head on it. What could it be? She shifted the glass and pulled the lamp closer to the page, but she couldn't make it out.

On Monday morning she was grimly exhausted. She left home later than usual, loath to return to work and encounter her colleagues, some of whom, though shocked of course, would not mourn for Rita.

Palmer and Kray were in the history office when she arrived, checking their mailboxes.

'Had a bad weekend?' Kray inquired, looking at her.

Gillian nodded.

'I'm very sorry about Rita,' he said gruffly. 'It shouldn't happen to anybody, and we've lost a real scholar—one the department would have been proud of.'

'Yes,' she replied, faintly surprised. Rita had never had much to do with Kray, so he must be responding to what others had said of her. Perhaps the department had appreciated Rita more than she knew.

'It's a shame,' Palmer said. 'Motorcycles are dangerous enough without riding them on mountain roads. I tried to caution her once, but she didn't listen. She was a headstrong young lady. Still, a shame, really.'

Gillian turned away. She could just imagine Palmer 'cautioning' Rita. In the days when sexist epithets had had the free run of the language, he would have been called an old maid. What a Godawful day it was going to be.

Allie, at her desk, made a face at Palmer's back. Jane was busy at the coffee machine. Gillian fetched her cup. When she had filled it, Jane, whose eyes were puffy, handed her something wrapped in a napkin.

'Banana bread,' she said. 'I made it this morning...I thought you probably wouldn't have eaten any breakfast.'

'You're right. Thank you. My dear,' Gillian added, touched by Jane's kindness.

The department was extremely subdued all day. Jane and Allie crept about the office, speaking in near whispers. Charlie Rankin sought Gillian out and said how sorry he was about Rita; for once he made no jokes. People moved carefully and quietly, muting the rude noises of life that continued all about the silence of death. Death was a little hole that closed, quickly and inexorably. The students gathered in murmurous huddles in the corridor. Gillian was aware of Libby's absence, and Paul's.

Ridgeway, coming out of the elevator in mid-afternoon and finding Gillian waiting for it, put his hand on the door to keep it from shutting.

'I've just heard about Rita Gordon. What a pity,' he said. 'She did tend to take everything a little too far, so I suppose it's fair to assume she was going faster than was safe. But such an intelligent student. A turbulent personality, but quite brilliant.'

On impulse, Gillian said, '*Why* didn't she get the Carver? Was there something wrong with her recommendations?'

Ridgeway shook his head. 'No, they were topnotch. I can't really say, Gillian, but the Carver committee's judgements have been fairly sound over the years, you know. The Fellows have all gone on to do them credit. And the decisions aren't always easy to make. Anyway, water under the bridge now, I'm afraid.'

He dropped his hand, releasing the door. Gillian rode the elevator down to the main floor lobby, thinking about the Carver. So the recommendations—besides her own—were all right.

Nothing awry there. She shook herself. There was no point in pursuing it.

The two faculty who were most affected, besides Gillian herself, were Carole and John Honeycutt. The three of them had lunch together in Honeycutt's office.

'She wasn't easy to work with,' John said. 'She had her own agenda, and she didn't like taking direction from me. A couple of times she criticized my suggestions so thoroughly, I asked her if we'd reversed rôles. She could be arrogant and damned irritating. But I like a good chewy argument, and I've never seen a better thesis. I was really looking forward to having her as a colleague for the next couple of years.'

'So was I,' Carole said. 'The Carver was a lead-pipe cinch, I thought.'

'I made that mistake, too,' Gillian sighed.

'Didn't everybody?'

'Everybody except the committee.'

'My recommendation wasn't the problem, I know that,' said John. 'It was so glowing she could have started a fire with it. Could they have been such Neanderthals as to turn her down because she's not a man?'

Gillian shrugged. 'The dean says not.'

Carole said, 'Then it was the Rayne money. She put a spoke in their wheel—Bingham's and Frost's, I mean. Everybody knows they had their cosy little plans.'

'Maybe. But Stanley doesn't think so, and he's not on their side in that game.'

Honeycutt snorted. 'I wouldn't trust Stanley to know what they were up to.' He leaned dejectedly on his elbow. 'I'm going to miss her.'

'Me too,' said Carole. 'I just can't believe it. Neither can the grad students. They all look as if they've seen a ghost.'

'They've seen their own,' Gillian answered. 'Immortality has been snatched away.'

'Do you think,' Carole said hesitantly, 'do you think Rita was riding carelessly because she was so upset?'

'Maybe,' Honeycutt said. 'Or maybe she was angry. People drive like demons when they're enraged. And she had reason,' he finished sombrely.

'I don't know,' Gillian sighed. 'Maybe Libby does.' She dreaded seeing Libby. 'Do you think I should keep after the Carver committee?'

'A little hard on Paul, isn't it? It throws doubt on his worth as a Fellow, and you can't give it to Rita now,' Honeycutt replied. 'Besides, they won't tell you, and it'll upset the department. I'd drop it.'

'I disagree,' Carole said. 'It's a matter of principle. It *is* hard on Paul, but maybe you could talk to him about it.'

'Well, I'll leave it till I'm back from London.'

'Will there be a funeral?' Carole asked.

'Frances is trying to arrange something with the family.'

Gillian and Carole walked back along the corridor together.

'I wish we had her back,' Carole said. 'She would've been such a useful ally. I had already imagined her at department meetings. No more stupid comments from Rankin, for one thing. She'd have given him her Asshole-of-the-Week award, and he'd have shut up.'

'Yes, she could have squelched him—which I can't seem to do.'

Gillian slogged on with the day. In the afternoon, she went to the library briefly to verify a couple of page numbers for the footnotes to the paper she was giving in London. The air smelled faintly of stale sweat, like a disused gym. She descended to the bottom floor, below ground level. Despite the lighting, it was somehow murky down here, and Gillian felt as though she were deep under water. The many floors of books above seemed to press downward, as, like a diver, she cruised along the reefs of books. It wouldn't surprise her at all to find distorted albino creatures lurking in the dim recesses, waiting for dinner to swim past.

The alleyways between the metal shelves were narrow. She squeezed past a man squatting on his heels inspecting the bottom row of a shelf near the one she wanted. She excused herself, and he looked up and said hello.

It was Dick Rasmussen. He stood up, groaning gently. 'To squat is good for the back, they say, but my neck may never straighten out again. If men can land on the moon, why can't they design a bookshelf that won't cripple the reader? It's probably a conspiracy of the librarians. They don't really want us to read their books, do they?'

She answered at random, not wanting to talk to him. She tried to move on, but he had something he wanted to say.

'I heard that your star student was killed in a motorcycle crash. I'm sorry.' He sounded genuine, and she tried to conceal her surprise. 'A good friend of mine nearly died in a crash a long time ago,' he went on. 'My freshman year in college. I was in the same race and saw it. Our whole crowd used to go out in the desert and tear around. It wasn't the first accident, either. But it was the first time somebody nearly died. I sold my bike the next day. Poor Jamie. He was burned over half his body, and it was weeks before we knew he'd make it.'

'But he lived.'

'He lived. He never rode again, and he dropped out of college, but he lived. Not like your student. I didn't know her, but it hits home, maybe because of the memories. So I can imagine how you're feeling, and I wanted to tell you I was sorry.'

'Thank you,' Gillian said. 'I appreciate it.' She moved on to the shelf she needed. She felt a little better. If Dick Rasmussen, who had been a complete dink on Triumph Day, could be genuinely kind now, the world was not as bad a place as it had looked a few minutes earlier.

CHAPTER 15

During the next few days Gillian was very busy at home and at work organizing her departure. She made lists. She hired her neighbour's thirteen-year-old daughter to rake up the leaves and rotting apples in the yard; she also asked the girl's mother whether anyone else on the street had found a smashed pumpkin on the doorstep. No one had mentioned any problems. She had her raincoat cleaned, cancelled the newspaper, polished her shoes, telephoned her mother, paid her bills. At the office, with Jane's coaching, she managed to print out some copies of her paper. She graded and recorded the marks for the late essays and returned these literary gems to their owners, rescheduled the graduate seminar she would miss while in London, and tried to empty her correspondence basket. Frances stopped in to tell her that the family would not be coming over and didn't want the body shipped to England. Rita would be cremated, and there would be some sort of memorial service. She thought she might consult Libby. Gillian pressed grimly on with her tasks, too preoccupied to see either Laura or Murray, though they both called to ask how she was and offer to drive her to the airport. She did go to see Libby, who hadn't shown up on campus since the accident.

Libby lived in a tiny apartment under the eaves of an old house half way between the UPNW campus and downtown. The steps climbed ungracefully up the blue-painted shingle exterior, barely missing a corner of one of the second-storey windows. At the top was a small, unsheltered landing with a crude railing of painted two-by-fours freckled by dirty rain marks. A couple of large clay pots stood in the corner, one bristling with dead daisy stalks, the other trailing a slimy web of rotting lobelia.

A hollow-eyed Libby opened the door. Gillian followed her up a steep and narrow flight of stairs past an angular little storage room tucked under a corner of the roof. At the top, a single open space was squeezed under the slanted planes of the roof's peak. A desk, a bed, a couple of dingy beanbag chairs and a long, overflowing bookcase took up most of the room.

Libby's sleek bloom, her seal-like gleam, was quite gone. She looked ill.

'I'll make some tea,' she said.

The kitchen formed a small L at the other end of a low, cramped hallway. Used mugs and a couple of pots stood in the sink. Libby filled a dented kettle. An overflowing ashtray was on the counter, and the apartment reeked of cigarettes. Libby lit one from the stove.

'I didn't know you smoked,' Gillian said.

'I haven't for a long time.'

She dumped a couple of teabags into a heavy blue ceramic pot.

Gillian looked out of the window at a ratty lane and the rear of a row of wooden houses. Nearly every one of them had stairs and balconies tacked on, and new, awkwardly-placed aluminium windows. The back yards were parking lots rimmed with ragged grass. Family houses of the 'twenties, revamped for the rentals of the 'eighties. Old wooden poles marched down the lane, strung untidily with wires.

'I didn't hear about it until the next afternoon,' she said. 'Frances came and told me, otherwise I might have opened the newspaper and read it there.'

'Yeah,' said Libby. 'That happened to some people who knew her.'

The kettle rumbled gently on the burner.

'Where did the picture of her come from?'

Libby shrugged. 'UPNW, I guess. It's an old one, from when she first came here.'

'I didn't think it was much like her. Do you know what she was wearing around her neck? That medallion, or whatever it was? I never saw her wearing it.'

'It was a St Christopher's medal.'

'Really?' Gillian was astonished.

'Mary Mayhew gave it to her when she left England. Rita said it was supposed to protect her. I don't remember why.'

'He's the patron saint of wayfarers. But I wouldn't have expected Rita to believe in it for a minute.'

'She didn't. She wore it because Mary gave it to her. It was gold, or something, and Mary meant a lot to her. She got a longer chain for it pretty quick, so people wouldn't see it. She said it gave them the wrong idea.'

'Yes, it would do that. Well,' Gillian sighed. 'I knew so little about her.'

'She wasn't easy to know.'

The kettle was boiling. Libby ignored it. 'She lost the medal a few weeks ago. She was very upset.'

'Lost it? How?'

'She thinks—thought—somebody stole it. She didn't wear it every minute. Her place was burgled, and it disappeared.'

'I didn't know that.'

Libby coughed, her eyes watering. She stubbed out her cigarette. The kettle screeched. Gillian took it off the burner and filled the teapot.

'Did she lose other things?' Gillian asked, when Libby stopped coughing.

'She didn't think so. But she said someone had been through her drawers. That's so creepy.' Libby shuddered.

'Was that after Triumph Day, or before?'

'After. I know what you're thinking. We thought about it, too. But she said the medallion would be easy to sell, so it could have been an ordinary theft.'

Gillian shivered. 'Yes, it must have been creepy, especially with those telephone calls she was getting.'

Libby nodded. 'She started taking her police whistle to bed at night.' She wrapped her arms about herself, cradling her grief. 'I want her back,' she whispered.

'I know.'

Libby's thin body quivered. She turned to the cupboards and busied herself with cups and spoons. Gillian looked at the anguished set of her shoulders and wished for a comforting word to say.

Libby put the cups on the table. 'I guess we should have some tea.'

Gillian sat down. 'Libby, I'm going to try to see Mary Mayhew when I'm in England next week. And maybe Rita's family, too. Do you know anything about them?'

'Not too much. She didn't like talking about them. Her dad was like some kind of religious nut, and her mother was sick a lot. She felt pretty bad leaving home, because of her mother, but she said she had to get out. There was one sister she liked a lot; I've got her address, if you want it. Rita gave it to me once when I was going to Europe, but I never made it to Manchester.'

She picked up her address book from beside the telephone and handed it to Gillian. 'I told Frances about Rita's sister,' she went on. 'I thought she might come over, but I guess she hasn't got the money.'

'Her parents are still in London?'

'Yeah.' She carried her tea over to the window and sipped it, staring out at the lane.

'Do you think Rita was too upset to drive, that day?' Gillian asked after a while.

Libby shook her head. 'She wasn't like that. She was real calm on her bike. It must have been the ice.'

Gillian set her cup down on the counter. After the rush of emotion, she felt exhausted. A copy of the *Drum* from the previous Thursday lay there. Gillian had seen the picture—the editorial staff had printed a clear, sharp close-up of the signs in the windows and the battalions of buttocks—but she'd been too stricken to read it when it came out. She glanced at it now. A description of the protest and the response, followed by quotes from President Bingham and assorted faculty and students.

'Disgusting,' she read. 'Absolutely unacceptable. Breaches all standards of decent behaviour.' Those were Bingham's comments. She raised her brows.

'Sounds like Bingham has broken ranks with Frost.'

'He must have realized how it'd look if he took their side. It doesn't mean he supports us. He hasn't committed to women's studies, and I bet not one of those guys will be expelled.'

'Yes, but at least he's not calling this a prank—as Frost is still doing, I gather. And any split between Frost and Bingham should be all to the good.'

'OK, but how are we going to stop this stuff? The flashers, the phone calls, and now this—this blatant hatred in public. I even think my car was probably part of it. I feel really frightened. I'm nervous about being on campus at night now.'

'Has anyone else in the Union been troubled?'

'Everyone. Except with Marnie the calls stopped, because her parents answer the phone. But she got an anonymous letter. I won't repeat it, but it was really graphic.'

Gillian winced.

'Tell her to keep it, if she hasn't destroyed it already. It might be useful evidence. I've started a file myself, if she wants to give it to me.'

'That's an idea,' Libby said thoughtfully. 'I could keep my answering machine tapes, too. I erased the messages, but if I get any more, I'll keep them.'

'What about the memorial service?' Gillian asked before she left.

'The Feminist Union's going to have it. It'll be like the Quaker ones, where people who knew her will come and say something about her if they want to.'

'Good. When is it?'

'Around the end of the month. Right now it's too soon. We'd all fall apart.'

⁓⚶⁓

The day before her departure, Gillian received a note from Jessie Rayne. She very much regretted Rita's death, and would Gillian join her for lunch?

Gillian telephoned Frances. 'I have an audience with the Queen. What do you think it's about?'

'I don't know. But it can't be bad news. She wouldn't invite you to lunch if she were backing out of the proposal.'

'I suppose not.'

'It's the best memorial we could wish for, Gillian.'

'I know. I just don't have any energy for it right now.'

'You'll get it back. I know it's very cruel that life keeps going; you feel as if it should stop and mourn with you. Anyway, I'm glad she's in touch with you. The tension around the administration offices is so thick I can hear the air twanging.'

'I'll go as soon as I'm back from England. What do the police say about the accident?'

'Nothing, yet. I understand they believe she hit a patch of ice. She didn't hit anything else, according to the witnesses.'

'What about her brakes?'

'They run a thorough check on all vehicles involved in fatalities, they told me. But they're understaffed, so unless something has priority, it just waits in line.'

Gillian went home to pack. She shared the descending elevator with Paul Smith and Jim Jacobsen. They had been chatting in the corridor, but at her arrival they fell silent. Jacobsen stood as far from her as the confines of the elevator permitted and hummed under his breath. They hadn't spoken since their fight about the *Drum* article. Paul, between them, obviously wished he were somewhere else. He and Gillian exchanged remarks about the probability of more rain.

'Good night,' Gillian said politely, addressing them both as the doors opened at the main floor.

'G'night,' Jacobsen muttered ungraciously.

She walked quickly along the path towards her car. 'Oaf,' she said aloud. 'Some department head you'd make.'

When she reached the parking lot, she discovered that her car had a flat tyre. The cap was off the nozzle; someone had let the air out. She had a perfectly good spare, but she wasn't dressed for changing tyres in the rain. Exasperated, she rushed into the faculty club to telephone the AA. Jim Jacobsen and Paul were having a drink at the bar. She wasn't going to ask Jacobsen for the time of day, let alone help of this sort. Too bad they were together; Paul was wearing blue jeans, and might not have minded getting wet and dirty. On a night like this, the AA would be busy. She made her call and drank a glass of wine by the fire. Then she went out to the car to wait. She listened to the rain on the roof. It had been falling all day, but now it was coming down with a tropical violence that was startling. It hardly seemed possible that it could rain so heavily for so long. But the storms—'weather systems,' as they liked to say on the radio, had been abnormal this fall. She had to wait a long time for the AA truck.

CHAPTER 16

Air travel is such a levelling experience, Gillian thought, adjusting her pillow. The drone of the engines and the humming vibrations of the metal skin of the airplane passed through the thin padding of the pillow and circled inside her skull. She shifted her cramped knees and switched out the reading lamp, hoping for sleep. They flew on through the darkness, over the invisible coast of Greenland. Everybody's stuck in here for the same number of hours, she thought, we all breathe the same desiccated air; we line up for the same washrooms, our bodies' common needs on display as we squirm past each other in the aisles. The flight attendants refer to us as 'the herd', and that's what we are, here in our pen, even the corn-fed hogs in first class.

Her great-uncle had had his own open-cockpit airplane and fought with the RAF in World War I. There were yellowed photographs of him in the albums at her mother's house. He wore a leather helmet and stood next to his insect-like airplane, with a hand on the wing as if it were a friend's shoulder. 'Flying!' he'd exclaimed many years later, when she was a child, 'it's the most exhilarating thing in the world.' Obviously, he'd never been on a flight like this.

How many times had she crossed the ocean? She'd probably averaged two trips a year over the last twenty years; at two crossings each, that was eighty flights. At ten hours each, a rough average, considering flights from the east coast, flights to Rome and Amsterdam as well as London, that was 800 hours of her life. More than a month. God. In the future she was going to settle down somewhere and not budge. But where? The west, where she lived now? The east coast, where she grew up? London? She had a stake in all three—emotional ties, history, friends. She had a man in London, she had a house in the Hudson River Valley. Rather, her mother had it and still lived in it, but it would be Gillian's someday. A wonderful house. So far as she was concerned, even Cotswold stone couldn't compete. Edward said he liked it as much as anything in England, but that didn't mean he'd think of living there—he was indifferent to the finer points of domestic architecture.

'I'd rather be in Manhattan, twenty storeys up in a block of flats.'

'Apartment building,' Gillian said.

'Tee-vee,' Edward recited, sing-song. 'Gas station, truck, raincoat, drugstore, al-u-min-um.'

'Tomayto.'

'Tomahto.'

'Let's call the whole thing off.'

Gillian smiled to herself in the darkness. Only a few hours to go.

⏤

'Do you want to go down to Sussex tomorrow?' Edward asked over lunch, not far from his Pimlico flat. 'I've the whole day, so far as I know. Sunday's usually good for finding people at home.'

'Where does Mary Mayhew live?'

'Near Alfriston. You'll like it. It fairly oozes olde worlde charm.'

'Unlike you,' Gillian retorted.

'We could walk on the Downs, if you like.'

'That's a handsome offer. I accept.' She was touched. Edward did not find country walks particularly interesting. She glanced out of the window at the blustery street. 'I won't insist on a picnic.'

'Good. I'm ready to sacrifice almost anything on the altar of love, but not Sunday lunch. There's bound to be a pub somewhere about.'

She gazed fondly at him across her lamb tikka. 'This place is as good as ever.'

'Ravi was glad to hear you were coming. I've booked dinner for our last evening.'

'Good. I must thank him for keeping you alive when I'm not here.' Edward rarely dined at home. He often forgot to eat when he was working or dined absent-mindedly on quite dreadful food. But at least once a week he had a quick dinner at The Jewel, because it was very convenient as well as very good. When Gillian came, she wanted good food, and Edward seemed happy enough to be reminded of it, consuming steak and kidney pie at Rule's with apparent pleasure, or letting Ravi choose a special meal for them.

She still felt, when she was near him, a heightened physical awareness that was absent at other times. Her appetites awoke, her senses were keener, or so it seemed to her. The life of the body, a blurred background in her daily routine, came into focus. He had an intense, physical energy she lacked; his hard, compact body, tightly-knit, quick-moving, was charged with vitality. Possibly, Gillian thought, occasional danger whetted the edge of that vitality. And perhaps the thrill—yes, that was the word—she felt wouldn't last if they lived together, but she was unlikely to find out.

She had asked him once whether he saw anyone else when she wasn't in England.

'No,' he'd said. 'But I'm not tempted to.'

'Why not?'

'Are you?'

'No.'

'Well then.'

'Who says our reasons are the same? Why not?'

He'd sighed. He didn't enjoy this kind of talking. He thought of it as one of her Americanisms, but he no longer said so, since when he had, she'd replied that most of the British women she knew wanted to 'talk' too. 'To talk' was a verb that had acquired a new meaning, he discovered: it meant to talk about what women talked about. Men didn't like to 'talk'.

He'd tried to answer her question. 'Being alone is a habit, I suppose. And my mind's on the job most of the time. I don't think about it.'

She'd waited. He'd gone on, slowly, 'I met you by chance. This...attachment is what I want. Perhaps it works because it's not part of my life all the time—the sort of intimacy you want isn't easy, and domesticity doesn't interest me. I suppose I could be seduced, but it hasn't happened.'

'If you did have an affair, would you tell me?'

'If that's what you want.'

'I'd prefer to know.' Easy to say, she thought, but she actually didn't want to rehearse that particular conversation, even in her own head. They'd left it at that. He'd never mentioned the subject again, so Gillian assumed that he had nothing to tell her. His life was lived intensely in the present; he fretted less than she did about past and future, a quality that occasionally troubled her but which she most often found exhilarating.

'Right,' he said. 'Sunday in Sussex. It'll be a job getting you out of bed, though. By the way, since I'm indulging in this bout of tourism, do you think you might tell me why we're going?'

'I want to tell Mary Mayhew about Rita, because I'm sure she would want to know. I could write, but I'd like to meet her. She knew Rita, and I feel cheated of the chance to know her. I'm sorry if it's a nuisance, but I want to find out more about her.'

'Investigating?' Edward inquired.

'Not in that way. At least, I don't think so. What could anybody in England have to do with Rita's motorcycle accident?'

❧

Edward woke Gillian at nine on Sunday morning. She looked blearily at this bathed and shaven apparition in its plum-coloured Viyella dressing-gown. Steam curled about it. She groaned.

'Go away.'

'No. I'm waking you at your express command. Besides, I've made coffee, and I'm collapsing under a stone or two of newsprint.'

'Later.'

He got into bed beside her. 'I have a cold wet flannel as well.'

She opened her eyes to glare at him. Her brain felt like a lead grapefruit. 'You thug.' She held out her hands. 'Coffee.'

❧

He backed the car out of the garage. 'We'll take the Vauxhall Bridge and the Brixton Road,' he said.

Gillian unfolded the map and found Alfriston. She was still sleepy, but she was excited, too. England! She was really here.

'I see it. It's near Eastbourne. I haven't been there, but I did go to Monk's House years ago—that's not too far away. What's the name of the river?'

'The Cuckmere.'

'Cuck. I wonder where that comes from. A cucking-stool was what they used for dunking disorderly women. Cuckoos?'

The streets were quiet. The broad grey Thames curved gently beneath them. She could see the Tate over her shoulder. She sighed happily. Edward glanced at her.

'London. I'm realizing I'm here.'

'"Every drop of the Thames is liquid 'istory,"' he intoned.

'Whereas the Nile is merely liquid, I suppose. Not to mention the Ganges or the Mississippi, or the St Lawrence.'

'Mere H_2O...and other less benign substances. You may wallow in exotic riparian romances. Give me an English river.'

'I'll push you into the Cuckmere.'

They drove south under a cool, pale blue sky striped with high cirrus clouds, past streets upon streets of sad-coloured buildings, through the widening ring of newer suburbs and at last into patches of open country and harvested fields dun and velvety under the weak November sun.

They drew nearer the coast. As the soft greens of the south spread about them on the quilted hills, Gillian said, 'Downs—like a big puffy green duvet for a landscape.'

'Still on about sleep, are you?'

'My body isn't really in England yet.'

'I rather thought it was.'

'No schoolboy humour, please.'

'Why not? It's every Englishman's birthright.'

Gillian turned to look at him. He was driving down a country road with her, and he wasn't thinking about the Yard. He seemed perfectly happy.

'I'm always a displaced person when I first get here,' she said dreamily. They passed a particularly inviting sun-warmed hollow in the undulating country. 'Let's stop. We could lie down in that soft green bed—and I'm not thinking of sleeping.'

'The cucking-stool was obviously a failure.'

'I thought we might reinforce the reality of England.'

'You must be mad, my darling. This is a public road. Besides,' he said, driving on, 'it's November in England.'

This was true, but he would have thought she was mad even in June.

❦

They had crossed the Ouse a little way back and now passed the small settlements of Selmeston and Berwick. Edward made the turn before Gillian realized they were upon it. 'Your quarry is on the other side of the river, but I'll show you Alfriston first.'

'Oh,' said Gillian moments later, as they drove into the tiny triangular centre.

'There you are. English Village, complete with historic Star Inn. Note the half-timbered Elizabethan façade. Do not note the unhistoric extension hidden behind.'

Edward drove slowly through the village and circled back. 'Perp. church, the Cathedral of the Downs,' he announced. 'Fourteenth-century parsonage, first building acquired by National Trust!'

'Edward, you've been reading.'

'Cows!' he said. 'Thatched roof!' continuing to point out the sights.

'Shut up, my sweet. It's lovely.'

'I knew you'd like it,' he said with satisfaction. 'Wait till you see where we're going to walk this afternoon.'

'You mean you've planned it?'

'Yes. I thought you might need cheering up.'

❦

They went back the way they had come, crossed the river and drove south for a mile or more, the Downs sweeping up directly on the left and rising again on the right across the flat-bottomed valley of the Cuckmere. They found the cottage with no difficulty. It had a white-washed front, a steep-gabled slate roof and end walls of chalk rubble like pale layers of fruitcake separated by thin courses of darker brick icing. There was a garden in front, and behind, a few trees and then the gradual upward curve of the down.

Gillian had chosen not to telephone. She hadn't wanted to explain—on the telephone—why she was coming. There hadn't been time for a letter—Sunday was the only day she had free. If she's not home, Gillian had decided, we'll just have a nice trip to the country. Now that they were here, she almost hoped this was what would happen. She would rather not tell Mary Mayhew that Rita was dead.

'Second thoughts?' said Edward, as the car rolled gently to a stop. 'It's not too late. We can drift in the general direction of the pub.'

'No,' Gillian said, resolute. 'I think my instincts are right, and I'm not going to panic.'

They got out and walked up the path to the front door.

'Do you mind if I don't introduce you as Detective Chief Inspector Gisborne? I don't want to rattle her.'

'Not at all. I'm on holiday today.'

Gillian knocked, and the door was opened almost immediately by a tall, stooping, grey-haired woman.

'I saw you coming up the walk. You don't look like missionaries, so I thought I could safely open the door. What is it?' She looked them up and down with a shrewd but not unfriendly eye. 'Not a political party. Charity?'

'Er, no,' said Gillian, a little thrown by this unusual reception. 'You're Mary Mayhew, aren't you?'

The woman nodded.

'I've come to see you because you knew Rita Gordon—and cared about her.'

'Rita! Is she in trouble?' The woman's voice sharpened with anxiety.

'I'll explain. May we come in?'

'Yes, of course.' The woman stood back to let them enter, and shut the door. 'Lily!' she called. 'There's somebody here about my Rita.' She walked in ahead of them into a small sitting-room. 'We were just making some tea. Will you have some?'

She went to fetch the tray, leaving them alone together. Gillian looked at Edward. His face was impassive. He strolled silently about the little room. He's cataloguing, Gillian thought. The policeman's habit. She looked about her, too. Worn, comfortable furniture, a British India carpet, books. Books piled on the floor by the sofa, a wall of books opposite the entrance. Framed photographs on the end tables, a crewel-work firescreen, a couple of bad paintings. Landscapes. Gillian examined the nearest one.

A mountain view: hills dense with evergreens, and behind them, floating implausibly against the blue sky, the white cone of a snow-covered volcano. That's Mount Shasta, she thought suddenly, or maybe Rainier. She painted them. The signature confirmed her guess.

Mary Mayhew reappeared with the tea-tray, accompanied by another woman and an arthritic collie that inspected the visitors calmly and lay down, dropping its chin to the carpet with an exhausted grunt.

'This is Lily Firbank,' Mary said. She nodded at the dog. 'That's Shasta. Do sit down.'

Gillian introduced herself and Edward, who took a chair near Shasta and made quiet overtures. In a moment, he was scratching the back of her head. Lily poured tea. She was shorter than Mary, plump and pink and wrinkled, like a slightly shrivelled apple. Her eyes were pale blue; faded, but not vague. Her hand held the heavy teapot quite steadily.

'You know Rita?' Mary asked.

'I do. I did,' Gillian said. 'I'm very sorry. I have to tell you that she was killed in an accident a week ago.'

'Dear God.' She put her hand out. 'Lily.' Lily put down the teapot and took Mary's hand in both her smaller ones. 'What happened?' Mary asked then.

Gillian told her. 'I'm sorry if I was wrong to come—if I should have written instead,' she wound up, 'but I thought, from what I knew, that you might prefer...'

'You were quite right. It's a shock—but you can tell me about her, about her life these last few years. She hardly ever wrote. Lily, I'm all right now. Give us some tea.'

Gillian told her all she could about Rita's thesis, the Carver Fellowship, the Feminist Union, and the proposal to Jessie Rayne. She gave Mary a copy of the newspaper photograph.

'That's the medal you gave her, Libby says.'

Mary put on her glasses and peered at the picture. 'It's not very clear, is it? I'm glad she kept it. I gave it to her before she left. Not that I literally believed St Christopher would watch over her, although I was raised a Catholic, and when I lose things I do pray to St Anthony, and sometimes it works, but I thought it might protect her from loneliness, that it would remind her that I was still here, thinking about her. It was so lonely for me in the beginning after I married Tommy. I didn't know anybody here. He died twelve years ago. I would have gone home then, but Lily wanted me to stay.' She smiled at Lily. 'We've shared this house for more than seven years now.'

'Where do you come from?'

'Eugene. Eugene, Oregon. A wonderful place. Do you know it? Lily's been there with me. It's wonderful, isn't it?' She appealed to Lily.

Lily nodded. 'Wonderful. But that country's too big for me. I grew up outside Lewes, and I've walked the Downs end to end since I was a girl. I couldn't live anywhere else.'

'I didn't stand a chance,' Mary said easily.

'Will you tell me the story of you and Rita?' Gillian asked, as the teacups were refilled.

'Oh yes indeed. That started when I was teaching. Tommy and I lived in London for many years, and I taught school. I started at a fancy girls' school, but I didn't stay. I wanted to teach ordinary children—the ones who had no advantages to start with. I thought I could be more useful that way. Old-fashioned do-gooder, that's me. Rita was a pupil of mine. I saw right away that she was bright. I'd have had to be blind not to. University material, of course. She had a solid gold mind, I used to say that to her. And we had to dig her out or nobody would see her shine. I gave her extra work, I gave her books, and she read them. She was starving for books. I taught her to write. Grammar, spelling, clarity. She learned so fast, just with someone to teach her. After she left my class, she would still come back and visit me, just to talk, and to borrow books. I had plenty, and there were always new ones.

'We used to talk about other things too, about politics, and religion, and the different ways people saw things in other parts of the world. I'm Catholic, as I said, but in my own way. I don't let the Pope tell me what to do. Rita's family were Protestants. An obscure Nonconformist sect. They were awfully zealous. No drinking, that sort of thing. Her father was a tyrant. Women and children had to obey and not ask questions. Rita's nature wouldn't allow her to do it. She was always in trouble. He didn't like her coming to see me—a Papist!—and he didn't like her reading the books I gave her. He made her bring them back once or twice, I guess I should be glad he didn't rip them up—not that they were anything too shocking; I didn't send her home with D. H. Lawrence—I wasn't stupid, but I didn't realize how narrow his views were until he sent back *The Picture of Dorian Gray*. He said he didn't want her reading anything written by a pervert and forbade her to visit me again. She disobeyed, and I encouraged her. I don't think it was wrong, even if he was her father. He was a dreadful, violent man. Is, for all I know. I haven't kept track of the family.'

'What did he do? Work, I mean.'

'Meat-cutter. Enough to turn you into a vegetarian, isn't it?'

She paused to sip her tea. Gillian hoped Edward was all right. She didn't turn to look, not wanting to disturb the flow of Mary's narrative. Lily watched Mary with anxious, silent affection.

'Well, I thought Rita should go to Oxford or Cambridge. She might have gotten in, too, though they didn't accept girls like her as often as they do now. But her father had other ideas. He wanted her to stay home and look after the family. He didn't even want her to finish school. Her mother was bedridden at times, and there were four other children. She refused to stay at home, and he thrashed her for disobedience. That happened more than once. One of her brothers was also a problem. They were both extremely religious, but the younger one was violent, like the father. Always fighting in the schoolyard, and so on. Anyway, in the middle of all that, Rita got pregnant. Punishing her father, if you ask me, but that's just my opinion. She wasn't even in love with the boy. She came to me. She was terrified that her father would find out and force her to marry the boy. This was in her last year of school. She wanted an abortion, and I helped her get one. How could I not? Her life would have been ruined. I thought she might have the child and let it be adopted, but she was sure her family would find out, and they'd never let her give it away. They did find out about the abortion; I've never known how. Not about my part; I guess they thought a Catholic wouldn't have had anything to do with it, and Rita kept quiet, but they somehow knew what she'd done. Her father beat her badly, much worse than he ever had, and her crazy brother tried to stab her with a kitchen knife. She deserved to die for her sin, according to him. He was put away after that. Even his mother was scared of him.

'Rita left home and never went back. She didn't go to Oxford or Cambridge, she went to Durham—it was further away. She got a student grant, and I helped her as much as I could. But her family never did leave her alone. Every little while, they'd come bursting into her new life. One of her sisters would run away, and her father would come looking for her, her other brother would come and try to get her to come home and return to the faith. They made her feel guilty about her mother. Then, sometime while she was at Durham, she began reading about feminism. It gave her a whole new perspective on her life. I would have suggested it to her, but I didn't catch on to those ideas till very late. My age, I guess. Well, that was fine, but she sent a book to her sisters, I forget which one it was, and she wrote a letter to her mother explaining her new view of the family. That was too much for her father. He told her not to come home any more. And I don't think she wanted to. But she still got letters once in a while, terrible, bruising letters. She had to get away. Far away from them all. She went to Canada. British Columbia, near where I come from. That was about six years ago. She wrote me a couple of letters after she arrived, to tell me she was all right. And then she wrote once in a while. She travelled a lot. She went to California, and New York, and Mexico—I don't know where else. She came to see me when Lily and I went to Eugene three years ago, in the summer. She seemed fine then. She was shining, I thought. That solid gold mind was really shining.' Mary sighed. 'But I didn't hear from her often after that. She wrote me when she finished her thesis. She said she just had to defend it and she'd send me a copy when she was a doctor. I thought I'd see her again one day. But I won't now.'

⎯⎯⎯⎯⎯⎯⎯⎯

In the car, Edward said, 'That was worth a detour, as they say in the Michelin Guides.'

'Wasn't she marvellous? I knew she would be.'

'Yes, you got on rather well.'

'It was nice of you to sit through all that.'

'Not at all. It was interesting. If I didn't think so, I'd be in the wrong job. And I liked them, of course.'

'And the dog. I noticed you chumming up with Shasta. Terribly reassuring of you.'

'Cynic.'

They had had lunch with Mary and Lily, and now they were driving up the road to the footpath Lily had recommended.

'You want to see the Long Man, do you? It's not far. There's a footpath a mile and a half up the road. Or you could go to Wilmington Priory and walk up the hill from that side. Then there's a path that climbs up the far slope and brings you to the top of Windover Hill. It's lovely up there. And there's a goodish long barrow up that way. After that, it depends on what sort of distance you care to walk.'

As they left, retracing their steps through the little garden to the road, Gillian looked about, noticing the dry leaves crackling underfoot and a few last blooms of bright pink cosmos. A stone birdbath stood in one corner of the garden: a small statue of St Francis stood at the edge of the shallow pool, his hand raised in benediction. A sparrow flew up from the rim and disappeared into the branches above.

They left the car near the Priory and poked about among the gravestones for a few minutes before ascending the hill. The leaves had fallen from many trees, but not all. Bare branches cast skeletal, wintry shadows on the walls alongside patches of the deep leafy shade of late summer. The sun gave off a thin warmth, but the stones were cold.

'This country is so pretty,' Gillian couldn't help saying. 'If I were living in London I'd be out here every weekend.'

'Right. You'd buy some enchanting Elizabethan ruin and learn to thatch it yourself.'

'All right, lover of the Great Wen, let's go see the Man.'

They climbed up the broad grassy hill side by side. For the last several hundred feet, the hillside ascended at a steeper angle, though still not too steep for walking, and it was on this smooth upper slope that the Long Man had been cut—gouged into the chalk through its coverlet of grass. They traversed the lower, shallower slant of the hill until they stood directly below the great figure. A vast green rectangle of turf was shaved close to reveal the human outline incised in the bone-white earth. The Man was huge, a shape as tall as half the steep-sided hill. He stood head on, his feet apart, his arms bent and extended to either side, his figure framed by two long upright staffs passing through his hands. His feet were turned, as though he might be striding along the hill.

Gillian had asked if he was Celtic, from the Iron Age. Lily said he was either that or Saxon. 'He resembles designs on the Sutton Hoo treasure. You'll have seen that at the British Museum. They don't know which he is. I think he's Celtic, like the Cerne Abbas Giant.'

Nothing moved on the bare hillside. The Man was perhaps two thousand years old, Gillian thought. He had been here, a constant, through Roman times, the Norman conquest, the Tudors, the rise and fall of empire, the blitz. Edward stood silent, a thoughtful frown on his dark, bony Celtic face. For a dreaming instant, the particularity of time and place fell away, and she saw history as unity, and herself not separated from the Celts or Saxons by millennia, but only by some membrane of the mind which had momentarily fallen aside on this ageless hill. Then the moment was gone, and they went on their way.

After climbing Windover Hill and wandering peacefully about the summits of the Downs for a time, they descended and went in search of a pub.

Savouring her pint of bitter, Gillian said, 'I wonder what makes people sure it's a man. He hasn't got any parts, let alone a fire hydrant, like the Cerne Abbas Giant.'

'He's rather a colossus, isn't he? And what we know about the culture must indicate it's a male figure. You're the historian.'

'Not my period. But any historian can tell you that what we "know" often reflects our own assumptions.'

'Policemen will tell you that, too.'

'Rita was good at ferreting out assumptions masquerading as knowledge. It was one of the things that made her a good historian. But it's not a quality people like when it's more generally applied.'

CHAPTER 17

For the next four days, Gillian was busy. She attended the conference, spottily, in the mornings and afternoons, gave her paper, listened to other papers and various panel discussions and gossip about promotions (too few), pay (too low) and the interval between acceptance and publication of papers in reputable journals (too long); lunched with colleagues and acquaintances, and spent some reasonably profitable hours in the British Museum. In the evenings, she met Edward for dinner. Each day he was up and gone in the morning before she was awake. Sometimes in the night the telephone rang. He would wake instantly, catching it before it could ring a second time, and utter an economical phrase or two, or disappear into the next room, from which she could hear the faint murmur of his voice as she fell asleep again.

On Tuesday he asked her whether she was still intending to visit Rita's family.

Gillian grimaced. 'No, not after Mary's story. What would be the point? I wouldn't mind meeting the sister Rita was fond of, but I don't have time to go up to Manchester.'

She had already told him the story of the fall term.

'Libby's actually intimidated now, though she's not normally a fearful person. And she's not the only one. Even I feel a little frightened. There hasn't been much physical violence, but everything suggests it—seems designed to be threatening. Besides that, the campus is like a hornets' nest. The president's office is angry and defensive because of all the noise in the media, the engineers are mad about the Rayne money, and half my department is pissed off because I'm in the middle of it. What does it sound like to you?'

'It sounds like a good year for a sabbatical.'

'Seriously.'

'Let's look at the chronology, then.'

Gillian had ticked off the incidents on her fingers: 'The Triumph Day demo, then Libby's car, the Rayne news coming out, and then the witch dummy hanging in the office and the flashers; the *Drum* article and then the smashed pumpkin at my door. The posters in the windows when the protest march was mooned. I don't know exactly when the obscene telephone calls started, or when Rita was burgled. Not long after the demo, I think. Do you think everything's connected? To the same people who shoved the women around at the gate and put those nauseating posters in the windows?'

'I think there's a suggestive pattern, yes. Though perhaps not to every event you've mentioned. If we begin with the demonstration—I take it you're not considering the possibility that an Antonia Blunt has infiltrated your Feminist Union?'

Gillian gave him a startled look. 'It's never occurred to me.' She shook her head, a little indignant. 'Definitely not.'

'All right. I didn't say it was likely. Then we'll assume that nobody but your women knew about the demonstration beforehand. Do I think what's happened since then has all been planned? Not as a sinister sequence. But the three Hallowe'en incidents—the dummy, the flashers and the smashed pumpkin have the same MO. What counts as a plan? The Pakistanis here are intimidated by skinheads—is that planned? Groups of ruffians go out and bash Pakis, and you could say they plan to, but the general climate of fear that's created is the product of race hatred that's tolerated by the body politic, not of a vast conspiracy.'

'Do you think we should be afraid?'

He didn't reply immediately. They were wedged into a couple of corner seats at an unpicturesque pub half way between Edward's flat and Victoria Station. The pub was crowded, and they had to lean close in order to hear each other. Edward gazed absently at the throng, his heavy, dark brows drawn into a meditative frown, his deep-set brown eyes slitted against the smoky air.

She thought of her dark driveway and the bushy paths across the campus, and the winter afternoons when it was already dark at five. She thought, too, of how safe she felt with Edward. When she walked in the streets at night with him, she was relaxed, free to move without the slight but constant tension, the need to be watchful she felt when alone. In bed with him at the flat, she wasn't disturbed by the night sounds that when she slept alone could rouse vivid fears of burglary and rape. It wasn't just that he was a man, or his policeman's practical skills. It was an extraordinary awareness he had, a sense that she and other people she knew seemed to lack, or had never developed. With no apparent effort, he was alert to what was going on about him, as though he could read the streets of the city as an animal reads the jungle. The scents of the predators, their whereabouts and intentions, so indistinct to her that she, like other women of her acquaintance, simply took precautions and hoped, were plain to him. He always knew before she did when someone was behind them, and how far, and what sort of person it was. He knew the night noises at the flat: the hisses and creaks of the heating, the grate of the key in the neighbour's lock, the way footsteps should sound. Twice, during the many times she'd been there, he had gotten out of bed to investigate a sound. Both times they had been dead asleep, and she, leaving her safety to him, hadn't awakened until he left the bed. The first time, he'd heard a muffled thud in the street below, and had called the local police in time to nab a car thief. The second time, scarily, he had pulled on his trousers and padded stealthily across the floor; she'd opened her eyes and in the faint glow from the streets had seen his shadowy shape leaving the room. She'd whispered his name, and he'd made a gesture for her to be silent. Her heart thumping, she'd lain still for long moments, hearing only a change in the silence, as though the space had grown larger. She'd nearly screamed at the crash that followed. Edward had caught a burglar leaving the top-floor flat.

'What woke you?' Gillian had asked afterwards.

Edward shrugged. 'I'm not sure. Something sounded odd.'

To feel so secure was a delicious reprieve. She sank into it, behaving in the city streets like a passenger in a limousine, not thinking at all of the road, but only of the scenery. It was irresponsible but she hardly cared. Then, when she was home again, sleeping alone, out alone at night, the anxieties, the need for vigilance and care returned. This made her very angry.

'I think your administration should take these incidents seriously,' he said at last. 'Whoever the perpetrators are, if they find that no one cares except their victims, they'll think themselves at liberty to carry on. I don't like your tale about the pumpkin. On the face of it, it's more silliness; the dummy was much more dramatic, but it didn't entail the same risk of bodily harm. You could have cracked your skull, falling in the dark. At best someone didn't consider that, and someone mayn't have cared. There are people who are excited by the sort of atmosphere you're describing—who want to push things further.' He hesitated. 'You've made me aware that telling women not to go out at night is no solution to the dangers they face. So don't bite me if I say be cautious.'

Two days later, after his question about her visit to the family, he said, 'I've checked up on that brother Mary Mayhew mentioned. He's been in and out of the institution several times since that incident nine years ago. He's been out for quite a while now. He even held a job for two years, but he was laid off in August. There's something else you should know.'

'What?'

'He's not only out of the mental hospital, he's out of the country. He left on September twenty-fifth.'

'Where did he go?'

'He had a seat on a flight to Vancouver.'

Gillian mulled this over. If he knew where Rita was, how had he found out? From Ruth—the sister in Manchester? She could telephone Ruth and offer her condolences, and ask...but what would she ask? 'Did you tell your brother where to find Rita? Where was your brother when Rita died?' The death was an accident, so what did it matter? But he hadn't come forward to claim Rita's effects, or represent her family. It was bizarre. Maybe he hadn't found her. But maybe he had. Then what was it like for her to find him on her doorstep when she'd fled half way across the world to get away from her family? What had they said to each other?

On the final evening of her stay, she impulsively called Ruth's number. If she didn't get through, well, she'd tried, and she wouldn't have to try again. Her desire to meet Rita's family, even her sister, had entirely evaporated. She was waiting for Edward to come home, drying her hair before venturing out into the damp cold of the November evening.

She punched the buttons of Edward's state-of-the-art telephone. The message button of the answering machine was winking, as usual. After five rings, there was an answer.

'Hullo?'

A child's voice.

'Is Ruth there, please?'

'No.'

'Will she be back soon?'

'About nine o'clock.'

She'd be out by then. The child sounded sensible enough for her to try leaving a message. She explained that she was a friend of Rita's visiting London and had called to see if there was anything she could do when she went back. She was going back tomorrow afternoon, but if Ruth wanted to call her in the morning—she gave the number, and the child apparently wrote it down.

She put on the dress she'd been saving: a soft, delicate mohair that clung to and yet clouded with its silky fuzz the outline of her body. It was a smoke grey, like her eyes. Like my hair, she thought wryly. It wasn't really true yet. There were grey streaks in its charcoal colour, that was all. Her mother had been quite grey by fifty-five, so Gillian supposed she would be the same. Would people treat her differently? Would she suddenly be dumped in the category 'old'—meaning no longer sexually attractive? Her confidence wavered. 'Old', then, could be less than a decade away. Perhaps the dress was too bold a claim. It was neither girlish nor vulgar, but it certainly alluded to sexuality. It was safer to be less direct. More dignified. She was thinking about what she might wear instead when Edward came home. He didn't ordinarily comment on her clothes, but seeing her from the doorway of the bedroom, he said, 'I haven't seen you in that. You look marvellous.' He came in, stripping off his coat, and slid his hands up her arms to her shoulders, then more slowly down her back to her hips.

'Mmmm.'

He was only a little taller than she, but while she perceived herself as light and thin, he, although not bulky, was heavier, denser, more solid, as if composed of a different, weightier element. She delighted in this difference, in the feel of it in shoulder and thigh as their bodies met. His hair was dark and smooth and thick as fur.

He stepped towards the telephone on the table beside the bed, pulling her with him. He ignored the blinking message light and dialled.

'Jewel Restaurant, good evening,' she heard, in a soft Indian accent.

'This is Edward Gisborne. Tell Ravi we'll be a little late for dinner.'

⌐T⌐

Thirty hours later, she was home.

It was late afternoon, and cloudy, and the daylight was already dim. She roamed restlessly about the house, her mind and heart not yet caught up to her body but suspended in some twilight region over the Pole, where night was six months long. She couldn't hope to see him again before May.

She picked up her mail from the floor of the hall and laid it on the table unread. She wasn't hungry or sleepy. She unpacked, threw a bundle of laundry into the washing machine, put on a CD of Brendel playing some Beethoven sonatas, and poured a glass of wine. Was this 'attachment', as Edward called it—he was nice in his choice of words—what she wanted? The partings, the severing of flesh from flesh, grew no easier. *Au contraire*. He said so too. The dumb misery of the long journey, this dislocation of the self in her own house. Was it worth it? And yet, he was there. She could pick up the telephone; so could he. And did. He would continue to be 'there for her', as people said on this side of the ocean. And much of the time, she liked being alone—liked living as it suited her, without needing to consider someone else, without wondering, like Laura, whether anyone would be home for dinner. But these hours and days after her visits to Edward were dreadful. Withdrawals from an intoxicated state. She shook herself, as if to throw off the burden of unwanted emotion. She'd been through this before; she'd be all right in a few days. The best thing to do was to pick up the threads of her daily life as fast as possible.

She telephoned Frances to see whether there had been any new developments while she'd been away.

Frances sounded cheerful. 'No catastrophes, thank God. Except the floods, of course. It's been positively Biblical around here. We were practically washed into the sea. It rained and rained and rained, and all the main highways were cut. People in the valley were rowing home. So now everybody's blaming the clear-cuts—of course the logging companies say there's no connection, but nobody believes them, they're such liars.

'Things have been quiet on campus, though. The Student Discipline Committee and the Academic Discipline Committee are both looking into those offensive signs in the windows of the Applied Science Complex. About twenty-eight or thirty engineering students were involved, and nobody knows quite what to do with them. Dean Frost is against suspensions; he says they shouldn't be punished for their ignorance. I've told Bingham that if nothing is done I'll resign.'

'Frances!'

'Oh yes. But I know Bingham wants to be seen to do something. He realizes it can't be given the usual boys-will-be-boys treatment. There's been such a stink about it in the media. Get this, though: Frost thought the engineers should send flowers to the Feminist Union as an apology. Can you believe it?'

'Really? What did he think would be suitable? Red hot pokers?'

A loud squawk of amusement came over the telephone. 'Thank God for a laugh, Gillian. I needed that.' Then Frances grew serious again. 'Another thing you should know: the story going round about the Carver is that the committee turned Rita down because she was emotionally unstable.'

'What do you mean?'

'That she had the best academic credentials, but that she wouldn't make a suitable Carver Fellow—wouldn't make a good colleague, might crack up before she could complete her book. I heard a rumour about this before the accident, but now it's talked about like a fact—as if the accident proved it.'

'Who started this rumour? What's it based on?'

'I don't know. Something in the file, I heard.'

'But all we know about the accident is that there was probably ice on the road. That says her motorcycle was unstable, not her. Or have you got a report from the police now?'

'Not yet. But there've also been some angry letters to the *Drum*, saying these rumours are part of a plot to discredit the Feminist Union.'

'I can't let this lie. I'm going to get to the bottom of it if it kills me.'

'Try Bingham. He's vulnerable right now, and he's the President. He might show you the file. The others wouldn't dare break their Cosa Nostra code.'

CHAPTER 18

Two days later, first thing in the morning, Gillian walked into the President's office. It smelled of new carpet. Walter Bingham, a balding sixty-year-old physicist with a deep, rasping voice and hooded eyes, had been president of the university for four years, and Gillian had spoken with him on a number of occasions. Folds of pinkish, inflamed-looking skin drooped below his chin, and in repose his face had a patient, almost mournful expression. He reminded her of a buzzard.

She had gone over in her mind a dozen times what she would say. She would say that UPNW was being embarrassed by a series of public displays of discrimination against women, that in this poisoned atmosphere the Carver decision was suspected of being another example of this discrimination, and the rumours were aggravating the suspicions. The secrecy of the committee was contributing to the problem and bringing discredit on itself. She would tell Bingham about the witch dummy and the other incidents. She was prepared to go further: she still had the witch dummy in her locked file drawer. It would look very striking on television.

In the event, the meeting at first ran more smoothly than she had expected. The President listened. Rather than denying the existence of the problem, he agreed with her, although he was inclined, she noticed, to blame the tension on the media.

'Those posters were disgusting, no doubt about that. Grotesque. I've no intention of writing them off as a prank, though in a sense that's all they were. But all the attention in the newspapers and on television isn't an asset to the remedial process. We get distortions and exaggerations—fuel to the fire. We need to get out of the spotlight and take a look at solutions.

'So far as the Carver is concerned, I don't think its deliberations should be a matter for public disclosure. But the sequence of events in this case has been most surprising and unfortunate. Rita Gordon's politics and the divisive atmosphere surrounding the Rayne gift have combined with these other events to create unfounded suspicions. I agree these suspicions are destructive. And the young woman's untimely death has naturally generated a lot of emotion. I'm quite willing to show the contents of her file to you, but I don't think it should be made public, and when you've seen it, I think you'll agree with me.'

He spoke into his intercom and asked for the file, and his administrative assistant brought it in. He took the file and handed it to Gillian.

'You're welcome to look at everything in the file, but the relevant document is a letter from the candidate herself.'

Gillian opened the file. She glanced rapidly through the sheaf of papers, skipping the CV and the forms from the History Department which she'd already seen in the departmental files, as well as the application form, which had been shown to her by Rita herself. She read the recommendations. There was Honeycutt's letter, as glowing as he had said, and her own, of course, and the external examiner's comments on Rita's thesis (*Cultural Dowries: Post-Secondary Education for Women in Britain, Canada and the United States, 1840–1875*). All unexceptionable, as were two more letters from members of her committee. At the bottom of the file, stapled to a memo from the Dean of Arts, was a photocopy of a short letter. Gillian read it.

She was dismayed. The letter was addressed to the Dean, in his capacity as chair of the committee. It opened with a bald statement that Rita was the most deserving candidate. It then referred to the exclusively male membership of the committee, and the male sex of all previous Carver Fellows. It went on:

The Carver committee has ignored wimmin candidates
for too long. We won't wait any more; we won't be good.
We will speak out and demand justice. If you refuse to award

the Carver Fellowship to the rightful candidate, the university will suffer the consequences. The Feminist Union will mount a serious, skillfully orchestrated publicity campaign to embarrass UPNW and the Carver committee. There will be protests, demonstrations and more. Remember: *you* don't have a monopoly on the use of force. The Triumph Day demonstration was just the beginning. We'll string you up by the balls, and the cameras will be rolling.

Gillian's eyes widened. She stared at the typeface as if it were Martian and then began to read the letter over again.

'Revolting, isn't it?' said Bingham. His rasping voice had an aggressive edge. 'And yet this nasty letter is from the same young woman who led a protest against a silly parade and who doubtless would have insisted that the engineering students who made those posters should be kicked out of the university. I'm sorry she's dead, but she was a very wrong-headed young person.'

Gillian found her voice. 'But who wrote it? It's not signed.'

'Oh, there's no question about who's responsible. Rita Gordon hand-delivered it to Cynthia—Dean Stanley's secretary—the day that applications had to be complete.'

'Where's the original?'

'In Stanley's file.'

'I don't understand it. I can't believe she would have done something so self-destructive.'

'Yes, that's the point,' Bingham said, more cordially. 'It was foolish. So foolish as to indicate a...lack of balance, shall we say? There were one or two members of the committee who wanted to take some sort of action in regard to the letter, but it's not at all clear what could have been done. And any reaction on our part would only have made things messier. She'd passed her thesis examination, so without the Carver she'd have been leaving the campus very soon. To be perfectly honest, it seemed wise to let sleeping dogs lie. Naturally, we reserved our right to give the letter to the media if the Feminist Union followed through on their threats. I'm fairly sure they would have lost a lot of public sympathy.' He gestured at the letter, still dangling from Gillian's limp hand. 'But it wasn't an act we cared to respond to in political terms, unless we had to. All it could ever have accomplished—and did accomplish—was to ensure that she not receive the Carver.'

'Would she have, otherwise?'

'I think it's safe to say she would have. Two committee members thought there was little need to discuss the candidates this year— she was obviously the best. Then I had to show them the letter Stanley had reluctantly brought to me. It was an unpleasant occasion, but there was no disagreement. The committee will not be blackmailed.'

'But why didn't you ask her about it?'

'To what end? Stanley and I both questioned Cynthia carefully; we were perfectly satisfied that Rita Gordon gave her the letter. Politics was clearly more important to her than scholarship, and the letter was hardly evidence of a collegial temperament. She wasn't right for the Carver. She couldn't have presented an explanation that would have salvaged her application.'

Bingham's voice dropped. In a confidential tone he went on, 'In fact, the committee was quite suspicious that we were *expected* to interrogate her—giving her an opening to politicize the Carver Fellowship in a way we thought would be most unfortunate.'

'Do you really think she would have sacrificed her chances even though she knew she was the best candidate?'

'I'm not a psychiatrist. But my opinion—the opinion of the committee—is that she held a greatly exaggerated notion of the extent to which sexism permeates the university. Perhaps you could call it an obsession. She applied just to show sexism in action, with the intent of sabotaging the process. She was convinced she wouldn't win, so she had nothing to lose.'

Gillian shook her head, unpersuaded. 'This is not the Rita I know. And I don't believe the Feminist Union could have endorsed such a foolish ploy.'

'Really?' Bingham said sharply. 'A group that thinks nothing of barging into a long-time relationship with an important benefactor, upsetting research plans that have been years in the making and depend heavily on the generosity of the donor—a group that stages incidents to attract the media and damage the reputation of a prestigious institution of learning rather than negotiating in good faith with a sympathetic administration? From where I sit, they're either extremely naïve or extremely irresponsible. We know women are having problems on the campus, and we take those problems seriously. The so-called Feminist Union is not making it any easier for us to arrive at solutions.' He folded his arms and looked at her from under his heavy eyelids. 'Frankly, I'm surprised you would allow yourself to be associated with them. I'm assuming you had nothing to do with this letter, of course, but I know you were in the bunch that lobbied Jessie Rayne.'

'Yes, I was, and plans or no plans, I still think the Rayne money would be better spent on women's studies. And I don't agree at all with your view of their activities. But I'll be surprised if the Feminist Union had anything to do with this letter.'

'Then she wrote it by herself. In any event, I think you see now why I don't wish to put a stop to the Carver rumours by making this document public.'

Gillian did see. It would cause another swell of scandalous publicity. For Rita's sake, she didn't want it published either.

'I'm not pleased about those rumours,' Bingham went on. 'Something leaked. I don't know who's responsible. But I'm sure we can stonewall this one. If there's no confirmation, the rumour will die down. Meanwhile, if you have any constructive influence on the Feminist Union, I suggest you use it.'

'I think you ought to know,' Gillian said slowly, 'that Rita was having a very bad time this fall. It wasn't just with the flashers in the parking lot, there were also obscene telephone calls, and threats, and her apartment was burgled. She's been under attack, even more than the other members of her group.'

'That is terribly unfortunate, and nothing can be done about it now. But if you're suggesting that this is why she wrote the letter, I can only say it would have been more productive to talk to the Dean of Women and the campus police.'

'I'm not saying that's why she wrote the letter. I'm saying that what's in it doesn't come out of a void. She's not the only woman on campus with good reason to be angry. And afraid, for that matter.'

Bingham sat back. 'Yes, I know that. As I said, we do understand that there's a problem. We're not ignoring it. We're upping campus patrols, and looking into more lighting. These things cost money that might have been spent on other projects, but we're prioritizing safety for women on the campus. And Bob Frost has agreed to bring pressure to bear on the organizers of the Triumph Day parade. There will be no slave wagon in the parade from now on.'

'Really? How did you get him to do that?'

'Let's just say he's realized that it's no longer appropriate.' Bingham didn't smile. 'Do you have any other specific suggestions?'

'Yes,' Gillian replied. 'If your administration is sympathetic to women on this campus, then get up on a platform with Jessie Rayne and tell us about the new women's studies department.'

⊰T⊱

On the way down the stairs, Gillian tried to think about Rita's letter. She was perplexed. Had Rita lost her mind? Had she actually imagined that there was something to be gained by trying to bully the committee? Or had her politics, imperceptibly to her friends, become a cracked mirror of what she despised, making ugly threats acceptable if they served the cause? Maybe she'd been carried away by the impact of the media after Triumph Day? No, that was grasping at straws.

Gillian considered Rita's deep dejection after she'd lost the grant. It hadn't been like Rita to sink so low. Maybe she'd realized she'd made a terrible mistake with long-term consequences. She wouldn't have told Gillian that, of course; she would have said, as she did say, that she'd expected to win. Had no one seen that something was wrong with her? Had there been no clues to her state of mind? To this apparent impulse to martyrdom? She thought how inadequate the university was as a community if a member of it could disappear over the edge so fast without anyone noticing. She had only begun to know Rita, she'd thought before meeting Mary Mayhew. But maybe she'd known even less than she supposed.

And that dreadful brother of Rita's, what about him? If she'd been unstable, his visit might have made a difference. Rita hadn't mentioned his visit to anyone, at least Libby hadn't said anything about it. Gillian, angry and sorrowful and uncertain about where the responsibility for this tragedy lay, walked back to her own building. The lobby looked bleak and unfamiliar. It was queer how disoriented she felt. Or perhaps it wasn't, she thought. She carried a picture of the world with her, a set of perceptions which she could in the abstract acknowledge as partial and flawed, but which in her concrete, everyday existence she had to believe in order to function. Everyone had such a picture; life was not possible without one. When the picture was disturbed, when the assumptions were shown to be wrong, one became confused. Even angry and fearful. Consider the people, she thought, who find out after ten or fifteen years that their partners have been habitually unfaithful. Half the pain is caused not by the acts themselves but by the betrayal that shatters their confidence in their picture—in their own ability to see straight. She felt a little like that now, as if her possible failure of perception about Rita had cast doubt on all her ideas about the world.

She stopped in the women's room on her floor. In the bank of mirrors lit by overhead fluorescent boxes she looked green-faced and haggard. She squeezed out a tissue in cool water and laid it against her eyes. Why had Bob Frost caved in, she wondered. Did Frances know about it?

She pushed open the door of the nearest stall. There was a scrawl on the inside of the door, large letters in black felt pen.

FEMINISTS MUST DIE

Her mouth dry, she opened the other stall and looked at the door. She saw the same scrawl. Her immediate impulse was to efface the inscriptions as fast as possible. She scrubbed at one with a wet paper towel, but the ink was waterproof. She hurried out to the office and questioned Jane and Allie, but neither of them had used the stalls that morning. Yesterday afternoon, just before she left, Jane had gone in, but hadn't seen any graffiti then. Neither of them had noticed any activity around the women's room that morning.

'So it probably happened last night,' Gillian said. 'The students shouldn't be a captive audience for that message; Jane, would you call maintenance and get them to scrub it off with solvent or paint over it today? Meanwhile, let's stick an out-of-order sign on the door.'

She went into her office and sat down. Rita was dead already. Were they all targets, as she had once suggested? No, that was crazy, she had died in an accident. The slogan was just a slogan. Words will never hurt me.

The next day she had lunch with Jessie Rayne. She was tempted to cancel; in her present state she didn't feel up to any negotiations or interrogations that might be in store. But she went. She had liked Jessie, and she was unlikely to have many opportunities to become better acquainted if she turned this one down. Besides, the best she could do for Rita was to try to keep women's studies on track.

They met at The Lilacs, a staid and expensive restaurant of a sort Gillian did not frequent. It was spacious and quiet, with a lot of mirrors and smoky lavender banquettes. She followed a well-upholstered hostess past several tables occupied by men in suits, all talking about money.

She was dead on time, but Jessie Rayne was waiting for her at a table near the windows. These were tall and flanked by heavy curtains. The bleats and rumbles of the city barely penetrated the double layers of glass, and the view was indistinct, like a grainy photograph, behind a gauzy screen printed with pale lilac blooms. A pleasant mauve light filtered through.

'This is my favourite table,' Jessie said as Gillian sat down. The soft leather seat was remarkably comfortable.

A waiter hovered. 'Your usual?'

'My usual is a dry sherry. What will you have?' Jessie asked Gillian.

'This looks like martini country to me.'

The drinks came, and the menus, and warm bread. They talked about food.

'I like red meat,' Jessie said. 'A lot of people I know hardly eat it any more, but for me, there's nothing like a good, thick bloody steak to improve a person's outlook on life. The beef here is excellent.'

Now and then she nodded to someone at another table; she was as much part of these surroundings as Gillian was of the UPNW faculty club, Gillian thought. And she got better service, since she paid more for it.

They talked about Cambridge. 'I was never so damn cold in my life,' she said. 'Those awful little shinburners were the only heat. A couple of times I went down to London just to stay in a good hotel where I could get warm.'

'It was exactly the same when I was there. I froze.'

'It still is. I looked at my old rooms, and they hadn't changed a bit...They think freezing is normal, I guess. There was a girl from India,' Jessie said, laughing. 'I thought she would *die*. She solved the problem by buying a huge mink coat—it went all the way down to her ankles. She could have used a couple of ladies-in-waiting to keep the hem off the ground. She wore it all winter—and spring. I remember she even slept in it.'

'Why did you go to Cambridge?'

'My mother was at Girton, but in her day they wouldn't let girls take degrees. You're looking at Marjorie Rayne's revenge.'

Not before they had nearly finished their steaks—which lived up to her recommendation—did she bring up UPNW and the women's studies proposal.

'There's been more fuss than I anticipated. More than you counted on, too, I expect.'

'Yes. There've been several unpleasant events which seem to be related.'

'I've heard about them, of course,' Jessie said crisply. 'You need not worry that I'll back out on that account. What's going to be done about those engineering students?'

'The disciplinary committees are deep in thought.'

'The students need their bottoms smacked. I told Bob Frost that whatever happened to women's studies, the applied science faculty wasn't getting any money from me.'

'You did?' Gillian's fork stayed in mid-air.

Jessie smiled grimly. 'I did. I told him I held him responsible for the atmosphere that allowed such incidents to occur. And unless attitudes changed, he wouldn't see another penny from the Rayne family.'

'What did he say?'

'He said important research programmes shouldn't be jeopardized by the actions of a handful of immature undergraduates. So I told him that large financial gifts weren't just practical help, they were a form of public approval—and that I couldn't give.'

'Whew,' Gillian breathed. 'He must have been livid.'

'He would have liked to give me hell,' Jessie said. 'But he couldn't afford to.'

'When was this?'

'The same day those posters went up.'

Gillian set down her fork. The same day Rita died.

'Why are you telling me this?'

Jessie grinned. 'Because you're the only person I know who would enjoy hearing about it as much as I enjoyed doing it.'

'I'll drink to that,' Gillian replied and picked up her wine glass. No wonder the slave wagon was finished.

'Besides,' Jessie added, cutting a shiny red sliver of steak, 'I may have a taste for blood, but it's a pleasant change to talk to an ally. I'm fighting on several fronts. My brother doesn't approve of what I'm doing—thinks our father wouldn't have liked it. No doubt he's right, but the company was left in my hands, not his. He can't stop me himself, but he's muddying the waters, and my financial advisers are whining. Frost and two of his department heads have been to see me. And Walter Bingham has made it clear that it would be a lot simpler to stick to the traditional family pattern. In the nicest way, of course.' She smiled maliciously. 'He wouldn't want the money to go to some other institution.' She set down her knife and fork.

'So how are we doing?'

'We're in a holding pattern right now. UPNW has to come up with money. My impression is they've been stalling, hoping they'll patch together an alternative I'll buy into. Bob Frost has offered some token concessions. Since I've told him there's nothing doing, things may speed up. He's a tough opponent, though. And of course the governors have their fingers in the pie. The dickering may go on for a while.'

They skipped dessert and ordered coffee.

'You know, I saw Rita Gordon on TV before we met,' Jessie said. 'I was watching the news, and she was speaking after the Triumph Day parade. I must admit, I thought she was making a mountain out of a molehill. But she started me thinking. There's been such a lot in the news about what's happening on our campuses, and the other problems women have in this world. Then I got these letters from the Feminist Union. They were so interesting, and I began to be intrigued by the idea. I never associated Rita with the letters—I didn't remember her name from the news. Then you all walked in, and there she was. It was a surprise.'

'Did you like her?'

'I'm not sure. But I was impressed, which I didn't expect. I thought she'd be too extreme, but everything she said made sense. I said so when I talked to Bob Frost about the proposal—I had to tell him first, of course, out of courtesy. He practically spat nails. I'm terribly sorry she died in that unnecessary way. I wish I knew more about her. Did you know her well?'

Gillian found it difficult to talk about Rita. She didn't want to discuss the letter in the Carver file, but it was there in her thoughts, casting a distorted shadow over the picture she would have sketched for Jessie. Impulsively, she said, 'If you want to know more about her, come to the memorial service. It's this weekend.'

'Maybe I will.'

CHAPTER 19

That evening Edward telephoned.

'You're up early,' Gillian said, realizing that it must be barely after six in London.

'I haven't been to bed. Just got in. How are you? No unexpected vegetable matter on your steps when you got home?'

'No. Nothing of that kind, I'm glad to say. But there are some new developments.' Gillian told him about Rita's letter. 'I can't believe she wrote it.'

'People are full of surprises,' Edward said. 'I have some news for you, too. Her sister Ruth rang up. Apparently her child—the one who took your message—did write it down but forgot to give her the bit of paper. She just happened to find it yesterday. It fell out of the *Radio Times* when she was tidying up. She rang up immediately, and happened to catch me. I told her who you were. She wants to read Rita's thesis—Rita promised to send her a copy when it was finished. She didn't think to ask when the university telephoned her about arrangements. I understand they haven't much money. She said she loved her sister, but she couldn't afford to fly over just to pack up her books and carry her ashes home in a cardboard box. Not a sentimental type.'

'What about John, the crazy brother? Did you mention him?'

'No. She just said no one from the family was going. I don't believe she knows he's over there.'

'Did you ask her?'

'No. Think about it. I would have had to explain what I knew and how, and that I'd made an unofficial inquiry on your behalf.

People get rather excited when they hear the name Scotland Yard. And if your chaps need to ask any questions about Rita's death, they might be a little shirty if I'd been blundering about, interrogating witnesses without any official standing. It's not my patch.'

'Oh. Yes, I see. Should I not have made that call from your number?'

'It doesn't matter. But you've got to understand that there are things I can't do, even if I appear to be the logical person to do them.'

❧

When Gillian had spoken to Ruth, she knew what Ruth wanted, but she was no wiser about John's motives or whereabouts. Cautiously, she had mentioned her contact with Mary Mayhew.

Ruth was apparently not a fan of Mary's. 'She'd talk both your ears off, that woman. Always did. But she was good to Rita. I'll give her that. Did everything she could for her.'

She volunteered little about the family.

'No one's coming over, I understand,' Gillian said neutrally.

'What for? Rita's dead,' Ruth said harshly. 'I'm the only one who she would have wanted, anyhow, and if I couldn't afford to visit her when she was alive, I can't see the point of going into debt to see her body.' What Gillian could do was to send the thesis, and mementoes or photographs if there were any. 'There won't be much—she wasn't the packrat sort. Neither am I.' She was interested in the memorial service. 'I would like to come for that, but it's not on,' she said. Gillian said perhaps she could write and describe it, and Ruth said, with more warmth in her tone than before, that she'd like that very much.

Gillian talked to Honeycutt. Had Rita corrected her thesis since the examination and prepared copies for the library? She had. They hadn't been bound, and he had taken it upon himself to attend to that. He would have an extra copy made.

She talked to Libby.

'I have a better idea,' Libby said. 'I already asked Tony to videotape the service, so why don't we send her a tape?'

Gillian recoiled slightly, then thought it would have been a natural enough idea to Rita. She was too old to be videobred; they were not.

That night she woke at three, starting up from a dream in which her airplane to London was hijacked by Dean Frost. He was waving a letter and shouting. She rolled over and tried to fall asleep again. She tried to relax her muscles one at a time, but her brain, bored with this, skipped towards wakefulness. The glowing numbers on the clock silently registered the passing minutes. November 22, three weeks since Rita died. Rita's letter, she thought. How strange it was. Something was wrong with it. She tried to picture the words on the page. Maybe if she saw the original she would know. But she already knew. She had detected a flaw, if only she could think what it was. 'Internal evidence has conclusively demonstrated...' she imagined, as if in a scholarly report, but what was the evidence?

When she got to the office in the morning, she went straight to the files and looked through Rita's. She picked out a letter or two and a couple of Rita's grant applications. Honeycutt had come in early, so she was able to borrow an unbound copy of Rita's thesis. She didn't know what she was looking for, exactly. She leafed through it, reading sentences here and there. She had read it once already and knew the substance of it. After fifteen minutes or so, she set the pages down on her desk and picked up the grant applications. She read them through and then looked at a couple of pages of the thesis again.

'So!' she exclaimed aloud.

'What's up?' said Jane, who had just arrived.

'Come in and I'll tell you. Wait a second.' Gillian got up and fetched coffee for both of them and shut the door.

Jane sat down, her face expectant, like that of a child invited to share a secret. A fortunate child, Gillian thought fleetingly, for whom secrets have connoted treats, not terrors. Yet Jane had been served her portion of misery. Where did her resilience come from?

'I'd like to consult you about a highly confidential matter,' she said to Jane. 'Rita was turned down by the Carver committee because they received a threatening letter about the political consequences of refusing her. They think she wrote it. I've seen the letter and I don't believe it. I think it's a fake.'

'Holy newt,' Jane breathed, horrified. 'How do you know?'

'I don't *know*—yet—but I'm quite certain. When I first read it in Bingham's office I couldn't make sense of it. This isn't Rita, I thought. But Bingham told me that she'd delivered it herself—handed it personally to Cynthia. So then I thought I must have been all wrong about who she was. I twisted everything around, trying to make it fit. Last night, though, I woke up and I knew it was the letter that was wrong. And now I've got something more concrete. Look at her thesis.' Gillian handed Jane the first page of the second chapter. 'Three lines down. See the word "skilful"? It's spelled the English way, with one L. In the letter it's spelled with two—the American way. Rita's spelling isn't perfectly British any more, but it's sure as hell not American. There's more, but I'll have to show you the letter, if I can get my hands on it.'

'What're you going to do?'

'That's what I want to talk to you about. I've got to see Cynthia and find out more about how the letter was delivered. Bingham told me Rita gave it to her.'

'She'll talk to you, why wouldn't she?'

'I don't know who wrote the letter. Someone who had it in for Rita, but that hardly narrows the field. Stanley told Bingham Rita gave Cynthia the letter. But who opened it? He could have opened the envelope alone and substituted the letter for whatever was in it.'

'You think Dean Stanley...' Jane was scandalized.

'No, but I don't know that he didn't. Obviously, the person with the most to gain was Paul Smith, but I can't start accusing people without any proof. Questioning Cynthia would be difficult. It would look so pointed. If she tells Stanley, he'll have a fit. And I don't believe the police can help. I have to have more to go on, but I can't let this turn into grist for the gossip mill before I've got more information.'

'But how can you prove it?'

'I don't know whether I can. But I need the letter to try.'

'You're really sure about it? What if that L was a typo?'

'It wasn't just the L. There are other differences, and one of the things a historian does is question the authenticity of documents and notice such differences...Jane, I'm positive she didn't write it.'

'Well, OK. Then I think *I* should ask Cynthia about opening the letter. I'm having lunch with her anyway, and if I tell her you saw the letter and are worried about it, it won't seem weird if I'm curious. Then you can figure out what to do next.'

'I'd be grateful, Jane.'

'Libby put up a notice about the memorial service, did you see? It's on the bulletin board.'

'Did she? I should have thought they'd want to keep it private.'

'Libby said they wanted everyone who cared about her to have a chance to come. She put a notice up in the student union, too.'

After lunch, Jane came right to Gillian's office, slipping in and shutting the door like a conspirator.

'Cynthia opened the letter herself. She said she was really shocked—she almost tore it up because she knew it would ruin Rita's chances, but that wouldn't have been right.'

'Was Rita there when she opened it?'

'Nope. Cynthia said she had forms and stuff coming in all day. She got everything together at the end of the afternoon—for the files to be sent to the committee members—and she opened it then. That's what I would have done. You can't fiddle with things like that all the time when they arrive, you'd never get anything finished.'

'I know.'

'She took it right to Stanley, and he was shocked too. He said not to copy it for the committee, that he'd show it to Bingham and they'd decide what to do.'

Gillian thought aloud. 'I have to do something. I'll cross Stanley off my list, since he didn't open the envelope. I can't see why he would have written it, and if he had, he'd have just put it in the campus mail. He couldn't have given Rita a letter to deliver to his own office. The question is, if I tell him what I think, will he give me the letter?'

'Why wouldn't he?'

'Bad PR.'

'But you could threaten to tell the papers anyway.'

'Yes, but I don't think that would work. The committee would close ranks, and the atmosphere in this department would be about as hospitable to human life as Pluto's. No, I think I'll just have to count on Stanley's respect for scholarship. If he didn't write the letter, he won't have destroyed it, at least.'

Allie tapped at the door and then stuck her head in. 'Hey, did you hear the news? Thatcher's stepped down! Whoop-dee-doo!' A stray ray of sunshine gilded her blonde spikes as she twirled in the doorway. She looked from Gillian's face to Jane's. 'Secrets?'

'For the moment,' Gillian said apologetically.

'I'll survive. It isn't exactly *Twin Peaks* around here.' Allie winked and shut the door.

'Well I don't know,' Gillian said to Jane. 'Maybe we could use Agent Cooper.'

⚜

'Well?' said Stanley when she arrived at the administration building in the middle of the afternoon. Cynthia was on her coffee break, reading the paper. She looked curiously at Gillian but merely gave her a friendly hello as Gillian greeted her and sailed past into Stanley's office. Stanley had Rita's file on his desk.

'Bingham told me he showed you the letter. What more is there to say?'

'He showed me a copy. I'd like to see the original and take it away with me.'

'What for?'

'To prove it's a fake.'

'*What?*'

'I believe Rita was framed.'

'Gillian, for God's sake. You've championed the girl, fine, but this is past the point of sense. She brought it here herself. You're wasting your time.'

But Gillian had come armed with pages of Rita's thesis and photocopies of her letters from the History Department files. She handed him one, showed him the spelling. 'And look,' she added, 'Rita never says "don't have". She's consistently British in her usage: she uses the verb got, or says "have no". You've got a Ph.D. in Eng. Lit.—you know what I'm talking about.'

Reluctantly, Stanley took the thesis and flipped open the file on his desk. He leafed through it until the letter appeared, then looked at it without touching it or offering it to Gillian. His eyes swivelled back and forth from document to document. Holding them by the edges, Gillian handed him the rest of the photocopies. He leafed through them, then read them one by one.

'This is very unsettling,' he said after a few minutes. 'How did you come to notice it? Had you just read her thesis?'

'When I saw the letter, I'd just come back from England. Perhaps I was especially aware of the differences.'

'But she brought the letter herself.'

'In a sealed envelope. What if someone gave it to her?'

'Who?'

'Another candidate, a faculty member—anyone who had the opportunity and a plausible reason for sending you something urgent.'

'Are you suggesting that Paul might have done it to get the grant?'

'It's possible.'

'My God,' yelped Stanley. 'If that comes out...' He looked aghast.

'Would you rather he got away with it?'

'No, no, of course not. But I would rather he resign quietly than wash all this in public.'

'If it was Paul.'

'If it is a fake,' Stanley retorted. 'Who would take such a risk?'

'Risk? What risk? The committee treats all documents as classified.'

'Suppose we'd asked her about it!'

'But you didn't, did you? And whoever did it knew you wouldn't. You assumed that she and the Feminist Union were responsible, and you acted accordingly.'

Stanley squinted uncomfortably, acknowledging her point. 'But that doesn't prove we were wrong. I'm not tarnishing the committee's reputation on your mere supposition.'

'Then give me the letter,' Gillian replied quickly. 'I know someone I can take it to, an expert who will be perfectly discreet.'

'What sort of expert?' Stanley asked suspiciously. 'Who is he?'

'He used to work for Scotland Yard.'

'Really?' Stanley said, on a sudden note of boyish curiosity.

The romance of the Yard, thought Gillian. Even here it casts its spell. She pressed her advantage.

'Yes. He's retired out here. I've met him before, and I know he'd do it.' She didn't, but she'd ask Edward to call him if she had to.

'Do what?'

'He's a fingerprint expert. Who's handled that letter?'

'Uh, Cynthia, of course, and Bingham and myself.'

'Well, wouldn't you think it pretty peculiar if Rita's prints are *nowhere* on that letter? If she wrote it and then handed it to Cynthia, she wasn't hiding anything—her prints will be all over it. If she didn't write it, they won't be there.'

'Well, but what if someone else in the Feminist Union wrote it? That would explain both the spelling and the absence of prints.'

'The group wouldn't concoct such a letter without showing it to her. You can't let this slide, you know that.'

Stanley hesitated. 'I'm not at all sure I should let this leave the office,' he said, his arm curling protectively around the file.

'What would I do with it?' Gillian said impatiently. 'Burn it? You'd be relieved.'

'The university doesn't need any more bad publicity right now.'

'If I took this letter to the newspapers, as a fake, without knowing who was guilty, it would be grossly unfair to Paul. He'd be bound to be the prime suspect. I won't do that. And I won't let anyone else do it. And I promise, if Rita's prints are on the letter, I won't say another word about it.'

'All right. I don't like it, and I still think you'll find that the letter came from Rita herself. But it wouldn't do to ignore the problem you've raised.' He frowned unhappily. 'There must be absolute discretion. I suppose an ex-Scotland Yard man will understand that. And he won't be busy, like our police. When can you have the letter back to me?'

'I'll have it in your office on Monday if I can.'

'And I have your assurance that you won't show it to anyone else?' Gillian agreed.

His hand hovered over the letter.

'Don't touch it,' Gillian said. 'There are probably too many prints on it already. I've got a file clip.'

She pulled the clip from her pocket and nipped one corner of the letter with it. She had brought a clean manila envelope, and she slid the letter into it. The telephone rang, and Stanley picked it up.

'Hello? Yes, put him on.' He put his hand over the mouthpiece. 'Sorry, I've been waiting for this call.' He rubbed his fingers and thumb together, then blasted a jovial greeting into the telephone.

Gillian gathered up her photocopies, mouthed a goodbye and made her exit before he could change his mind. She carried the file out to Cynthia. Behind the letter, she had noticed, was an envelope datestamped PM 6 October, like the letter. She showed it to Cynthia, in whose face curiosity had won the battle with decorum.

'I'm taking the letter away with me. Is that the envelope it came in?'

Cynthia nodded, her straight pale hair swinging.

'May I ask you something? Are you sure you couldn't have been wrong about who brought it?'

'I'm sorry. I don't make mistakes about things like that,' Cynthia said calmly.

'Why did you keep it?' Gillian asked. 'You don't usually do that, do you?'

'No, normally what happens with grants is I stamp every envelope that comes in; that way, if an item is datesensitive, or if I don't open it myself, I know exactly when it arrived. I even know if it came in the morning or the afternoon. I started doing that after a student submitted an application and was disqualified for missing the date by two days; he swore he'd handed it in on time and that I must have let it sit around before I opened it. Now there can't be any arguments about that. I have a routine. I usually open whatever's come in after the second delivery of the campus mail, then I stamp the letters and throw away the envelopes unless there's a problem. I didn't have a real reason to keep this one...it was just a feeling. The letter was going to cause trouble, I knew that.'

'If you have a yen to become a historian, let me know,' said Gillian. 'You've got all the right instincts.'

'Actually, I'm saving a lot more paper now, even envelopes, but it's for recycling. Jane told me about the bin in your department.'

Round-eyed, Cynthia watched Gillian use her file clip to pick the envelope out of the file.

'You really think Rita didn't write it?' she asked.

Gillian nodded and handed over the rest of the file.

'Why?'

Gillian opened her briefcase, carefully extracted a second set of photocopies and explained. Cynthia looked them over.

'I see what you mean,' she said. 'If you handed me a file of letters from the admin people, I could tell you who wrote some of them without seeing the signatures—just from the way they put things.' She handed back the photocopies. 'I wish I *had* torn the darn thing up.'

'You couldn't.' Gillian sighed. 'But so do I.'

CHAPTER 20

She walked down the hall and stopped at Frances's office. Frances was looking out of the window, her back to the door.

'How about a drink at the faculty club later?' Gillian started to say, but Frances interrupted her. She barely turned her head.

'Gillian. I've just heard from the police. That accident Rita had—it wasn't an accident. Somebody tampered with her motorcycle.'

'I thought so,' Gillian blurted. She stopped, shocked at herself.

Frances swivelled around. 'You did?'

'I didn't know I did. I've just realized it now.' She shut the door and leaned against it. 'What did happen?'

'I don't understand exactly, I don't know a thing about motorcycles.' Frances's voice was husky. 'But apparently, when they lean sideways the way they do when they go around curves, the first thing that touches the ground is the footpedal. So the pedals are hinged, somehow, and bend back when they hit the street. Otherwise, if they were rigid, they'd drag like a brake on only one side, and the motorcycle would go out of control.'

'Yes, I see, I think.'

'When the accident squad examined Rita's bike, they found two tiny little bolts attached to the footpedals—they were hardly noticeable, but the hinges on the pedals couldn't bend up. When she leaned way over on her favourite curve, one of the pedals hit the road and the rear wheel lifted right up. That was the end.' She cleared her throat.

'Do they know who did it?'

'No. But they have a whole team of people working on it, since it's a homicide investigation now. The major crime squad. They'll be interviewing you pretty soon, I'm sure.'

Good, Gillian thought. She was oddly calm. The news was horrible, yet it was almost a relief. Rita hadn't been unstable or desperate. There was no mystery about the 'accident'. Instead there was a crime, and the resources of the police would be brought to bear on it.

'Who could have done it?' Frances asked. 'One of the engineering students?'

'It seems likely. It would have been easy for them.'

'But why? What would they get out of it?'

'Why? You mean a practical reason? Maybe there wasn't one.' Gillian was suddenly consumed with rage. 'Maybe most of them will stop at shoving or flashing women in dark parking lots, maybe some of them think a contemptuous display of bare asses is enough, or giving us a few scares. Pornographic jokes are just normal, aren't they? Obscene calls are just a prank, the slave wagon's a hoot, threatening letters, well, they don't actually do any damage, do they? And they may serve to put us in our place. It's a continuum, that's the point. Whoever got Rita just had to be further along it. Rita had some notoriety, she was a leader, she was even on television. Imagine how she was talked about by those guys: "the witch", "the bitch", etcetera. She became a focus for the general hostility we all experience every day. And some guy waiting to go off like a bomb suddenly had a target. Maybe he thinks he's a hero now.'

'Do you think that was what happened?'

'Well, it can't be some scheme to do with the Rayne money. They wouldn't get it back because Rita was dead.'

'No, but maybe revenge?'

'Who?'

'I don't know. But those bullies who put up the posters are still walking around scot-free, thanks to Frost. The committees haven't made any decisions. I may have to resign after all.'

'No!'

Frances smiled wanly. 'I did tell Bingham I would, remember, if nothing was done about them.'

Gillian moved towards the door. 'Don't resign. Not yet. This isn't over. Let the police start digging.'

In the meantime, she thought, I'll see what I can find out about the Carver problem. She picked up her briefcase, conscious of Rita's letter. Thank God for something to do.

CHAPTER 21

Idling in the line of cars at the Point Roberts border crossing, Gillian thought about the absurdities of history. She hadn't waited for the weekend to visit Malcolm Birdseye, the retired fingerprint expert from Scotland Yard. The matter was too urgent now, so she had telephoned and driven out the same afternoon. On the highway south of the Oak Street bridge, she'd realized that her driving was erratic. She'd parked on the shoulder for a few minutes, taking deep breaths to calm herself. When she pulled out again she deliberately forced her mind away from Rita's murder, keeping herself occupied by reviewing the history of the landscape she was driving through. How many of the commuters who daily cursed the Deas Island Tunnel knew that John Deas had been a Black entrepreneur, one of the first salmon canners on the Fraser?

The Point, a tiny peninsula only a couple of miles long, dangled from the forty-ninth parallel like a forgotten sock on a clothes line. North of the line was Canada, south was the United States. Because Point Roberts lay to the south of the straight line drawn by treaty in 1846, it was American—part of the state of Washington—even though the mainland was Canadian. It was as though Cape Cod were Canadian, she thought, or Land's End were French. In effect, it was a political island, surrounded by water and Canada. This senseless arrangement might have been rectified, but for some macho posturing over a dead pig...even the Kaiser had heard about that pig eventually.

The Point was a backwater, a sleepy stretch of rural coastline with a few hundred year-round residents and a tatty fringe of weekend cottages owned by Canadians. Hanging in the air, as in many border towns, was an odour of the shabbily illicit. When Gillian had first moved to Vancouver, the Point was known for pornographic movies and bars that were open on Sunday. Now, Sunday drinking and red-hot videos were available north of the border, and Point Roberts was known instead for cheap American gas. Groceries and alcohol too. The wine store did a land-office business with Vancouver's œnophiles; wine, like gas, was cheaper in America. Bargains and rarities were almost unknown in the BC government liquor stores, and the absence of wine merchants was a sore point with most wine drinkers. Not a few of Gillian's colleagues shopped regularly at Liberty, as the Point Roberts wine store saucily called itself, smuggling their finds across the border in the glove compartment or under the groceries, their otherwise law-abiding hearts thumping wildly as they submitted to the laconic inquiries of the Customs officers.

These days, the traffic at the crossing was growing heavier. More gas pumps had been added, and the grocery store was packed every weekend with Canadians and their loaded carts: forty-eight rolls of toilet paper, a dozen quarts of milk, eight packets of hamburger rolls on special, ten pounds of ground beef. Gillian moved another car length forward. Someone was talking about Kennedy. Of course, it was November 22nd. Twenty-seven years ago. She'd just come out of class when she'd heard. She'd telephoned her grandparents as soon as she got home, so they wouldn't learn about it on the six o'clock news. Her grandfather had answered. All he'd said was, 'Oh no!' And then, 'Let me tell your grandmother.' But she'd been so upset she'd blurted it out as soon as her grandmother said hello, and her grandmother had started to cry and hung up. The memory was still painful.

Gillian heaved a sigh and looked at her watch. Malcolm Birdseye was expecting her soon, but she had allowed time for the border. Birdie, Edward called him. He was nearly seventy now, with a bad case of emphysema. He'd moved to the Point to live with his daughter, who ran a seafood restaurant and bar. Gillian had liked them both.

'Just like an English village,' Jenny had said about the Point. 'Nosy and clannish. The people who've lived here the longest expect to run everything their own way, and some of them don't hesitate to tell you so. It's a funny old place, but I like it. I can walk to work, and I can shut the bloody place in the winter if I feel like it.'

Gillian crossed the border at last and turned left towards Boundary Bay. Birdie lived in a small house by the water, on Bayview. He liked it there, he'd said, because the bay was an important stop on the Pacific flyway. 'I'm not named Birdseye for nothing. Been a birdwatcher all my life. Living here, I'm like an opera-lover with a box at Covent Garden.'

Edward said Birdie was the best. He knew a lot about forensics as well as fingerprints. She hadn't forgotten what Edward had said about the basic premise of forensic evidence: the theory of interchange. Any person at the scene of the crime will take something away and leave something behind.

Gillian found the house, a one-storey cottage across the road from the beach. The driveway was empty, so presumably Jenny was busy at the restaurant, as one would expect on a Friday afternoon. There was a pungent smell of tidal flat in the damp air, and gulls wheeled overhead. Birdie opened the door, looking pleased to see her. When she'd telephoned, he'd brushed aside any suggestion that she might be putting him to too much trouble; indeed he'd said he would enjoy having a look at the problem.

'I don't miss the job,' he'd wheezed, 'the grind and the late nights, I'm too old for that now. And my lungs are dicky. But I miss the conundrums. Now and then, people get clever, and then it's a pleasure beating them at their own game.'

'I don't think this letter will test your ingenuity,' Gillian had felt obliged to say, but he'd urged her to visit anyway.

He took her into the living-room, where a sofa and a pair of comfortable armchairs were set by the window looking out on the bay. Field glasses and several bird books lay on a low table between them. A door opened on to a planked terrace and rough grass. The beach was right across the road. He opened the door.

'Come outside for a moment.'

She followed him out to the terrace and looked at the bay. It was wide and calm under the cloudy sky of late afternoon, the far shore dim in the distance. The water slapped gently at the stony beach. Gillian heard a heavy, rhythmic creaking sound overhead.

She looked up. An enormous blue heron flew over the roof, its wings lifting and falling slowly, thumping the air.

'There's a heronry on the Point,' Birdie said. 'The largest in these parts. Marvellous places, heronries. Bizarre, you might say. The birds nest high in the trees in colonies, and if you stand underneath, you know, you can hear them honking and screeching and see them flying in and out. With that big wingspread and long neck they look like a flock of pterodactyls. Quite remarkable.'

He led the way inside. 'Of course there are speculators here who want to cut down the trees. They don't give a damn about the herons. Money, that's what they think about. They want to cover the Point with golf courses and hotels and more petrol pumps than Saudi Arabia, and sod the flyway. We've got more than fifty pumps now—the border traffic's so heavy we're marooned here on weekends. Funny how there's always some berk ready to foul his own nest.' He leaned on one of the armchairs, breathing audibly. 'I wish I could take you out to Lily Point, but it's too far for me now.'

'I remember it,' said Gillian. 'Jenny and I went last time, when you and Edward were too deep in shop talk to notice. It's beautiful.'

Tall, eroding cliffs of clay, naked earth gleaming ochre and gold in the afternoon sunshine, the twisted silver shapes of driftwood on the stony shore, leaning trees and the distant blue shapes of islands humped against the sky: she hadn't forgotten Lily Point.

It was a long slow business, becoming attached to a new landscape, a part of the world unknown in childhood. The countryside where she grew up—the familiar fields and pastures, the crumbling stone walls, the oak-crowned hills—was rich with meaning, like a native language, in which the words are not flat and bare of association, but velveted over with one's own history and coloured by literature. She had felt quite at home in the English landscape, but then she had visited it constantly as a child, in books. The western coast of North America, however, had scarcely crossed her mind. When she got there, she was a stranger. Everything was too big; the forests were too dark, there was no harmony between land and buildings. The trees were the wrong shape—too many evergreens—and the steep-sided mountains rose around her like walls. Now, many years later, she had attached herself: to the late golden summers and the long soft springs, to the blue light on faraway islands, to water-worn rocks and the smooth russet skin of the arbutus tree. At certain moments she had been conscious of the process, as though, spider-like, she had thrown out a new filament. Her visit to Lily Point had been one of those moments.

Birdie had gotten his breath back. He turned towards a bare table in the corner of the room. 'You've brought your little problem along, then?'

She opened her briefcase and pulled out several manila envelopes.

Birdie held out his hand. 'Let's have a butcher's.'

He switched on a gooseneck lamp over the table, and a strong light shone on the clean surface. Gillian talked while he laid out the various pieces of paper, handling them by their edges.

'I brought these photocopies because they have identified prints on them,' she explained. 'No one has touched those except the Dean, and these are the secretary's. And this is a note from Rita which I believe only she and I touched, and these are some papers she handled in a recent meeting with me.' She had brought the envelope as well as the infamous letter. Cynthia's comment about recycling had reminded her of the scene between Rankin and Verne Palmer. Most people were still careless with envelopes; there might be something helpful about this one, even if they got nowhere with the letter itself.

Birdie gave her an interested glance but didn't comment. He opened a grey metal box like a toolbox. Inside Gillian saw cannisters of powder, little brushes in clear plastic tubes, tape, and a big flashlight. 'My clobber,' Birdie said. 'Not much use for it now.' He took out a cannister of dark powder. 'Dark for light surfaces, see, so the patterns show up better.' He took a brush that reminded Gillian of a small shaving brush, dipped it in the powder and swizzled it over Rita's letter. 'Don't expect too much,' he warned. 'If several people have handled the letter, the prints'll be all mixed up.'

'What are the powders made of?' Gillian asked curiously.

'Mostly graphite nowadays. They used to be made of terrible things—lead and aluminium, and such. A lot of fingerprint men didn't live long.' He gave a wheezy chuckle. 'Most of 'em were smokers, too, so their troubles were blamed on that.' He dusted the envelope and Rita's note to Gillian about the Rayne meeting. 'Now then. Press your fingers on this bit of paper here, and we'll see what yours look like.'

Gillian spread her fingers and pressed down on the paper. Birdie rolled each one from side to side a little, then dusted the prints. 'Nice. Too bad they don't come like this every time. They'd be even better if you were nervous. You see, when a bloke's where he's got no business to be, he's scared. So he sweats. The acid and oil leave a strong pattern—*if* he touches a good smooth surface, and doesn't smear it, and it isn't a doorknob or some other bit of hardware that every Tom, Dick and Harry puts his bloody hand on.' He examined the papers one by one and then compared them.' Gillian looked too. Some prints were clear, the whorls and ridges plain to her inexperienced eye. Others were smudged, or faint, or mutilated by overlapping marks. Birdie showed her some points of identification in the patterns: the whorls and bifurcations and short, isolated ridges he called islands that were the unique marks of each human being. Then he told her what he could see. He saw Gillian's fingerprints on Rita's note, along with a number of clear prints that weren't hers. If those were verified as Rita's, then her prints were also on the envelope that had held the letter. There was an especially fine thumbprint on the back that matched a thumbprint on the note. He turned the envelope over and showed her that there were also prints belonging to at least two other people. One of them, thanks to Gillian's photocopies, was identified as Cynthia's. The letter itself now looked as though it had been passed around in a coalmine. It bore the prints of three or four people, laid one over another. There were a few clear prints, including Cynthia's left forefinger and Stanley's thumb. Others were unknown.

'With a bit of luck, we'd find enough here to identify those, but proving a negative is another matter. You want to know whether Rita touched this letter. If she did, either she wore gloves, which doesn't make a lot of sense, from what you've told me, or every print she left has been obscured by subsequent handling. Here and now, my dear, I can say she probably didn't put a finger on it. But I wouldn't swear to it in court.'

CHAPTER 22

The next day Gillian had an interview with the police. The major crime squad detective who had taken over the case as a result of the accident squad's investigations was close to fifty, she guessed: a burly man with ruddy cheeks and crinkly grey hair cut very short. He had an outsize nose with a bridge that jutted aggressively from the broad plane of his forehead. His grey eyes, under heavy brows, were neither friendly nor unfriendly. His name was Frank Bacon.

Do they learn that stare in school, Gillian wondered, or through years of on-the-job practice? She hadn't been nervous about coming, nor was the police station designed to intimidate. It presided over the sleaziest corner of the city, but the lobby was panelled in wood and laid with a floor of ceramic bricks of the type people often used in their kitchens. Despite the bricks, the station was unmistakably a male precinct. You might say it was studded with symbols of authority, she thought, eyeing the uniformed men and the guns. Not to mention male authority figures, like Bacon. Were there any women at all in the upper ranks of the police force? Upstairs, there was the predictable warren of windowless offices, each with its computer terminals and swivel chairs. There was no corporate luxury here, rather the contrary, but the building (at least the parts she had seen) wasn't grim. Nevertheless, she was now aware of tension in her neck. She couldn't tell what Bacon was thinking about her activities. She had explained briefly about the Feminist Union, the Triumph Day demo and the Rayne money, while Bacon listened and another policeman took notes. Bacon knew something about these matters already, he told her; he had interviewed Libby the previous evening while Gillian was driving back from Point Roberts. Now he wanted to hear her version of events. She had brought along the inflatable dummy she had found hanging in the history office and the roll of film with the pictures she had taken of her vandalized porch light and the jack o'lantern. She hadn't gotten around to developing them.

He was interested in the scrawls she had found in the women's room, having heard nothing about them from Libby.

'You mentioned them to no one besides the two secretaries?'

'No.'

'When did you find them?'

'It must have been Tuesday. Yes, in the morning, fairly early. So they had to have been done Monday night.'

'And did you connect them with Rita Gordon's death?'

'Naturally I thought of it. But I believed her death was an accident. I concluded the scrawl was just another form of harassment.'

'And what do you think now?'

'I'm not sure. Maybe my first idea was the right one—but there could be someone with a list—and Rita's was just the first name on it.'

'And you think these incidents are deliberately organized?'

'That's what I've been asking myself all term. I think a lot of things that happen to women on campus happen at random—I mean they're just part of a generalized hostility that society thinks is normal. But the Feminist Union stood out—as feminists, as disturbers of the established order. I think that there *has* been organized harassment of the Union, and especially of Rita.'

'And if so, who's doing it?'

'A bunch of male students. I can't prove which ones, but I believe there's a core group of engineering students who are responsible for most of it.'

'Why?'

'Triumph Day, the Rayne money…and their Dean is a macho idiot, so the atmosphere in their faculty isn't exactly discouraging.'

His face was impassive. He gestured at the folded dummy.

'This dummy that you found hanging in the department office. You hid it. Why?'

'I thought it would frustrate the intentions of whoever put it up.'

'Which were?'

'To scare people—Rita, or the whole group. Maybe to make Jessie Rayne withdraw her support from women's studies.'

'Libby Hosmer said you had suggested she record the obscene calls she was getting. Why did you do that?'

'In case someone could identify the voices. I—

He didn't wait for her to finish. 'You don't seem to have been eager to contact the police.'

Gillian's heart sank. He was suspicious of her, and she hadn't even told him about her fingerprint researches yet, or Rita's brother. She said nothing. He drummed the fingers of his left hand on the arm of his chair.

'Well? Why were you gathering evidence on your own?' His stare, if not precisely hostile, was challenging.

'Two reasons,' Gillian said after a pause to frame her reply. 'The events and their effects were cumulative—none of us knew they would keep on the way they did, and I had no idea that Rita's death had anything to do with them. Any one of these incidents, even a series of them, is perfectly ordinary. Women live with this all the time. In my experience, the police aren't able to do very much about the sorts of things that happen to women every day, unless a particular pattern is prolonged and predictable. The police can't be everywhere at once, and nobody likes living in societies where it feels as if they are. It seemed more useful to gather enough evidence to force the university authorities to do something.'

'And your second reason?' He was still sceptical, but some tension had gone out of the atmosphere. He'd apparently found the first part of her answer reasonable and wasn't offended. Gillian was relieved. He was comfortable with his own authority, then. She had been afraid when he asked the question that he was resenting her investigations as invasions of his territory, which would have made it very difficult to proceed. Now it appeared more likely that he was routinely curious about her motives. Or perhaps he was just impatient with amateurs. He was still waiting for the second half of her reply, looking at her from under his brows. Lowering his big head, she thought, like a bull. Well, she would take the bull by the horns.

'Secondly, my main efforts at investigation were aimed in another direction—a matter of a university grant which should have been awarded to Rita and wasn't. This didn't appear to be a matter for the police at all.' She explained about the Carver Fellowship. 'It now appears that the letter she brought was written by someone else; I took it to a retired fingerprint expert and he couldn't find her prints on it. He—'

Bacon interrupted her for a second time. 'Who? What expert?'

'Malcolm Birdseye. He lives in Point Roberts.'

This had an electric effect. 'Birdie? How the hell do you know him?'

Gillian reddened. She could have mentioned Edward as soon as she arrived, but she hadn't wanted to—she'd thought it would look like asking for special status. Now why was it embarrassing to explain about Edward? Because the Yard had a peculiar celebrity. And because there was no word to describe their relationship. This might be the only reason left for getting married. Then you could say, comfortably, 'husband' and that was that.

'I have a very close friend,' she could say. Too coy. Damn it. She should have solved this one by now. People she knew who lived together mostly said 'the man/woman-I-live-with'—a mouthful—or 'partner'. Neither seemed apt for a relationship that was constructed of holidays and telephone calls—even if it had been going on for years. She could hardly call him her beau, as her mother sometimes did. 'Lover' was too physical, 'constant companion' was too Hollywood, and anyway, if there was anything Edward wasn't, it was a constant companion.

'The man in my life,' she said, gritting her teeth, 'is a detective at Scotland Yard. His name is Edward Gisborne. He and Birdie are friends.'

Bacon regarded her with new interest, as she had known he would.

'So.' He sat back. 'That puts a somewhat different light on things.'

'Does it?' Gillian asked. She was put out. 'I still could be a busybody—or even a murderer.'

Bacon laughed good-humouredly. 'Now don't get on your high horse. I didn't mean to insult you. You've been something of a surprise, you must know that. Well, well. Birdie.' He sat back. 'You'd better tell me the rest.'

She went over the details of the Carver episode. 'I couldn't bring you the letter—it's in Dean Stanley's files again—in a sealed envelope, because I'd promised to return it. But I did say, when I brought it back, that I was going to tell you about it, and he had to agree.'

'Do you think it's connected to the case?'

'No, I can't see it. The idea was to prevent her from getting the grant—and that was achieved. Even so, I didn't think concealing the matter from the police was a good idea.'

Bacon looked at her alertly. 'But Stanley did?'

'He thinks it's a purely university matter, and there's no point in troubling the police.'

'Why did they assume she'd written it?'

'Because she brought it herself, and her politics made a committee of conservative males perfectly ready to believe she would behave irrationally.'

'So when exactly did you go see Birdie about this?'

This was the question she had been anxious about. She'd gone to see Birdie after Frances had told her the news of Rita's murder. She should have gone to see Bacon instead. But she wasn't going to lie about it.

She told him.

The friendly atmosphere evaporated. What was she doing running off to Birdie when she knew the major crime squad would be interested?

'I didn't think it was relevant,' she said.

'Didn't think? It's my job to decide what's relevant. You know that, better than most people. You must have had another reason.'

'Yes. I did. I already had Stanley's OK to see Birdie. Frances, by some miracle, heard about the murder before he did. I knew he'd never let me have the file after he found out. He would have sat on it unless the police asked for it.'

'Which is exactly what he should do.'

'But you might not have wanted it!' Gillian cried. 'Suppose you'd caught the murderer right away because he'd done something stupid or someone saw him tampering with the motorcycle. I wanted to see those files.'

Bacon grunted. 'I phoned Frances Romano. Was that a miracle? I thought the person most concerned would be the Dean of Women. Was that wrong?'

'No. You were right, but the pyramid usually dispenses information from the top down.'

Bacon leaned on his elbow, considering her. 'At least you didn't botch it up trying to dust the prints yourself,' he said at last. 'But from now on, anything like that, you bring it straight to me. Understood?'

Gillian relaxed a little. The worst was over. She then recounted her doings in England, aware all the while that Edward's reluctance to interfere had been well founded. It would have been awkward explaining to an angry homicide detective why they'd been questioning Rita's family. Bacon expressed no surprise when she mentioned Rita's brother—but then he had talked to Libby.

'Do you know where John Gordon is now?'

'No.'

At the end of the interview Bacon said he would be in touch when he had further questions. He rubbed his hand over his jaw and moved his shoulders as if to unstiffen them. He ruminated silently, then said, somewhat abruptly, 'Research is something like detective work, I'm told. You've been chewing on this for weeks. What's the flavour of the day?'

'That a bunch of engineering students joked about killing her and one of them turned it into reality. But I haven't any proof. I don't even know their names.'

'Any other ideas?'

'Her brother, I suppose. He did try once before.'

'No enemies in her own little group that you know about? Rumour has it that feminists can get pretty hot under the collar when they don't agree.'

'That's true, and a person like Rita did raise hackles. Tact wasn't her long suit. But this group has only existed for a few months. It represents a certain point of view and is still close enough to operate by consensus. There's no bitter infighting that I know of. Besides, statistically speaking, the killer must be a man, right?'

Bacon sighed. 'A man who knows her. What about your department? What's-his-name—Paul Smith—who received the fellowship?'

'If she'd been killed before he got the Carver, it would make sense. But what would be the point later?'

Gillian, exhausted and overwrought, drove home in a blinding rainstorm, left a message on Edward's tape and had a hot bath. She turned on her radio. The rain was flooding the highways again. And there was another slide blocking the Squamish Highway. A small one this time, the announcer said cheerily.

Not long after that, the telephone began to ring. It was Libby. When she hung up, it rang again. By nightfall, everyone knew that the accident hadn't been one.

CHAPTER 23

The memorial service was held on Sunday afternoon. The church was not far from the university gates; a small, modern building with plain white walls and a single stained glass window above the altar. The seats, which weren't fixed in place, had been arranged in concentric squares. The people who came would face each other.

Gillian was early, but she wasn't the first to arrive. Libby and Marnie and Denise were there already, as well as six or seven other women whose faces Gillian recognized from the Triumph Day demonstration. In the centre of the square was a table covered in a white cloth. Flowers were strewn over it—roses, narcissi, freesias—and a tall candle stood unlit in a silver holder.

Libby came across the room and drew her into a corner.

'I've decided. I'm not going to talk about it.'

'Fine.'

'I want everyone to think about her, not about him—whoever the fuck he is.'

'Yes, I know.'

'But he might come today.'

Gillian had thought of that. 'Maybe. But Frank Bacon will probably be here too—looking for him.'

Libby chewed on her thumbnail. 'What if something happens?'

'Like what?'

'Like something bad.' Libby fidgeted with the beads she was wearing. 'Last night I started thinking, you know, what if some guy with a machine-gun shows up, like in Montreal? A guy who wants to kill a lot of feminists. I almost chickened out,' she said uneasily, embarrassed by her own fear.

'I don't believe we have to worry about that,' Gillian said with conviction. 'Think of *how* Rita was killed. This villain wants to keep himself intact.'

'You think so?' Libby relaxed a little. 'I feel kind of dumb, being freaked out, I mean.' She laughed unhappily. 'But it's like they say—just because you're paranoid doesn't mean you're not being followed.'

'I'll keep an eye on who comes in,' Gillian said.

'OK. God, I can't stand to think he'll be here watching us.'

They grimaced. It was a nasty thought: Rita's murderer sitting among the mourners, watching the effect he was having.

Gillian took a seat facing the door. The room filled up. Many people who had taken part in the protest march were there, women and men, students, staff and faculty. Laura and Frances both came; they sat with Gillian, but no one wanted to talk much. Gillian realized she hadn't spoken to Laura in days—not since the day after she'd returned from England.

The History Department turned out in respectable numbers. Gillian saw Honeycutt and Carole Stein together on the other side of the square, and a little later Kray arrived. Kittredge sat with Jane and Allie. Rankin and Palmer did not appear, nor did Ridgeway. Much to Gillian's surprise, however, Jacobsen shuffled in and took a seat in the back row near the door. He was followed by Cynthia, and then a little eddy of students, perhaps from one of Rita's tutorials. Behind them was a man who looked vaguely familiar. Gillian stared, but couldn't place him. He was alone, and he sat down at the end of a row at a distance from other people.

As her eyes swept the crowd, Gillian saw another unexpected face. For a moment, she couldn't think who the woman was, and then she recognized the cleaner who mopped the floors in the History Department at night: a small, tired-looking Bengali woman whom Gillian had occasionally seen when she stayed very late at the office. Rita must have made her acquaintance during the months she'd often worked all night on her thesis. Gillian could picture them having tea at three in the morning. There were also many people whom Gillian didn't know at all, and who, she suspected, hadn't known Rita. The event hadn't been publicized off campus, but on campus, Rita had had some notoriety.

Last to arrive was Jessie Rayne. It was a pleasant shock to see her there. Unlike many of the crowd, she wore black; she looked formal in her little hat and a dark fur jacket. Gillian fluttered her hand, and Jessie made her way across the room.

'I nearly didn't come because I thought only close friends would be here. But after I heard the news I realized that there were bound to be some curiosity-seekers.'

Gillian nodded, distracted by a glimpse of Paul Smith sitting in one of the back rows. She hadn't seen him come in.

In a shadowed recess at the back of the church, Libby was talking to Tony, the young man Gillian had seen with the video-camera at the Triumph Day demonstration. He had his camera now.

'The media?' Jessie asked, her eyes following Gillian's.

'No, they've been asked to stay away until it's over. He's a film student.' Libby's hand touched Tony's arm in an intimate gesture. 'They're taping the memorial service for Rita's sister. She couldn't come.'

She looked around for Frank Bacon. She'd been sure he'd be here. But she saw no sign of him. He would have been conspicuous, she realized. He looked like a cop, and the few middle-aged men present were familiar faces on the campus.

Libby stepped away from Tony and made her way towards the table at the centre of the square. Marnie followed her, and then came Denise wearing a long skirt and an embroidered magenta blouse, and carrying a guitar.

Libby stood still at the table, the candle in its silver holder in front of her. She cleared her throat and shivered a little, though the church was warm. The crowd ceased shifting in their seats and murmuring and became still. Tony emerged silently from the shadows and trod quietly behind the rear row of seats. Gillian looked from Libby's strained face to the assembled mourners. Her eyes went to the end of the row, to look again at the man whose face was vaguely familiar. His glance crossed hers without recognition.

Libby said, nearly whispering at first and then lifting her voice as she gathered confidence, 'We are here to mourn our dear friend Rita Gordon, who died on the first of November. We loved her,